SARA HOLLAND

evermore

ORCHARD

ORCHARD BOOKS

First published in the US in 2018 by HarperTeen
First published in Great Britain in 2018 by The Watts Publishing Group
This edition published in Great Britain in 2019 by The Watts Publishing Group

1 3 5 7 9 10 8 6 4 2

A CIP catalogue record for this book is available from the British Library.

ISBN 978 1 40834 952 6

Printed and bound in Great Britain by CPI Group (UK) Ltd, Croydon, CR0 4YY

The paper and board used in this book are
made from wood from responsible sources.

Orchard Books
An imprint of Hachette Children's Group
Part of The Watts Publishing Group Limited
Carmelite House
50 Victoria Embankment
London EC4Y 0DZ

An Hachette UK Company
www.hachette.co.uk

www.hachettechildrens.co.uk

To my siblings: Rachel, Ben, and Hannah—
I can't wait to see where your journeys lead

The Sorceress saw a silvery shadow rise from the Alchemist's broken body, and dart away across the earth, too fast to chase after. Within the silver, something glowed dark red and pulsing. Too late, the Sorceress realized that the Alchemist had indeed tricked her—he had stolen her heart.

—From *Sempera's Classical Histories, the Myth of the Alchemist and the Sorceress*

But what if the Alchemist did not die, not really—what if she had found a way to live?

—From the personal notebooks of Liam Gerling

THE SORCERESS

Tonight, I will make the Alchemist's blood—Jules Ember's blood—into a weapon.

I stand in a room deep below the ballrooms and balconies of Shorehaven. A timelender hunches across from me, sweating as he mixes powders at his workbench. He's the latest in a long line of timelenders I've commissioned to lure the Alchemist out of hiding. All have been inadequate so far; all have died for it. But something tells me tonight will be different.

The air prickles with danger. With promise.

The people of Sempera are so uncreative with their precious time, their blood-irons. When they don't drink them like beasts, they fritter them away to make their flowers bloom, or feed them to their fires to make themselves warm in the winter.

But the right blood-iron could burn down the world.

When the timelender tips the vial of Jules Ember's blood into his little cauldron, light flashes through the room—as if we're not far underground, as if day has come early and all at once. The ash and grime billow around me before the *boom* knocks us both off our feet. For an instant, flight. I think of the world as a hide stretched taut across the frame of a war drum, the kind I remember from centuries ago. Someone's just brought the mallet down.

Even as my back hits the floorboards, my blood sings with triumph. An image burns behind my eyelids: a landscape of flames, the outline of a decrepit town with a pathetic name: *Crofton*.

I laugh to myself as I stagger to my feet. The timelender is lying prone on the floor, knocked there by the impact, gasping like a fish. "So it *is* you," he murmurs. My true name, *Sorceress*, dies on his lips.

Never mind that. Inside the bronze cauldron, giving off its own faint light, is a shifting, sparking liquid. No color and every color at the same time, the magic is hard to look at directly with these human eyes. The man dying at my feet has created it out of Sempera's finest diamonds and only one year of the blood-iron sweet Jules Ember left behind at Everless.

I bring the small cauldron to my lips and drink the Alchemist's time. Just a little.

I have plans for the rest.

Pain lances my throat.

I breathe, alive, grip the edge of the table as my weak body shudders. I wait for the time to coalesce into a thousand daggers like it did that night at Everless, the night I finally realized who Jules Ember was under her skin, in her heart. I wait for her time to fight its way out of me like something alive.

That doesn't happen. Instead, power seeps into me.

Energy courses through the room, magic in every particle just waiting to be unlocked and set loose on the world, snarling like a pack of wild dogs.

I pour a few drops of the liquid into a bottle, dark green to hide its contents' diamond quality.

Aboveground, I hand the bottle to the Everless boy Ivan Tenburn. He's afraid of me now; he holds it like it will bite him. Good. I need him to be careful. I need our creation to make it to Crofton intact.

Where it will deliver the Alchemist to me.

"Make me a fire," I whisper into Ivan's ear.

TO THE CITIZENS OF SEMPERA

A NOTICE for the capture of Jules Ember of Crofton, murderer of the First Queen, the late Savior of Sempera, the Lady of Centuries; and of Lord Roan Gerling, beloved son of Lord Nicholas Gerling and Lady Verissa Gerling, devoted brother of Lord Liam Gerling.

A reward of five hundred years of blood-iron is offered for the murderess's living capture and delivery to Queen Ina Gold's soldiers.

1

When I wake, my hands are covered in blood.

It's only a trick of the moonlight and shifting shadows. Still, I frantically scrub my palms against my damp cloak, as if such a simple gesture could wipe away the red that stains my memory.

I sit in a corner of my friend Amma's shed right outside of Crofton, my teeth chattering more with fear than cold, as her aunt's three chickens cluck softly at me from their pen. Spring rain taps against the roof. When I was a girl folded in Papa's arms, the sound of rain was a lullaby—it sang of new life, of fledgling wheat that would soon be harvested, kneaded, then baked into bread on a blazing hearthstone. The rain lulled me to sleep, as soft and real as the voice of someone I love.

Now it's a faint drum becoming louder with every gust of wind. The sound of doom approaching.

The shape of Crofton drew me in from the woods—the broken line of rooftops against the sky that I've seen so many times before. Our cottage is only ten minutes down the path, I realize, then there's a pang of grief as I remember that it no longer belongs to Papa and me. I would trade all the splendor and luxury of Everless for one more evening by the fire with him. But even Everless is lost to me—my first real home, now forever forbidden.

I didn't mean to stop after fleeing Everless, but when I caught sight of the familiar shed jutting from a recently plowed field, I couldn't stop myself. My feet moved of their own accord. As if by ducking into this familiar darkness I could turn back time itself, weeks and months of it, and undo everything that's happened.

Say good-bye to Amma, if I were lucky.

That was hours ago, in the dead of night. There are soldiers out searching for me. Jules Ember, the Queen's killer. I've heard them at times, crashing through the undergrowth and clumsily breaking branches, always giving me plenty of time to seek shelter in a cave or up a tree. Now I'm here; now I'm safe—

Something *snaps* outside. It's loud enough that I hear it over the sound of rain and low rumbles of thunder.

I press my eye against a crack in the old boards that make up the wall I'm leaning against, fearing some soldier or wandering bleeder has stumbled upon my hiding place. I'm not sure which would be worse. A bleeder roaming the woods would likely cut my throat, drink all my years for himself without pausing to glance at my face. But a soldier would throw me in chains and drag me to the palace in a prison carriage. It turns out not to matter. All I see outside are the trees as they sway with the wind, their branches bending into whipping, shadowy arms that seem to point to me, whispering—

Murderer! Alchemist!

I swallow. For a moment, I swear that I glimpse the face of the girl who hunted me in my childhood nightmares, outlined in a flash of lightning. Pale animal eyes that wear kindness like a mask. Hair dark as the night sky. Her white teeth bared in a grin.

When I was a child, Papa told me my dreams could never hurt me—but he lied. Two weeks ago, the girl tore out of my nightmares and stepped into the world.

Caro. The Sorceress. My ancient enemy.

I breathe in. Out. I close my eyelids, trying to calm my racing breath, listen to the rain make steady *taps* on the roof. I hug my knees to my chest, letting the sound fill the darkness around me—but it's not enough to dispel the knot of anxiety gathering in my chest. In the woods, I was able to ignore my fear. Shove it aside and let my attention be taken up by the task at hand: walk, hunt, hide. Get to Ambergris, the dock city where a ship waits to take me away from the land of Sempera, at Liam Gerling's arrangement.

But, now that I'm here, how could I leave without saying good-bye to Amma?

Every day after the sun rises, she comes here to collect eggs for her and her sister Alia's breakfast. Soon she'll discover me, and there's nothing I can do but wait. Wait to see if my old friend will scream at the sight of me, if she'll run for the soldiers who surely patrol Crofton at every hour of the day and night, hoping to drag me away.

Just as I think this, the door creaks open. I've been expecting it, but fear still rips through my body and my head snaps up.

Amma is silhouetted in the doorway, a blanket over her shoulders and a woven basket over her arm. She looks well, and joy flickers briefly through me at the sight of her red-flushed cheeks. I gave her the blood-irons that Liam Gerling sent me in secret after Papa died just outside the gates of Everless. I'd hoped that the heavy bag of coins would help her build a better life for herself and Alia.

My friend rubs a hand over her bleary eyes as she steps inside—then catches sight of me and freezes.

I'd meant to stand up, but I'm frozen too. I stare up at Amma, trying to arrange all the words flying around in my head, but she speaks first.

"*Jules?*" she breathes.

"Amma." My voice cracks on her name, unused to speech from my silent week spent in the woods between Crofton and the Gerling estate. I press a hand to the wall and use it to push myself unsteadily to my feet, but I don't take a step toward her.

Not yet. Not until I'm sure she won't run from me, screaming.

Amma's mouth opens, then closes in shock. Finally, she whispers, "Please tell me you didn't do it."

She doesn't have to say what she means by *it*. Word of my crimes has spread to every corner of Sempera. That I seduced Roan Gerling while a servant at Everless and used him to gain access to the visiting Queen's chambers. Then cut Roan's throat and stabbed the Queen through the heart.

"I didn't," I say. My voice comes out hoarse, pleading. "I didn't, Amma."

Amma stays stone-still in the doorway, her eyes boring into mine, round and glistening. Then she takes a cautious step toward me, moving into a pool of light that bleeds through a hole in the roof. She's trembling. "Then what happened? Who killed them?"

"Her name is Caro," I say, my voice wavering a little, even though I've practiced the speech in my head. It's hard to force out her name, like the word itself is a stone wedged in my throat. All of Sempera thinks me a murderer. Standing there, helpless and trembling in front of Amma, I realize that I need someone to believe me. I need *Amma* to believe me.

If my friend doesn't see the same Jules she's always known— doesn't see me for who I am—I think I'll shatter.

"Caro was the Queen's lady-in-waiting," I continue, fighting to keep my voice steady. "She killed the Queen and Roan and

5

blamed me for it. Now everyone thinks I'm guilty."

I almost say, *Everyone except Liam Gerling*, but I stop myself.

Amma blinks and then closes the shed door behind her. My heart skips a beat as her lantern throws flickering shadows over the shed walls.

"Why?" she whispers, her face pale. "Why would the Queen's lady-in-waiting kill Roan?"

My eyes burn suddenly, fiercely. "I don't know," I lie, swallowing down the tears that threaten to spill over. "They say she has the ear of Lady Gold. Maybe Caro thinks she'll be more powerful with Ina as queen."

I desperately want this statement—this partial truth—to be enough. For the line between Amma's brows to disappear, and for the tension in her shoulders to slide away. But as the crease and tension remain, I realize how foolish that hope is. Amma has always been able to tell when I'm lying, ever since we were girls and my lies were about things like spilled soup and broken dolls.

"They're saying you're a witch. That only a witch could kill someone as powerful as Sempera's queen." Amma's voice is small.

My stomach sinks with dread at the idea of telling her the truth: I'm the ancient Alchemist, the wicked Alchemist, reborn. I brace myself, inhaling deeply. "Do you remember the stories I used to tell? About foxes and snakes?"

Amma's eyes flicker. "I suppose so."

More to buy myself time than anything else, I reach into my bag. Amma starts a little and tracks my movements with her eyes. I ignore the small stab of pain this gives me.

In slow, steady movements, I take out the leather-bound journal that I stole from the vault at Everless. The book that I remember from my childhood, left behind when Papa and I fled the Gerling estate, filled with stories and drawings that I first thought to be just the ramblings of a little girl. Until Papa died trying to retrieve it, in the hopes of keeping the information within safe—keeping me safe—from the Sorceress, my oldest enemy. It seems to warm my hands now, brimming with secret knowledge—and more than that, a link to the castle that holds so many of my memories within its walls.

You were right, Papa. I was in danger, I think sadly, holding the journal out in the space between Amma and me. He thought the Queen was the threat. But the real Sorceress was waiting, watching from the shadows all the while. I befriended her, just another servant girl. I revealed my secret to her before I even knew it myself.

Fox and snake. Sorceress and Alchemist.

Amma lifts her lantern to see the journal, and her mouth flattens. But she takes a cautious step forward and opens it with one hand, holding the lamp close with the other.

"Your stories," she murmurs, turning a few pages. Then looks up at me. Concern and suspicion chase each other across that face that I know so well. "You wrote them down? What is this, Jules?"

"They aren't just stories. They're a key. A key to things I've forgotten." Nervousness dries out my tongue. "The snake . . . that's what I called myself. And the fox, that's Caro."

Amma's eyes flick up to me. "The girl who killed the Queen."

"We were friends a long time ago, before I met you. At least I thought we were friends."

"You mean, when you and your papa lived at Everless?" Something shimmers in Amma's eyes—the look of the little girl who would beg me for every scrap of detail I could remember about the Gerling estate, who would let tales of lords and ladies carry her away.

"Sort of." I take a shuddering breath. "Amma, I learned something about myself when I returned to Everless. It's going to sound mad when I tell you, but please just listen. And then after, I'll leave. If you want me to." *But please let me stay*, I add silently. I've lost so much in the past weeks—Papa, my home, my friends, even Everless, the place I both hate and love. I can't lose Amma too.

Liam Gerling flits across my mind again, the complete belief in his eyes when he stood in an open field and told me I was the Alchemist. I wish he were beside me, if only to show Amma that I'm not mad. Not yet.

"Do you believe in the Sorceress?" I ask.

"Of course." Amma's answer comes without hesitation. I remember the wooden girl statue she keeps in her window, the leaves and berries of ice holly, the Sorceress's sigil, carved above the doors. The same motifs decorate shrines all over Sempera. To Amma, to everyone, the Sorceress is a benevolent being, and the Alchemist the evil thief who stole her heart. Anger brushes a finger along my throat. Caro has had centuries to shape her stories, while the Alchemist—while *I*—have to start anew with each incarnation, shrouded in ignorance of what's come before.

"The Sorceress is real," I say. I close my eyes so I don't have to see Amma's reaction to what I say next. "I've met her."

Amma gasps softly. "How can that be?" Her voice is awed, reverent. Her eyes are the widest I've ever seen them.

"Caro—Caro is the Sorceress." The words sound strange out loud. "She disguised herself as a servant girl to the Queen, to be close to power without being noticed. She's not as strong as she once was, so she has to hide behind the guise of a handmaiden."

I shudder, remembering the words Caro screamed at me, right before killing Roan Gerling in front of my eyes. *I want to be timeless again. . . . No fear of aging or death, without having to drink peasant blood like a damned wolf.* Liam told me that when I stole Caro's heart, I stole her immortality, breaking it up into twelve pieces—twelve lives. But still, the Sorceress lives. Even without her heart, she's more powerful than anyone walking the earth.

More powerful than me, though I don't understand how or why.

"Jules . . ." Amma's looking at me uncertainly, her head tilted, like this is one of the riddles we passed back and forth as children. "I don't understand." One of the chickens gives a soft, inquisitive-sounding *coo*. "How do you know this Caro is the Sorceress? And why would she kill Roan?"

"She told me." Even though I knew these questions would come, they get harder and harder to answer. I feel the beginnings of tears sting my throat as a memory flashes: the Queen slipping from Caro's control, falling to the floor like a puppet with cut strings. "She wanted to hurt me. She was trying to break my heart."

"Why?"

My voice comes out in a soft, pleading whisper. "Because she thinks that's how she'll get her power back."

What little color was left in Amma's face drains slowly away. Her eyes dart to the journal and back to me. The old tales and her friend before her. I know the pieces are starting to come together. "But the stories—"

"The stories say that the Alchemist tricked the Sorceress." I hear Liam's voice in my mind as I think of the two stories, the truth and the legend, entwining over the centuries. Where they differ, where they intersect. "He"—most people think the first Alchemist was a *he*—"offered her twelve stones, saying they were pieces of the heart he had stolen, and she rejected them."

Amma nods along to the familiar tale. "And she forced him to eat them instead." Her eyes are wide in the dark. She's released her clenched fists, and drawn a little closer to me. For a moment, I can almost pretend we are children again, trading stories as we huddle close to a fire, desperate to ward off the chill and gloom of winter.

"The stones *were* the Sorceress's heart—her life, Amma, her time." I whisper now. "And when the Alchemist swallowed them, it all flowed back into him. But instead of living on like the Sorceress, the time was broken up into pieces. The Alchemist would live for a while, then die, then be born again." I stumble a little over the words. It's a story I still don't remember living, though I feel the truth of it.

"Jules, you're not making any sense." Amma lets out a strangled laugh, and I can tell she's trying for her usual briskness. "Stop this. You can eat and rest, and tell me when you're feeling better what's going on."

"No, Amma, listen." I reach out for her without thinking. She flinches—my heart twists—and I drop my hand to the journal, take the reassuring weight of it in my hand. I take strength from the soft, aged leather cover, the stories that overflow from the inside. I've leafed through it many times while walking through the woods. At moments, it's been the only thing convincing me that I am not mad. "I am the Alchemist."

Tears brim in Amma's eyes and overflow down her cheeks.

They catch the faint morning light and call up tears to my own eyes. "Why are you telling me this?" Amma whispers.

It's the first question that I didn't see coming, and it makes my breath catch. I realize I'm holding the journal over my chest like a shield. I put it down, and it falls open where a rough drawing has filled the page: a fox lashing out at a rearing snake, claws and teeth and fangs.

"Do you believe me?" I ask, my voice shaking. It's not what I meant to say, but it's what comes out.

Another long silence passes, and Amma takes the journal into her hands and opens the cover. "I never thought you were a murderer," she says softly, her eyes flitting up to meet mine almost shyly. "I knew you had no love for her, but Roan . . ."

His name breaks the dam on my tears, and they spill out silently. Amma inhales sharply, and she lurches half a step to embrace me before pulling back.

"I didn't want any of this to happen. I never wanted—"

My words are cut off in a gasp as Amma crosses the floor and wraps her arms around me. I think I might break apart—but from relief now, the first happiness I've felt in what seems like an eternity. I lean into her, and she hugs me tight, not seeming to care that I'm coated in forest grime. Her scent is familiar, the scent of home, and for a long moment I do nothing but breathe it in.

"You're my best friend, Jules," she murmurs. "Of course I believe you."

At these words, my tears flow stronger than ever. They fill my eyes and run down my cheeks, cutting through days' worth of dirt. "Thank you, Amma."

Eventually she pulls back, her face thoughtful. "So Caro's the fox, and you're the snake?"

Her voice—patient but skeptical, like she's questioning one of Alia's wild stories—makes me choke out a laugh. "So it seems."

"My Jules, the Alchemist of legend." Amma's face grows more serious. She lays the journal carefully on a crate and drops her hands to hold mine. "You'll have to forgive me if I take some time to understand."

"I still don't understand."

"Even when the messengers from Everless came with the news, I didn't believe it." She looks down, her eyes going sad. "That's why she killed Roan? To break your heart, since . . . it was hers to begin with?"

I nod around the lump in my throat. "But it didn't work." Even though I feel broken, I'm still alive, and I cling to that like a lifeline. Amma's hands are warm around mine. "Maybe I didn't really love him. Or just . . . not enough."

"It's not your fault, Jules," she says. "Perhaps your heart is stronger than you think."

I shrug, though deep in my gut I know it's not true. Even now I feel fragile, like a blow in the right place would shatter me utterly. Amma takes a step back—I feel a pang of loss as her hands leave mine—and guides me by the elbow to a bale of straw, making me sit. She plops down next to me and takes the journal into her lap. Slowly, she flips through the pages.

"It says here . . ." Her eyes flit to me, her brow creasing. "It says here . . . *Fox will hunt Snake, always and forever.*"

"She always has." I try to sound offhand, but inside, my stomach twists. "Eleven lives, and I think she's killed me in all of them."

Amma taps the page with her finger. "What are you going to do then?"

I can see the fear in her tight shoulders, but her voice is so matter-of-fact. It's almost reassuring, like all I need to do is think things through, and I can survive this. "I'm on my way to Ambergris, the dock city," I say hesitantly. "I'm leaving Sempera." *That's why I needed to find you.*

Amma's lips tighten into a line. "Well, you know best, I suppose . . ." She sounds doubtful.

"You don't agree?"

"It's just . . ." She crosses her arms and uncrosses them again, a nervous habit that means she's thinking. "No disrespect to your papa, but that's what he did all these years, and it doesn't seem to have worked."

"I'll come back soon." I don't know if it's true, but I can't bear the thought of the alternative. "When I'm strong enough to face her."

"Seize the day, Jules, before it seizes you first." Amma's eyes are bright when she looks at me. I laugh; it's one of her favorite expressions, though it has a dark significance. Live now to the fullest, because when you're poor in Sempera, tomorrow may never come. "I suppose I'd better do my best to get you ready for that day. What do you need?"

I shake my head, thankful tears still in my eyes. She just gave me everything I needed and more, and I feel like her faith in me could fuel me all the way to Ambergris and onto Liam's ship. But of course that's not the case. "A little food, if you have some," I say, smiling like a fool. "And maybe I could stay here today . . . ?"

"Of course," Amma says, bending to gather the eggs. In the course of a few moments, she's assumed the brisk efficiency that she's always had, that's allowed her to take care of her sister all alone. "The soldiers already came through this morning, so I'd think you could stay as long as you need."

My chest aches with gratitude. "Thank you, Amma."

"I'm due at the butcher's in an hour, but I'll be able to sneak out after the morning stampede at the market. I'll come back with food as soon as I can. And maybe some soap and warm water, while I'm at it." She grins at me. "You look like a forest fairy, with mud for clothes."

The sound of my own laugh startles me. "Soap then, and I'll do my best."

Amma turns to look at me one last time before bustling out of the shed. Now that she's started smiling, it's like she can't stop, the edges of her lips tugging ceaselessly up.

"I'll be back before you know it."

Despite the cramped shed and the company of the chickens, I sleep well throughout the day for the first time since I left Everless, made whole again by Amma's presence and comforted by her talk. I don't have nightmares of the Sorceress, a girl on a dark plain or running through the woods, chasing me or being chased by me. Instead, my dreams are filled with the more pleasant memories of Crofton: playing in pollen-soaked fields with Amma in the summers and sitting at the kitchen table with Papa, the proud smile that he doesn't attempt to hide from me. In my dream, we are happy and content, warm, our little cottage redolent with the smoky smell of venison that I've brought home from a hunt, cooking over the fire.

Something is wrong though. Somewhere beyond the walls of our cottage, there is shouting, screaming. Papa tenses, the smile slipping from his pale face. The smell of smoke is too strong. There's a strange, acrid edge to it.

When I wake up in the cramped dark of Amma's shed, the smell is still there.

A feeling of unreality grips me as I sit up and look around. Amma's chickens are squawking in panic. The far side of the shed is outlined in flickering orange light, glowing fingers of it reaching through the cracks in the planks. I scramble to my feet and snatch up my bag just as a broken line of fire reaches through and alights the hay scattered across the floor.

For a moment, I am seven years old again, seven and rooted to the ground as the forge at Everless burns down around me.

But this time, there is no Papa to protect me, to carry me away. There's only me.

I don't give myself time to think. Clutching my bag, I turn around and kick the wall behind me, once, twice, three times until the rotting wood gives way, then yank open the hen coop so the hens can scurry out behind me, vanishing into the woods.

But any worry over losing Amma's chickens or burning down her shed vanishes as I turn around, following with my eyes the river of fire that has flowed into my hiding place.

Because Crofton is in flames.

2

Panic grips my heart. Smoke is everywhere.

In the near distance, fire blooms over the blunt edges of Crofton's rooftops. I run across Amma's grandfather's fields toward the smoking heart of the town, heedless of how I stumble over the old, loose cobblestones and mounds of freshly tilled earth. I need to find Amma. A picture forms of the squat butcher's shop where she separates meat from bone, the market stall where she and Alia spend their days.

All those people, all those flames, all that wood.

My lungs are raw, my limbs already aching, but I push on, leaping over the broken-down wall that separates Crofton proper from the outlying farms. I reach the main road, then race toward the huddle of buildings, vaguely noting the clusters of people flowing in the opposite direction. I could be recognized, but that seems like the least important thing in the world as I race into town. Orange light flickers across the sides of the pale houses, brilliant as earthbound lightning. Thick smoke blurs out the sky above.

Sorceress, help me find Amma, I think desperately, absurdly, a child's panic seizing control of my limbs. But *sorceress* is not a blessing anymore. It's a deadly curse.

Soon I'm forced to slow, heat searing my face, burning my eyes. All around me, the wooden buildings smoke. Down the road, the schoolhouse is already a heap of rubble. Smoldering debris clutters the streets, the remains of furniture and market stalls. I have to jump over burning pieces of this or that as I pick up a jog, looking around desperately for any sign of life. The road is narrow, the flames close, and my hair begins to curl with the heat. An odd smell hits my nose—I jerk my head up to see that only a few steps away, the timelender's shop is ablaze. I swear I can hear blood-iron bubbling as it melts.

A memory hits me of a garden party at Everless, a lifetime ago. A fire in the middle of it, contained in a bronze holder but reaching outward, fed by blood-iron, by hours and days and years, so that the flames burned hot in winter. A new wave of panic crashes against my skin.

How long will this fire burn?

"Help!" I cry out, though I can't see anyone who would hear me. "Amma!"

No human voice answers my shout, but the fire ripples suddenly, as if a breeze has swept through it, and sparks land on my sleeve. I yank my arm back—

And stop. There's something strange about the fire, even stranger than if it were only feeding on blood-iron. The flames, twisting yellow and red, shrink and grow with a rhythm as steady as breathing—controlled, constant, *alive*.

A crash behind me tears me from my thoughts, and I spin around. A man's just burst from a house some yards ahead. Sparks fly out the door behind him.

He sprints in my direction, the fire following him into the road, flowing from the building. It's not spreading as fire should but flows in his footsteps like a living thing, licking at his heels, advancing down the street in small, wild leaps. As he nears, flames inches behind, I remember a pack of coyotes I saw once when I hunted in the woods—half a dozen of them chasing down a wounded deer, yipping and jumping with something like joy as they closed in.

"What are you doing? Run!" The man grabs my arm as he passes, pulling me down the road, back in the direction of Amma's farm. The flames seem to fall back from the man when I'm beside him. I don't let myself think about what that means.

"What happened?" I gasp as we run, my voice hoarse from smoke and terror.

"Tenburn—" the man shouts, but he's cut short by a cough.

With his other hand, he clutches something to his chest: a small copper statue of the Sorceress, meant to bring luck. He goes on. "Something unnatural; it won't die. My wife ran for the Readeses' farm, the creek—" He squeezes the statue in his hand, a silent plea for aid.

Unnatural, I think, and then: *Caro*. This is her doing. It must be.

The Sorceress statue in the man's grip is unburned, perfect. Mocking me.

I grind my heel into the dirt, attempt to rip my arm from his hold. "Let me go, please, I have to go back. My friend—"

"Larys!" A woman jogs down the road toward us. Even with the dark smudges on her cheeks, I recognize her: Susana, the local farrier, who would often visit our cottage when she needed my father's blacksmithing knowledge. At first, her fearful eyes are fixed on Larys—but then her gaze falls to me, and I watch her face stretch into a mask of horror. She halts and stares, like I myself am made of flame.

"Snake," she spits. Her expression is unmistakable—hatred. The man, Larys, drops my elbow and jumps back, his arms wrapped protectively around himself. As if I might pounce and take a bite out of him, given the chance.

Before I can think, the woman's in front of me, her hand closing like a vise over my arm. "My brother is dead because of you. His home collapsed on him. You've brought this on us," she hisses, trembling in terror or rage. She glances rapidly left to right. Looking for someone else to tell. *"Murderer."*

And she shoves me backward, into a bed of flames.

I fling my arms out, but there's nothing to grab hold of. My ankle catches on what remains of a wall, and I fall back into fire. The pain is blinding, all-consuming—and then it's gone.

When my vision clears of its red haze, I see that the flames have retreated and re-formed into a ring that encircles me where I'm sprawled in the wreckage of a building. I can feel the heat from the flames, but the coal under me is cool. Larys and Susana stand in the street, gaping at me.

"Help!" Susana shouts suddenly. "Soldiers!"

"No, please—" I start, but the words die in my throat. My vision blurs with tears, making me feel like I'm in one of my dreams. I imagine the people I grew up with seeing me and screaming, *Snake, witch, liar, how dare you show your face here.*

You know me, I want to scream. *I'm just Jules Ember. Pehr's daughter. This is my home.*

But there is no *just* about me anymore. Caro's stories have spread through Sempera like a cloud of poison. I am the demon in a girl's body who murdered the Queen and Roan Gerling, enemy of the Sorceress, the crown of Sempera itself. I don't understand what Caro has wrought here, but I know that it is meant for me.

She will kill everyone in Sempera, if that's what it takes to break me.

Amma. With the thought of her, it's like the fire has jumped into my heart and ignited there.

I plant my hands in the coals and push to my feet, and Larys and Susana curse and turn tail like their worst nightmare is behind them. But I don't care anymore. Just like the moment when I saw Roan fall into Papa's hearth as a child, I don't think. I *can't* think. Something larger has taken hold of me, filling my chest, moving my limbs from the inside.

I turn and charge toward the flames, throwing myself deeper into Crofton as it burns.

Smoke coats my lungs like sand. My eyes burn with it, and it's becoming hard to see. But on the street, fire parts and flows near my feet like river water around a stone. It doesn't touch me as I pelt toward the center of town, toward the familiar narrow path that leads to Amma's butcher's shop. Maybe she ran out already and is safe outside the town, watching it crumble, fearing for me.

The creak and snap of burning wood fills the air around me. A clothesline on fire, its shirts and blankets transformed into blazing flags, falls in front of me, floating to the ground like leaves in autumn. Coughing and screaming Amma's name, I turn onto the street where she spends so many of her days.

And stop short.

Most of the buildings have already been reduced to ashes. This must be where the fire started. And the street—Amma's *shop*—is a smoking ruin, the tallest part of it rising just over the top of my head. The interior structure is exposed, the storage rooms open to the air, their jagged shapes shimmering faintly with embers.

A plume of smoke rises into the sky and, for a heartbeat, seems to take the shape of a slender girl. My delirious mind imposes features on the smoke: beautiful but with a sinister smile. *Caro.*

I hear her voice in my mind. *I will break your heart, Jules.*

For the longest moment, I can't move, can't think, can't breathe. Caro couldn't know. She couldn't possibly know that Amma was my friend. Could she?

Then a fresh surge of adrenaline floods my limbs, and I'm moving forward—through the heat and the thick smoke that permeates everything, billowing up in gusts of wind, searing my throat and skin, stinging my nose and eyes. I crash my way through the rubble of the butcher's shop, the snapped wooden beams and splintered workbenches, the charred remains of the room where I loitered for hours upon hours, exchanging gossip and stories with Amma. A curtain eaten away by flame, half of a broken teapot with its ceramic surface singed. No sign of people. Maybe Amma was able to escape.

Then a ceiling beam falls from its place with a heart-twisting crash. In the hole in the wall it leaves, I see something that makes my heart stop.

Amma sits slumped against a fallen beam, her eyes wide and unseeing.

"Amma," I breathe.

I rush to her and drop to my knees, taking her gently by the shoulders. Her chest is still. There are no burn marks on her skin—but her side is smeared with blood. My eyes fly to a streak of deep purple hardly visible on her filthy red-and-black-smeared dress. The unmistakable color of mava dye, left behind by a royal soldier's weapon, and—

The handle of a dagger jutting out of her back. Though the polished silver is smeared with blood, I recognize it immediately: it belongs to Ivan Tenburn, commander of the guards at Everless.

Caro has already started to make good on her promise.

Rage at Caro rushes up in me, and with it, power. I fling out my hands, grasping at the threads of time, asking it not just to stop but to unwind, turn back, just like I did to save Roan Gerling when we were children at Everless. *Save Amma*, beats a rhythm in my head.

Slowly, the smoke around me billows inward and shrinks toward the ground. The gray churns, swirling in ways unconnected to the breeze. In the distance, I think I see some of the flames flicker and die. The pool of blood seems to shrink, flow back into Amma.

But then a deep, sick sense of wrongness fills me, a soul-deep nausea that makes my knees go weak. My body shudders as the strength drains rapidly out of me, and before I even realize I'm sinking, I'm on my hands and knees in the rubble, heaving with sobs, ash-black tears dripping down my face.

And now, I do scream: in grief, in frustration, in rage.

The ruined walls of the butcher's shop crash down, burying half of Amma's body in twisted wreckage. Behind them, in the now-exposed alley, a dozen soldiers in deep purple royal uniforms stand in formation. Their faces are covered in cloth masks.

"Seize her!" one shouts.

I drop my head as they close in, limp as a doll, the strength gone out of me. I barely notice something flash silver by my hand—a butcher knife glinting next to Amma's loosened fist. I close my fingers around the handle and take it up my sleeve just before the masked soldiers descend.

They haul me from Crofton. The Alchemist of legend, bloody-handed and hollowed out with grief. My toes drag over the ground and leave trails in the dirty rubble. Everything swirls around me as if I'm in a dream, the soldiers' words sounding like they're coming from the other side of a pane of glass. The only thing I can glean for sure is that I am being taken to the palace, Shorehaven. To Caro.

A faint voice in my mind whispers, *Fight them.* If I tried to muster the magic in my veins, to summon the Alchemist, I might stop time long enough to slip their hold and run.

But I don't. Because I know by the way they wrap chains around me—tight, tripled around my arms and waist as if I had the strength of ten people—that the soldiers are afraid of me.

26

They don't touch me, so they don't find the knife. Their fear hushes my mind even as they toss me in a metal-walled carriage and close me in darkness. Amma's death mask is seared onto the pitch-black canvas inside.

Caro took her from me, even if she didn't wield the blade herself. She razed Crofton to the ground. She reduced my home to a pile of ash.

Now it is my turn to invade hers.

Seize the day, Amma whispers in my ear.

I will not fight. Not yet. Not until the soldiers take me to Shorehaven.

3

The carriage door has a small rectangular opening, subdivided by rusty iron bars. For the next three days, it becomes my window to the world. The soldiers cart me across Sempera—avoiding the towns, keeping to the woods or the plains. I imagine the mob that would descend on the prison carriage carrying the Queen's murderer.

The soldiers shove food and water through the slot, but I scarcely eat. There's no room for anything else in my body but anger and a low, constant dread. And a growing sense, as we go farther east, toward the rising sun, that something is aligning within me, as if the Alchemist buried inside me knows the way to the palace on the shore—and longs to be taken there.

After two sunrises, in the foggy morning light, the sliver of the outside world that I can see changes: the woods and plains give way to low, rolling hills, scattered with scrubs and sand. The roads get wider and smoother. Where our path converges with another, there are suddenly more covered carts heading in the same direction as we are, each brimming with crates of apples or bleating livestock. Even the air is different—laced with the scent of brine, heavy and buzzing with something that feels like power.

We are close to Shorehaven. To the Sorceress.

It burns my blood to think of my things—the leather-bound journal especially—bouncing along in a soldier's bag. Though they keep their voices down, I sometimes hear the guards speaking through the metal walls of the carriage.

"I don't like this," a female voice says at one point. "Bringing her to Shorehaven during the coronation. The palace will be crawling with silly nobles wanting to get a look at her—"

"We're almost there," a male voice cuts in. "One more day and she's the Queen's problem, out of our hands." He chuckles darkly. "I need the blood-iron. My wife is expecting a little one any day now."

Their voices wash over me until they stop making sense, the words carrying no more meaning than the rhythmic stamp of their footsteps. The hours stretch on. Whenever the company stops to let me out to relieve myself, a full half-dozen women soldiers trail my footsteps, their daggers and rifles out. Their wide eyes and trembling hands give me a faint, perverse satisfaction.

They're right to be afraid of me—they all are—even if it's not for the reasons they think.

Unease blooms in me at the thought. Since when have I delighted in others' fear?

On the third night after the fire in Crofton—after the death of my oldest friend—when the moonless dark is bleeding into dawn and I think I'm going to explode from the anger roiling under my skin, I hear it: the sound of waves breaking against cliffs. I pull myself up to the window, ignoring the pins and needles racing up my legs, and look out just as the carriage rolls over a narrow wooden bridge crossing two huddling cliffs.

The sea is at the bottom of a hundred-foot drop. Glorious and unending, the ocean stretches, black and calm in the distance, white and frothy near the shores. It makes my breath catch—I'd always felt that there was a cage around Sempera, walling us off from other lands that I've only read about in the pages of books. Here it is: all that water, trapping us here to eat one another alive.

From Liam's map and the cliffs flanking the water in the distance, I know that this is a cove and not even the ocean proper. But it's as close as I've ever come to the sea, at least in this life. I can't help but stare—first at the water, and then, at the shape that looms at the end of the road. From a crown of rocks, Shorehaven, Sempera's palace, rises up from the cliffs, outshining the moon.

The castle of pale stone is dripping with light. It looks

strangely natural, beautiful in its asymmetry, as if it's been pulled from the cliffs that surround it. The sight of it sends a fierce pain through my chest. I've never seen the palace before. Of course I haven't. But when my eyes travel across its hundreds of windows lit up like a chandelier against the night sea, I realize that's not quite right. I know the castle, know that if I draw nearer it will reveal itself to have strands of ore veining its marbled sides, along with coal and gold and rubies and sapphires so subtly woven into the stone that you scarcely notice until the sun sets or rises. Then, the castle appears to be afire.

The memory rises to the surface suddenly, like when a sudden familiar scent plunges me back into the memories of childhood. I have been here, to Shorehaven. Suffered here. Not as Jules—as the Alchemist.

The images, sounds, feelings barrel through me: Caro had captured me. Was keeping me prisoner in the castle dungeons. Then, as now, she tried to break me. I remember blades, fire, pain. I pull the collar of my shirt up over my face so the soldiers don't hear the half gasp, half sob that I can't hold in.

The smell of smoke from Crofton still clings to my clothes, even after days of travel. It anchors me to the moment, reminds me what I have left to do. Amma is dead; Roan is dead; Papa is dead; but there are still people living, people who Caro might cut down to get to me.

She's the Queen's problem, the soldier said. Ina's face takes form in my mind as she was the last time I saw her, smiling and happy, before I found out the truth about Caro and the Queen. And about Ina—that we were born together to a woman named Naomi in a town called Briarsmoor, in the midst of fire and screaming. I learned she was my twin, just as everything fell to pieces. Ina must think— My *sister* must think me a murderer now.

Unless—would she believe me, as Amma did?

Together, could we destroy Caro, dismantle her invisible reign?

I take a deep breath, trying to stay clearheaded, to temper the rush of hope that cuts through my grief and anger.

As we get closer, a larger, main road comes into view, packed with carriages that crawl along like shiny black beetles. The procession is illuminated by oil lamps hanging on the end of the tall iron poles that line the road. These must be the nobles of Sempera, arriving for Ina's coronation. Is Liam somewhere within those walls?

For a second, I see his face—his midnight-dark eyes, his lips parted as he breathes a word. *Alchemist.*

The name jolts me. Because even in my daydreams, that's what he says. Not *Jules.* If neither of us had ever learned the truth, if I was just another farmer's daughter from Crofton, would he have even learned my name?

I shove the thought away. It doesn't matter. It can't matter—not with Caro hunting everyone I care about. I conjure Ina's face instead, intelligent eyes in a pale freckled face, framed by cropped dark hair, familiar to me before I knew why. She's the one I need to find. Assuming I can escape the guards.

Rather than joining the glowing parade of carriages streaming in through the front gate, ours turns sharply along one of the narrower roads that spread from the main path like spokes on a wheel. I stand by the gated window, my fingers wrapped around the cool bars.

The palace is ringed on its land-facing side by a seamless, pearl-colored wall—deceptively low, but smooth and uniform as metal. Above, I can see golden light through glass, flowered balconies lit up with strings of lanterns. Below, enormous waves batter at the base of the cliffs, their spray almost reaching to the lowest of the windows that dot the palace sides. The ocean water leaves the stone wet and shining.

I repeat what I need to do to keep myself calm as the palace grows outside. One way or another, prisoner or free, I need to find Ina. Stop Caro.

I touch the butcher knife still tucked into my sleeve, as if I could draw strength from it.

The small, dark shapes of guards pace along the top of the wall, most watching the main gates. Even above the sound of the waves, I can hear the laughter and joyous chorus of rich, fluted voices. To the left, the smooth palace wall slopes off with the ground, so that there's nothing between the palace and the ocean but a sheer drop—a height of at least thirty or forty paces. Below, huge, sharp boulders poke treacherously up through the waves like the metal-gray teeth of a sea monster, jaw gaping open to swallow the palace whole.

Fear crashes over me as we pass through a narrow gate set into the northern wall. The gate shuts behind us with a groan, shutting out the sound of the waves. Quiet falls, broken only by swells of distant music and wind swishing through trees.

I think of Amma's burned butcher's shop, the forlorn shape of her body. Anger and grief surge through me, pushing down the fear as we roll into a moonlit garden.

The doors open, spilling moonlight over me as thick as blood. Leather-gloved hands reach in. I scramble out before the soldiers can take hold, swallowing a whimper when my legs cramp and tremble. I collapse into a heap on the cool grass. Beyond the wary soldiers surrounding me, the garden blooms with thickets of flowers and slender trees. I peer up, surveying the glittering spread of windows, hoping to find some clue of where Ina might be.

And then— "Hello, Jules," someone says.

My scream freezes in my throat.

Caro stands deeper in the garden, still as a statue. Her face is in shadow, but I would know her anywhere. How she stands, the way her dark hair whips in the breeze. I want to back away, but it's like my body has frozen, the air turned to ice in my lungs.

She makes a gesture, and the soldiers file away out the gate we came in, as quick and silent as mice trying to avoid capture. One hands her my bag before departing. She opens it and withdraws the journal, which she pinches between her fingers before flinging it to the grass. Anger blooms in me, but I remain still. Papa died for that journal.

"Jules," she says again, her soft words carrying across the space between us, wrapping around me like she's whispering in my ear. "It's good to see you." She steps forward, stopping just feet from me, and withdraws a long dagger from her belt. A shiver runs over my skin, which tightens, expecting a blow.

But Caro doesn't strike. Worse—she smiles with a languid, luxurious movement that seems to stretch seconds into minutes, like a noble sipping blood-iron from a steaming teacup.

She offers me the knife, handle first, her fingers delicate on the blade.

Moonlight catches her face, so familiar from my brief days at Everless—and, somewhere deep in my mind, from centuries of engraved memories. She's smiling as if we are schoolgirl friends reunited after a few days apart. Her teeth shine in the dark.

I rise to my feet as steadily as I can and pull Amma's knife from my sleeve instead of taking the one she offers me. She shrugs and turns it around in her hands, her fingers closing lightly around the handle.

She's not afraid of me.

Still, I brandish the blade between us, hoping Caro can't see how my knife hand trembles. The knife isn't what Caro should fear. I call out to the time in my blood, will it to respond, and then gasp in almost pain as it tears out of me—more time magic than I've ever wielded before, making the earth beneath my feet tremble.

And yet—nothing freezes. The air in the garden seems to shudder, but time doesn't stop, doesn't freeze. My blood shivers in my veins. Something is holding me back, preventing me from stopping or even slowing time.

Caro doesn't react except to sigh, "Oh, Jules."

"How are you doing that?" I grit out, furious.

Her laughter rises like bells in the night, mixing in with the faint melody from inside the palace that falls around us, steady as rain. Caro takes another step toward me, close enough that I can reach out and touch her. "You left a few year-coins behind at Everless. You shouldn't be so careless with your blood."

An involuntary shudder passes through me. I'd completely forgotten leaving the coins behind on that awful night she engineered an accusation of theft from the Gerling vault, and manipulated me into selling time for her. When I had tried to feed her my blood-iron, she couldn't consume it; it re-formed and stuck in her throat. That was how she knew, finally, that I was the Alchemist, and not Ina.

Caro seems to read the memory on my face. "I found a way

to consume it, which has had interesting effects to say the least," she says, a smile crawling across her face. "You consumed my whole heart, Jules. Surely you wouldn't begrudge me a little of your—"

"*Enough*," I growl. The knife handle is hard and cold and rough beneath my white-knuckled fingers, a reminder of what I've lost, why I'm here. In one heartbeat, I drop the attempt at time-bending and lash out at Caro with the knife, a wide swing.

Immediately I regret it and back away as Caro ducks, her own knife sweeping through the air. Not rough and scorched like Amma's knife, but jeweled and gleaming and sickeningly sharp. "I thought you were above trying to fight me, Jules. You've failed in every life. What makes you think you can succeed now?"

Because Amma told me I was strong, I think wildly—but the truth of Caro's words cut me, making me feel impossibly small next to the vaulting towers of Shorehaven. In front of me, Caro's power radiates in waves. I try not to show my fear. "I stole your heart, didn't I?"

I'm pleased to see her jaw clench in anger.

"And even diminished, I beat you easily," she growls. "And when I break you, I will take what's left of it back, even though you've wasted it on"—she pauses, eyes raised to the blue-dark sky as if she's remembering—"*eleven* pathetic lives. I won't kill you now, Jules. And you shouldn't be so bold with me, considering you've only one life left." She sneers. "Instead, I'll hollow you

37

out and make you my puppet, just like I did the poor late Queen. All of Sempera will see what I can do with time until I can break your heart for good. Then I'll dispose of Ina, and Sempera will see what a queen worthy of her throne can do. What else could I bind to their blood, Alchemist?"

The words drop ice down my spine. Bind something else to blood? What could she mean—what else could be taken from us, from our veins? Fear makes me slow. When Caro lunges fiercely at me, I only barely dodge her blade.

"But I was hoping we could talk for a bit first," she says conversationally. "I've missed you. And we oughtn't disturb the coronation guests."

"You killed my friend," I hiss, a tide of fury rising inside me and pushing the words out. "You burned my home."

"I had to bring you here, didn't I? I couldn't let you keep lurking in the shadows." Caro scoffs, but her eyes gleam with something like hurt. Then the hurt is replaced with a beatific smile that lights up her face. "Were you there? Did you see it?"

"I saw it," I retort, slashing out again with the knife. I try to recall the sparring lessons Roan passed on to me when we were children, but it just calls up a wave of rage and loss. Caro dodges my swing without breaking my gaze.

"We can do wonderful things together when we combine our powers, Jules."

Her words burn inside me. I try to ignore them, to push them away—because what does it matter now what happened five centuries ago, facing her, knives clutched in both our hands? "Amma did nothing wrong," I hiss. "You should have left her out of this. Everyone in Crofton."

"They don't matter." Her voice is wild and joyful again. "They're ants next to us, Jules. Everyone is."

A combination of rage and horror makes my reply stick in my throat. I lunge forward at Caro again, raising the knife high.

She whirls away from me, her own knife a flash of silver in the air. "I know you better than anyone else," she almost sings. "You're just as impulsive as ever."

As she speaks, she dances out of the way of all my blows, her movements quick and graceful and efficient. She doesn't seem to be trying to hurt me, but I realize that we're closer together now than before. Caro is luring me to her—*just like she lured me here*, I think bitterly, foolishly. A storm of frustration crystallizes into movement, and I lunge forward with a grunt—and trip to my knees when Caro glides out of my path.

"Ina cries for him every night," she whispers, a malicious curl in her voice. "He wasn't worth a day-iron, and yet she *weeps* over that unfaithful Gerling boy."

The memory of Roan's blood burns behind my eyes, the shape of Amma's body crumpled in rubble. Papa too, and others, a sudden chorus of ghosts in my head. For a second, the grief feels bigger than me, like it's going to burst through my skin. I spring forward, a wordless snarl escaping my lips—

And bury my knife in Caro's side.

She doesn't cry out, but gasps, as if I've slapped her. Blood spills out of the wound. Triumph and shock and disgust crash through me. I let go of the knife and fall back, my breath coming fast. The world spins around me, but one thing stays in focus: the crude handle of Amma's butcher knife, protruding from the lacy fabric of Caro's dress.

Caro still grips her own knife, but her hand falls to her side, useless and slack. It's too dark to see much—but the blood shines like black oil in the moonlight, welling up around the blade. I can't tear my eyes from it.

"Jules," Caro whispers, touching a hand to the wound. Her smile is gone. Her voice is small and vulnerable and makes something twist painfully in my chest.

Then the Sorceress falls to her knees with a soft, pathetic thud.

I twitch, instinct telling me to go to her, to help her, but I steel myself. *No, no, no.* The clever handmaid I befriended at Everless was just an invention, a mask. Caro is the Sorceress. She killed Roan Gerling. She killed Amma. She razed Crofton to the ground. That's not changed by her ragged breathing, the blood dripping over her fingers, and the pained curve of her mouth like a gash across her face.

Her face. Something in it is wrong . . . something in it is

changing, subtly, in the light of the moon. I take a step closer. Lines are spreading over her chin, cheeks, forehead. Her eyes are sinking deeper into their sockets, becoming wreathed in violet shadows. Her skin is even paler than usual, becoming the color of parchment, then bone.

With a shock I realize that her black hair is turning silver, like the moonlight is a physical thing clinging to her and painting her braid, dripping down until the white sweeps over her shoulder. She lets out a keening moan and wraps her arms around herself.

Something makes me close the distance between us in two quick strides. Without knowing why, I drop my hand and press it to her chest, over her heart.

Or where her heart should be. Because there, at least, the tales are true.

Her skin is freezing through her dress, as if there is a lump of ice buried inside her, sending out, instead of a beat, waves of cold that immediately begin to numb my palm. Cold emanates through me, to my fingertips, which meet the skin of Caro's chest, the shiver traveling up my arm until I swear I can feel a claw of ice trace the undersides of my ribs and slowly encircle my own heart. The chill is cold as death. I gasp, then breathe out a cloud of frost. It hangs in the air between us, fine as a veil.

Though I've heard the story of the Sorceress's heart count-less times, I *feel* it now. On my skin. In my bones. Inside my chest. *I carry the Sorceress's heart.*

For a moment, my pulse pushes me closer to her, as if the heart imprisoned behind my ribs is vying to be back where it belongs.

"I remember this," she says faintly, more to herself than to me. Her hand, cold as bone, closes over mine.

Horrified, I look into her face. It's still morphing before my eyes, delicate lines fanning out from the corners of her eyes and mouth—fine against the furrows of pain carved into her brow, but growing deeper and deeper as I watch.

Then—

A violent tug at my core. I slam my eyes shut and hear the world remade around me: a single, quiet shout of noise. Light, even behind my closed eyelids.

And smell—wet cedar, incense smoke, tang of blood.

Even before I force my eyes open, I know I'm no longer on the palace grounds. I'm somewhere—somewhere else.

The floor under my knees is damp, hard. The moon has been swallowed too, replaced by a dim candle. Caro is in my arms, her mouth open in a scream. The sound is unbearable.

Except it's not Caro's scream—it's mine. The candle, the walls around us, Caro's form, all are frozen in time. I register that her dress is a filthy blue, not the midnight lace-furrowed silk that my knife tore through.

Then I'm reeling again. The next breath, I'm in the court-yards at Shorehaven once more.

Caro is in my arms, her eyes closed. But the blood that spilled over the fabric of her dress is retreating back into its wound, the gray shrinking from the black of her hair.

She stirs. Opens her eyes and looks up at me. Alive, and angry.

4

I shove the revived Caro away from me and scramble to my feet. The world smears around me. She stares at me, her eyes bright and dancing, and pushes herself to her knees. Nausea folds my stomach in half. In one motion, Caro closes her hand around the knife and pulls it out from her side, then lets it fall into the grass.

The sight of the blood on the blade is too much; it makes me dizzy. I look around, backing away from Caro as I scold myself for believing a simple blade would kill the Sorceress of legend. I should remember that I have never been lucky.

I can't kill her—

Ina. I must find Ina.

The guards brought me inside the palace gates when they discarded me at Caro's feet. I sprint for the closest entrance into Shorehaven, an archway leading into a narrow corridor, not letting myself look at Caro, though I can see her out of the corner of my eye, still lurching to her feet.

Each step jogs my churning insides, but I push on, tearing through what's clearly a servants' corridor. The hall curves gently to my right, mirroring the outside wall, and to my left I can see a bit of staircase through a stone archway. I veer in that direction, hoping that if Caro follows me she won't know if I've gone up or down. I choose *up* without thinking and pelt up the stairs, one floor, two floors, three. Soon my lungs and legs are burning fiercely, but adrenaline, and the image of Ina's face in my mind, keep me going.

Desperately, I recall any distant memory of Shorehaven, the knowledge that I've been here before. I know this place. So where would a young queen go while she waited to be crowned?

A pair of faint, low voices rises up to the vaulted ceilings— someone else on the staircase. Whether they're guests or guards or servants, I'm not sure. They'll hear my heavy footsteps, so I force myself to slow and climb the stairs at a normal speed. My heart is thudding so loudly in my ears, I can scarcely hear the chatter of servants in the hallways or the rustle of silk skirts as noblewomen are ushered into the palace.

When I get to a landing, I have to decide whether to keep climbing or go down another servants' corridor. This time, it's not my buried memories that guide my steps—it's my ordinary memories of Ina at Everless. How she chafed at the guards

45

outside her chambers and lied smoothly to the Gerling lackeys who wouldn't let her outside the gates.

If I know her, she will want to be somewhere alone. A tower, perhaps, as far away from the guards as possible.

Up.

I force my thoughts away from the coldness of Caro's chest. I pass a few gold-suited servants on my way up the stairs and through the narrow corridors where my feet take me—but they look almost as harried as I do and don't give me a second glance.

No guards. A small voice in me whispers that this is wrong— *it's another trap*—but I can't stop to consider, afraid that I'll look over the railing and see Caro's eager face looking back up at me. My feet take me up and up and finally down a window-lined hall, to a set of double doors at its end.

I push into an airy, high-windowed chamber, lit by a few lamps and much moonlight. Through the multicolored glass I see the gleaming slopes and spires of Shorehaven's roof, and beyond that, the glitter of the sea. Inside the room, there are stacks of books, cloth dolls, clothes scattered all over like flower petals.

But then I see her, and my heart contracts in shock.

Ina.

The new Queen—my sister—stands in front of a tall mirror, her back to me, powdering her face. The memory slams into me of the night I entered the old Queen's chambers convinced that she was the Sorceress, and seeing her making herself up like this, as pale as a ghost in the mirror. But Ina is not the old Queen. Not a shell, not doomed.

Pulse racing, I take a step into the room, eyes fixed on Ina. Taking in her slumped shoulders, her dull eyes, the way she moves, like every motion costs her. My friend.

My sister. Born to the same mother in Briarsmoor the day time splintered there, taken by the Queen and Caro to Shorehaven while Papa spirited me away. It hits me suddenly that now, she's the only family I have left.

Ina meets my gaze in the mirror. The powder slips from her fingers, hitting the polished vanity and bursting into a cloud of shimmering dust around her. Ina whips around, her eyes flying wide.

For a sliver of a moment, I think she's going to run and embrace me—I see the impulse flit across her open, trusting face—but then an icy-cold hatred floods into the white shock of her eyes. Her hand shoots to a silver bell sitting under her mirror. Her fingers hover over it. Ready to bring guards swarming.

"Ina." I stare at her, my mind slow, my mouth dry. "Please, just listen to me."

Ina moves slowly, almost as if she's in pain. She takes up the bell from the vanity as well as a silver dagger that I hadn't previously seen, and rises from her cushioned chair.

"Caro told me that you were captured." Her voice is calmer than I expected but colder than the coldest, darkest winter day

I ever experienced in Crofton, even when Papa and I were near starving.

My friend. My queen. My sister. Glaring at me with something like hate in her eyes. But it's the pain buried there, only half hidden beneath her fury, that I cannot bear.

"I'm sorry," I whisper without meaning to. A hoarse plea for mercy, for understanding.

"Why?" The word comes out in a hiss. "I know you've had a hard life, Jules. I can understand why you might have hated my mother, or the Gerlings. But I never did anything to you. Roan *helped* you." Her voice is shaking, but her dagger is steady. "I trusted you."

"Ina," I say brokenly, raising my hands palm out. "Ina, I didn't—"

I mean to tell her that I didn't kill Roan. But before I can get the rest of the sentence out, Amma's face flashes behind my eyes. The way she'd embraced me in the shed, and then dead on the burned ground of the butcher's shop, her blood pooling around her.

I convinced Amma to trust me. She believed me. And she was still taken from me.

My voice dies in my throat in a way that has nothing to do with magic.

Ina stalks closer to me, seeming to radiate cold. I can feel tears start to prick at my eyes. "I only ever tried to be kind to you, and you ruined my life. Caro always said people would take advantage of me for kindness. I should have listened." She stops a single pace away from me, the dagger held tightly at her side. Her fingers curl around the handle so tightly that the blade seems to be a part of her: a single, sharpened claw.

One tear, then another, tracks down my face, but I don't wipe them away. I didn't kill Roan or her mother, I'm not the monster she thinks I am—but that doesn't make her words any less true. They are dead because of me, both of them. And Ina is alone with Caro. With Caro, who's probably coming up the tower steps as we speak.

I swallow the speech I'd prepared for Amma. It's safer if Ina believes a lie.

Summoning an image of Caro, of Ivan, of the interchangeable Gerling faces that stole every blood-iron from my papa's belt, I twist my face into a mask of anger.

"Your mother and the Gerlings ruined my life," I spit. The old anger swirls in me, awakened by the barbed words on my tongue. "They killed my father just for stepping inside Everless. But only after they couldn't starve us, along with our entire village."

She hasn't yet mastered the art of hiding the feelings that cross her face. Even through my tears, I recognize them—confusion, anger, shock, anger again. Each one lands like a blow as I grope for words. Even now I want to take back what I've said, search-ing for something to say that will show Ina the truth without putting her in danger from Caro.

But there's nothing, no part of the truth that will keep her safe. I reach and reach, but there's nothing there.

"The Queen was a blight on Sempera, siphoning the blood of the poor. What are our years worth to you? To your mother? To the Gerlings? I watched people *die* while you and Roan gorged yourselves on feasts and the blood-irons of the starving," I choke, sputter, but I push on. "The Queen deserved to die."

Ina rings the bell.

The loud, clear chime cuts straight into me. I hear footsteps, many of them, thundering down the hallway outside. A high female voice cuts through the stampede with a shouted command.

Even though I told her I was the monster she was expecting, my throat clogs up with shock and betrayal as she moves forward—with more deadly grace than I knew her to have at Everless—and presses the tip of the dagger against my chest. But I meet her stare, longing to communicate the truth of me, of *us*, with only a glance. Remembering the silent language Amma and her sister kept between them as lovingly as a secret.

The muscles around Ina's mouth tighten. Confusion and wariness war on her face. The silence between us stretches, more deafening than the onslaught of footsteps on the other side of the door. I stare at her, tears trickling down, torn between pushing her away and betraying the truth in spite of all reason.

Finally, just as the door opens and shouting guards pour in—Caro's skirts swirling in the midst of them, a spot of deadly calm in the center of the storm—Ina draws the dagger away from my chest.

Then something strikes me hard in the temple, and everything goes dark.

When I come to, the shape of Caro's face swims slowly into view, her sharp features and green-glass eyes, as lovely as a poisonous vine. For a moment, I imagine that I'm back at Everless, collapsed in a bed with her after a long night, like the day she, Ina, and I went to Laista and drank madel to celebrate Ina's impending wedding to Roan. And for the space of a heartbeat, I feel happy. I feel safe.

Then the pain comes back to me, and awareness with it. The rest of the room clarifies around us. Tall windows show a star-spattered sky, reflected in the mirrors that circle us, so that everything seems to be silver and stars.

Still in Ina's room, then. But Ina is gone.

Caro—her face young and lovely again, no sign that I put a dagger in her side—is above me, cradling me in her arms. With one arm she supports me, half upright, and with the other hand she's trailing a finger across my brow. A chill goes through me. Caro holds her hand out away from herself, examining with fascination the blood on her fingertips, turned black in the starlight.

She whispers a word in a language I don't understand—and flames spring from her fingertips, flaring bright like candles, and then blink out before I can move, leaving her hands clean. Like the flame is feeding on my blood.

Dimly, I think how foolish I've been. I thought I was becoming a match for her, with my paltry control over time. But her powers are so far beyond my understanding. From the wild look in her eyes, I'm not sure even Caro herself understands them.

"Stop toying with me," I hiss through my dizziness. "If you're going to kill me, kill me."

Caro freezes, then tilts her face down toward mine.

"We've been over this, Jules," she says, and despite the eerie expression on her face her voice sounds normal, low and musical as always. A bit impatient. "I will never hurt you until I must."

"Until you can break my heart," I grit out.

"Exactly." Her eyes fix on me. "Now, tell me—"

A sudden, distant swell of music cuts off her words. It's such a foreign sound here, in the midst of this horror, that it takes me a moment to make sense of it. String instruments, many of them, muffled through walls. Distant drums that make the floor tremble, so slightly that I probably wouldn't have noticed if I were on my feet.

Caro draws in her breath, her forehead creasing in frustration. "The coronation. I'm afraid I must leave you for now, Jules."

She just reaches into her dress and brings out a vial full of what looks like brown salt. Before I can move or think, she holds it up to my nose—and when I draw breath, a kind of shimmering fog steals over me, sapping what little strength's left in my body. Then a sharp finger of pain runs down the center of my scalp, as if my mind has cleaved in two.

I can't resist at all as Caro slides me off her lap; I flop to the floor like a rag doll.

Through the throbbing pain, I hear Caro's voice, high and sharp and confident, call down the stairs. I can't tell what she's saying, but a moment passes and then she's gone, her footsteps receding away, her voice blending into the orchestra.

Two billowy, dark shapes approach—I see, through my blurred vision, two palace guards coming cautiously toward me.

I can't fight back as they pick me up by my arms and fasten my hands behind my back with a length of roughly hewn rope. I attempt to cry out, but I can only manage to mangle the words. It's as if Caro's cast a heavy shadow over my mind, hiding what I need to defend myself.

It doesn't matter, I think miserably, *because who would come to help a murderer?*

Liam's face flashes in my mind. *I should have listened to him*, I think dimly. I should have escaped to Ambergris. Now our plan is ruined.

My mumbled speech seems to give the guards confidence. Soon, they're hauling me to the door, down the stairs, down a hall; whatever drug Caro forced me to breathe makes my limbs weak and useless. All I can do is try to remember what paths we follow—down stone staircase after staircase, through halls that grow darker and narrower as we go—but there's a persistent whisper in my head that sounds half like Caro's voice and half like my own, and it asks, *Why bother? Why try? You'll never escape her.*

Even that falls silent as the guards shove me inside a cramped cell, then slam the door shut behind me.

5

In my dreams, I become a snake, my long muscles coated with scales that gleam like emeralds. I slip through darkness and shadows that reach out long fingers and try to catch me. Gold races past. A slender form, amber eyes. *Fox,* I think, my thoughts whittled down to nothing but flashes of sensation and feeling. Freezing air across my body, light ahead as the fox looks back. Fear, terrible fear, and a noise behind me, like the howling of a great wind, or a hound baying, its jaws snapping and snarling at the heels of its prey, getting closer—

Fear jolts me awake. At least I think I'm awake; it's too dark to be sure. I blink. My eyes focus on a strip of light cutting through blackness. The glow is coming from under my cell door. Adrenaline courses through me, left over from the nightmare. That awful howling.

I push myself up on my elbows, trying to shake the dream away. I blink again as my eyes adjust. These must be the dungeon cells inside the guts of Sempera's palace—the ground beneath me is the same ivory stone as everything else but dimmed by dust and grime. In the near darkness, I can make out tracks worn in the floor where prisoners have paced back and forth. My limbs cramp painfully as I lever myself into a sitting position.

It's quiet, but the quiet isn't absolute. If I listen hard, I can hear faint voices outside the door, see the light broken up when guards pace in front of my cell.

Time passes, slips through my fingers like sand. I stare out the small opening in the cell door for hours, willing my eyes to focus on its rectangle of light. I count the motes of dust that swirl in and out of shadow. I devour the guards' every word, each more muffled by the slab of wood that separates us. I try to hear the lilts of their accents and guess where each is from. Anything to focus my thoughts after whatever drug Caro made me inhale. Anything not to think about the glint of Caro's blade, Ina's ice-cold stare and the way her eyes have changed now that the light has gone from them.

When a new shadow disrupts the glow that spills over the floor of my cell and stops there, my whole body tenses, alert.

"You two are missing quite the feast downstairs," an unfamiliar female voice says. "You might as well go down, this one isn't going anywhere."

"Captain," one guard says, his voice gruff but nervous. "We have orders from Lady Caro to guard her here."

"She's dangerous," the other man adds, kicking the door with his boot. "Tried to go for the Queen with her bare hands. Saw it with my own eyes."

Gently, using an elbow to prop myself up, I shift toward the door to listen better. I feel anything but dangerous—but the drug seems to be wearing off, my senses returning, even blearily.

A woman—the captain?—cracks the door open as much as a chain will allow and peers into the cell. She cuts her eyes at me, appraising me critically. Then her face changes. She widens her eyes at me, mouths something.

I stare at her, bewildered. She repeats the silent words, and this time I recognize the shape of the words.

Stop time.

My mind is still dull, aching, but that means I don't pause to question why this captain is telling me to use my magic. My heart is beating fast. It's easy to press my palms to the floor and will time to slow around me. In my haze, I can almost imagine strands of it tunneling out from my hands, skirting the woman and winding up around the two men. They still, two windup dolls whose mechanisms have wound down.

I can't hold it for long, weak as I am. But I don't have to. The woman crosses the hall and pinches out the torches' still flames.

Her movements are efficient. Then she returns to her place, just as I lose my hold on time.

The world speeds up. The flames gutter out in the span of a heartbeat.

Dark falls, and she cries out in passable fear. Then there are two thuds, and then larger thumps. The second guard has time to cry out—a short, strangled noise—before he goes down too with a massive thud on the floor. My breath catches. I hear the sizzle of the torch being relit.

The woman's steps sound on the stone floor, and my cell door creaks open.

I squint against the light to see a Shorehaven guard with a long braid down her back, in the same uniform as my captors. I don't recognize her. As the woman stands there, breathing hard, someone else emerges from the shadows at the other end of the hall.

It's Liam.

I almost think it's a hallucination caused by whatever Caro gave me in Ina's room, but as he hurries into the cell, I know he's real. Liam, who told me I was the Alchemist, who spirited me away from Caro at Everless. I could never dream up that precise, efficient way he moves, the way a few locks of hair escape from their queue to curl around his face. He's paler and more drawn than he was at Everless, but polished in a bottle-green military waistcoat, gleaming with gold buttons and epaulets. The Gerling insignia glitters on his breast.

He nods at the captain, who vanishes silently down the hall, her braid the last piece of her to disappear around the darkened corner.

The old fear—of the Gerlings and especially of Liam—stirs in me as he crosses the cell in three long steps. I draw back a little. I'd known he might be here at Shorehaven, but that's entirely different from his standing in front of me, right now.

I swallow. Though my vision is still bleary, fraying at the edges, his face stands out against the wash of light. His eyes flicker from remoteness to relief to fear.

"Jules," he says, and it sounds like a breath he was waiting to exhale. "You're alive."

The last time I saw him, he helped me escape from the Everless dungeons and sent me on my way, with instructions to meet his unbound friend in Ambergris. He saved my life. He didn't have to, but he did. He crouches in front of me now and takes me in: my ragged clothes, the wound seeping at my hairline. Heat pours off him, and concern with it. "You never made it to Ambergris, like we'd planned. I thought—maybe bleeders . . ."

I cast my eyes down again. It hadn't occurred to me that he'd be worried. "I'm fine."

Show nothing.

There was a reason I left Everless without saying more than *thank you.* I scarcely know Liam—but I scarcely knew Roan either, and Caro still killed him. Too much has passed between Liam and me in the short time we've been allies. This silence feels heavy. Dangerous.

I put a hand on the wall for leverage and try to push myself up, not wanting to appear weak. Liam reaches out as if to touch me, and I flinch away without meaning to. If Caro finds out he's helping me . . .

"You shouldn't be here," I say.

A wounded look crosses his face but only briefly. "Well, that makes two of us. All the more reason to get out now." He takes my arm and helps me to my feet, then drops his hand quickly and busies himself with undoing the bonds at my wrists. "What happened? Did Caro hurt you?"

This time, I meet his eyes. I know he's referring to the wound on my temple, but that's only the start of what Caro's done. "She had Crofton burned," I say. My throat closes again, thinking of it—the cries, the smoke. The hate from the people who remained. Amma's body.

The color drains from Liam's face. "Burned? What do you mean?"

"Burned down." My blood seethes. "You haven't heard? No Gerlings were present."

His eyes flick to the ground in shame, but his voice is harsh. "I haven't been keeping account of Gerling interests. I haven't spared a thought for anything but you. Your safety," he adds quickly.

"Ivan was there," I say softly, my throat thick with old anguish. "There's nothing left."

Liam goes still, his hands motionless at my wrists. His chest moves once, silently. Then he seems to gather himself and the bonds drop to the floor. He checks the hall outside the door and then beckons for me to follow, looping a hand under my arm.

"We had a plan," he says in a low, brusque voice.

"*You* had a plan," I reply, wanting to push him away. I imagine Caro's eyes on me, watching from some unseen hiding place. The words come out louder than I intended them, annoyance swelling in my chest and pushing them from my lips. Even after all that's happened, his officiousness still irritates me.

Liam helps me out of the cell and into a dim, narrow hallway, his hand on my arm firm. "It doesn't matter now. We have to leave."

I lean against the wall while he drags the two guards inside the cell, lifting the keys as he does, and locks the door. His eyes meet mine for the briefest moment. Though his face is controlled, I see another flash of emotion there, like the glint of a coin at the bottom of a well. Fear, for me. It's gone in an instant, but it makes my stomach clench.

Liam unhooks an oil lamp from the wall and carries it as we

walk. "At least tell me Caro hasn't seen you."

My silence is its own answer.

Liam's voice is hard-edged. "Jules, Crofton was probably a trap for you."

Anger flares through me. "I picked up on that."

"She knows you—"

"She knows the Alchemist," I hiss, though the grain of truth sits uncomfortably under my skin. Caro did set a trap. She knew I'd come if Crofton were in danger. Only hours ago, knife leveled at me, she taunted me for my sentimentality. Still, I say, "She doesn't know me."

The nightmare from the cell flashes into my mind, the slices of my past lodged deep. Flashes of blood and magic and weakness and strength, fox and snake and something howling.

"What is it?" Liam asks softly. I've slowed without meaning to.

I pick up my pace again. "My memories are starting to come back. Of other—other lives." I try to sound detached. The truth still feels unnatural, wrong somehow. "How did you know I was here?"

"I found this on the palace grounds." As we hurry through the eerily quiet corridors, he withdraws something from his coat pocket and shows me. My journal.

"You shouldn't have carried this," I say, my voice shaky. "Someone could see you with it and know that you're helping me."

"Think, Jules," Liam says, slipping the journal back into his jacket pocket, over his chest. He slows, opens a door off to our right. We slip out into another quiet hall, lined by doors at wide intervals. A residential area. At any moment, one of these doors could burst open, and we'd be ruined. I can only pray that all the guests are downstairs celebrating. "There's another reason I would be looking for you. The story goes that you killed my brother. No one thinks we're allies."

A chill goes through me as his meaning sinks in. Caro and Ivan think Liam means me harm. And he *should*. He should hate me. I didn't kill Roan, but he would still be alive if it weren't for me and my childhood infatuation.

Liam doesn't speak again until we reach an upper level carpeted in plush silver and blue. Tapestries depicting Sempera's history line the walls. I follow Liam as the Queen's life plays out in thread around me, intricately woven battle scenes with swaths of glittering red blood, grotesque to look at in the low light.

But a figure in one of the pictures snags at my gaze. A middle-aged man seated on a black horse hoisting a green-and-gold flag while battle rages around him. A silver hound stands proud at his feet. The man is unremarkable enough, except for the expression on his face: even in miniature, he looks almost bored.

I stop. My hand lifts without my entirely meaning it to,

moving toward the tapestry. Then a woman's distant laugh snaps me back to reality, and I hurry after Liam.

Near the end of the hall, Liam fumbles with a key and ushers me through a blue door. We slip inside, and I finally take a breath of relief.

It's a noblewoman's room, littered all over with discarded dresses and trinkets, as if someone spent hours trying on clothes and tossing each reject mindlessly away. I nearly step on a string of pearls lying on the floor. Anger at the careless opulence pricks at me, but it's more muted than it once might have been, my head still full of fire and smoke.

I find a cushioned chair and sit down—my limbs are heavy and stiff—while Liam goes to a wardrobe on the far side of the room. It's open, vomiting velvet and silk.

Now that I'm still, the full weight of the danger we're in sinks down on me. "Why risk this, Liam?" I ask quietly as he rummages through clothes.

It takes him a moment to respond. "The fate of Sempera is tied to yours," he says at last, his back to me. I remember what he said when he took me from Everless and told me I was the Alchemist, when he tried to convince me to run.

If you die, we are all lost.

A shiver sweeps over me like a cloak, remembering Caro's voice, describing how she was going to break me, then inhabit me, just as she did the Queen—slipping on my magic like a glove

64

to bend the world to her will. I push the thought away and am almost grateful for the distraction when Liam turns around, his hands overflowing with something made of indigo velvet and lace.

"What is that?" I say, nearly laughing.

Liam blinks. He starts to cross the room toward me, then stops and lays the dress on a side table instead. "Shorehaven will be on high alert with you here," he says. "It won't be long until they find the guards we knocked out. The rest will be on watch for anything amiss, but Ina and Caro will be busy with the coronation for the rest of the night. They won't be expecting you to slip out among the guests, in plain sight. It's our best chance at escape."

"Ina's coronation," I echo. Even after seeing her, it's a strange thought: Ina—my friend, my *sister*—the new queen of Sempera. Then the rest of Liam's words catch up with me, and I scoff. "Do you think just because I'm in a gown, Ina won't recognize me?"

Liam lifts something dark and gauzy from the top of the pile of fabric. A veil, I realize.

"All the women are wearing these," he says quietly, with an undercurrent of emotion I can't identify. "A sign of respect. For what should have been a wedding."

Roan's wedding. I swallow down the sudden lump in my throat. "If we're discovered, even you won't be able to explain this away."

"Do you think I don't know that?" Liam's voice is testy. "I know I'm dead if this goes wrong. That's why you should trust me." He picks up the dress again and tosses it into my lap while avoiding my eyes. "Get ready, so we can get out of here and get you to Ambergris."

I fold my hand into the cool fabric, but don't move to put on the dress. "You should leave before we're caught."

I try to summon my old impression of Liam: of my days in Crofton and at Everless when I saw him as an enemy—his posture perfect, his face stone, his eyes cold. The old Lord Gerling, feared, invulnerable, a suit of armor made of flesh and bone, selfish and cruel.

It almost works, until he tells me, "I don't care about the danger."

"Don't say that to me," I snap, casting my eyes somewhere over his shoulder. He's close enough for me to reach out and touch him.

But I don't. I can't. I need to push him away, just like I did with Ina. It's the only way he'll be safe.

Words flow from my mouth like hot poison. "I just— I don't want more blood on my hands, even yours."

"No," Liam says quietly. "I expect not."

A cold weight settles on my chest. I pull my sleeves over my hands and clench my fists tight, focusing on the pain of my fingernails pressing into my palms instead of the thorn burrowing deeper into me with every word uttered. "I hated you for years. I was *afraid* of you. Can you understand why it's hard to believe you now?"

Liam's eyes search mine as if he'll find an answer there. But I give him nothing.

Finally, he says, "We aren't children anymore. Love me or hate me, we have a common enemy now."

I fold my arms to keep myself from visibly shaking. I hope Liam mistakes it for anger. "That's all we have."

I gather the clothes Liam gifted me into my arms and walk straight-backed to the adjoining washroom—forcing myself not to look over my shoulder at him, though that's all I want to do. On the way, I snatch up a slender dagger in a sheath sitting on one of the cabinets.

Not Amma's butcher knife, but better than nothing.

As I wash my face and arms and strip out of my traveling clothes, Liam gives terse instructions through the door. Ina is being crowned queen as we speak—the thought raises goose bumps on my skin—and after the ceremony, everyone will gather in the east ballroom to celebrate. The balcony there looks over the cove, and below that, at the bottom of a set of stairs, is a beach. We will go through the ballroom, down the balcony and the stairs, straight to the beach, where his friend Elias, another coronation guest, has arranged a boat to take us away.

As I pin up my hair and pull the dress over my head, I want to ask him if he really thinks it will work. And though the question feels like a blade pressed against my chest, I want to ask if he plans to escape with me, abandoning his ruse of loyalty and the safety that comes with it.

Instead, I let the veil fall silently over my face, and the world is overlaid with a translucent pattern of gray taffeta. It's only then—as Liam instructs me to say, if asked, that I'm a visitor from Connemor, a cousin of Elias's—that I can bring myself to look in the mirror.

The dress fits perfectly. It's velvet, the dark blue of the night sky at the height of summer, with constellations of white lace at my elbows and collarbones. A dipping back reveals my shoulder blades. With my face hidden beneath the veil, and my knife concealed, strapped to my calf with my traveling belt, I could actually pass for a guest at the coronation. As long as no one looks too closely at what's under the veil.

Liam is in the middle of describing the best route to take through the ballroom. But when I step out of the washroom, his words stop. His eyes go wide, and his lips part. For a second I want more than anything for this to be real. To be welcomed at my sister's crowning, to walk into the ballroom arm in arm with someone who looks at me the way Liam's looking at me now, to dance with him without having to hide my face.

But I have never belonged in that world. And even now,

Liam's look of surprise fades out into cool neutrality. He may be my ally, but he can't be anything else. I can't give Caro any more tools to break my heart. She's already taken enough.

I swallow and step past him through the doorway. With Liam in my wake, I follow the sound of music rising up from below.

6

When we get to the ballroom, all my fear and anger melts away momentarily into awe.

The floor and walls are the same pale stone as the rest of the castle, veined with shining strands of silver and black. The ceiling is a dome of glass, letting in a blazing spread of red and orange and purple—the sun setting over the ocean. It bleeds gold light down the walls, over the floor, making the people spinning on the dance floor—so many, surely more than two hundred—seem gilded, even through the translucent gray of my veil. I forget myself, and my grip tightens on Liam's arm.

But he is tense beneath my hand, reminding me that despite the smile on his face, he's afraid and we are in danger. Firmly, he takes my elbow, pulling me down the stairs, toward the crowd.

The hem of my dress sweeps the floor, the dagger beneath my skirt heavy in its sheath.

At the front of the room, the marble floor rises in a set of wide stairs, where an orchestra is arrayed over the steps. I've never seen anything like it: dozens of musicians are spinning out the melody on cellos and flutes and drums and instruments I can't even name. One long flute appears to be made of a human bone. The melody is beautiful, though I can't help but shudder. As we move forward, the music wraps around me like something tangible, a language I don't speak, that nevertheless tugs at me in ways I don't understand.

Above the orchestra, a throne carved from shining, dark wood sits empty.

Halfway down the stairs, Liam stops and turns to face me. He leans in close to whisper in my ear. I try not to shiver.

"The door. There. Do you see it?"

I follow his gaze to a set of glass doors all the way across the room, propped open to admit the sight of another lush garden and the faintest sound of crashing waves. It seems very far away, with a sea of people dancing between us and escape. I nod.

Liam smiles stiffly at a passing couple. "It leads to the balcony."

As we descend the stairs, I expect the heads of everyone in the crowd to snap toward me, veil or no veil, and for shouts of *murderer* to fill the room.

But it doesn't happen. The crowd—people in military dress like Liam, or sweeping gowns and veils, moving in pairs and complicated patterns, aren't looking at me. They're looking at one another, eyes gleaming beneath veils. A few glances land on me, and my heart begins to race—until I remember the sharp-edged gossip that used to wind through Everless, of the various wealthy prospects that Lady Verissa recruited for Liam, only to have him reject them all. A girl on his arm will draw attention, but it can't be helped.

A cluster of people with wineglasses in their hands walk close, chattering loudly about the offerings of the banquet table. One of them, a man in a deep purple jacket, breaks off and begins to stride toward us, his eyes fixed on Liam. A stone drops into my stomach as I recognize Lord Renaldi from my first dinner party at Everless. He was the man who'd threatened to bleed Bea a year for spilling wine on him, before Roan diffused the tension with his charm.

"Fascinating times we live in," he says, too loudly, words slurred. "Our first change of power in five centuries, and we get a little stripling of a thing for a queen." He grins at Liam and claps his arm, braying out laughter.

My spine stiffens. Ina may not trust me, but it pains me to hear her spoken of like this. It takes all my effort not to yank the drink from the nobleman's hands and throw it in his face for his tone.

"Isn't that right, Lord Gerling?"

Liam smiles. His eyes are pure ice, but I suppose Renaldi is too drunk to notice. "We'll see," he says. He nods, punctuating the conversation, and peels away from Renaldi, still guiding me lightly by the sleeve.

Chiming laughter rises to the ceiling. The group drifts away. As Liam looks down at me, I realize my fists are clenched, my nails digging into my palms. *Do you doubt Ina too?* I want to ask him, but it's not the time or the place.

"Like I said, no one will notice you," Liam mutters. He reaches out and puts a hand on the small of my back. No outsider looking at us would be able to tell, but his hand on my waist is light and impersonal, his smile hollow. Formal, distant.

A cluster of people mill about the bottom of the stairs, everyone who descends stopping to join them. Liam steers us in their direction as I tilt my head, trying to see what's at their center. And then my mouth goes dry.

A middle-aged timelender, dressed as prettily as the rest of us, in a forest-green gown with gold-lace trim, sits at a small table with her glittering instruments in front of her. Smaller and shinier than the tools of Duade in Crofton or Wick, the timelender who bled me of ten years in Laista, yet still sharp, still menacing.

But here, an odd, unsettled feeling sweeps over me. Something is different—because here, people come to her one by one, smiling and chatting as they willingly offer up their hands. In

Crofton, the line outside Duade's shop was long and desperate: heads were bowed, and low voices pleaded with the Sorceress to bless them with an extra hour or two. When I went to Wick in Laista, he drew a drop of blood from each giver, then measured their time by sprinkling a special powder into it and lighting it on fire—carefully counting the seconds of the flame's life to make sure he wouldn't overdraw and kill the giver. The timelender in green doesn't measure anything now. Everyone here can spare years, maybe even decades, if that's what she's taking.

A couple peels away from the table and passes by us. I hear the woman say, "Darling! Careful, you'll get blood on my dress."

"What is this?" My whisper is too fierce. Anger at the injustice boils in me.

Liam's eyes dart from side to side. He sees the same thing I see—that this line is between us and our escape. Whatever it is, we must go through it.

"A tithe for Ina," he murmurs, taking my arm and drawing me close. "Everyone is to offer a year of their own blood. It's meant as a gift of sorts. I'm sorry, I didn't realize—"

My stomach lurches. A *year*. And these people don't even care; they're laughing and smiling as they roll up their sleeves, exposing their arms and palms like fish bellies to the dancing candlelight of the hall. Their flesh is smooth. Unblemished. No signs of having been bled before.

A year is nothing to them. They've never had to sacrifice a single one.

As a silver-haired gentleman steps away from the table, I watch the timelender cork a vial of his blood, laying it alongside dozens of others on a bed of velvet. The man is more concerned about his finery, blotting a smear of blood with an embroidered handkerchief.

So much blood, sparkling prettily in vials like a nest of jewels. A man behind me catches my eyes and raises a brow. "In line?"

Liam responds for me. "Yes." He positions me next to him and speaks softly. "It's all right. I'll give another year in your place—"

"It's not that," I stammer, a half lie. "It's just—I don't think my time can be consumed. It hurt Caro when she tried to drink it at first, at Everless. Do you think it would hurt Ina too?" My words dry up as another, even worse fear sinks into me. What if Caro lays hands on my blood again? What dark magic could she wreak then?

Even with the veil between us, I see shock and then doubt flash across Liam's features. For all his years of study, he didn't know this about my blood.

Suddenly, he seems younger than he is, and I feel exposed for what we are: a boy who, even with all his intelligence and education, is only nineteen, and a girl who has centuries of memories and knowledge and magic but can't access them.

75

The line lurches forward—it's Liam's turn. He squeezes my arm gently and steps up, leaving me frozen, my head spinning with new information. This dark tithe. Liam's offer to give a year of life for my sake. The overwhelming fear of Caro having more of my blood, making me complicit in her havoc.

I see the blade open Liam's skin, and my vision fractures. *It's just his palm. Just his palm.* I look away so I don't have to see him bleed.

When it's over, Liam looks back at me, smiling indulgently as the timelender bandages his arm. "I hope you'll excuse my sweetheart," I hear him say, dripping charm. "She's quite unable to stomach the sight of blood."

"Oh, come now." The timelender's voice in return has the same easy, aristocratic charm, but there's a hard edge in it. "She can close her eyes, or have you hold her hand."

She raises her voice, addressing me, and I don't like how shrewd her gaze is. "Surely, my lady," she says, a dangerous insinuation in her voice, "you don't want to miss the honor of having your own time run through the Queen's veins? I also hear that she plans to fashion a blood-iron jewel for her crown."

My stomach drops as, all around, people begin to turn toward me. Heads tilt curiously. Their attention feels like a threatening breeze, ready to tear off my veil and expose my murderer's face to the whole ballroom.

So though my limbs are leaden with fear, I step forward. "Of course not," I say, making my voice whispery and timid as I roll up my sleeve. Liam puts an arm around me, and despite my earlier reluctance to let him touch me, I'm grateful for it now. As the timelender's blade parts the skin of my palm, Liam bends down, as though he's kissing my temple to give me comfort. Instead, his lips brush my ear.

"It'll be all right."

But just as the timelender reaches for a bandage, the room quiets, and all around me, heads snap toward the throne. The timelender drops my hand and dips into a low bow as a door in the wall behind the throne opens, and out step two girls in sweeping gowns.

Caro. And the newly crowned queen of Sempera: Ina Gold.

7

Fear spills into me—the protection of the veil seems flimsy with Caro in the room—but I can't tear my eyes from Ina. She wears a veil too, but it's translucent, threaded with small shining tear-drops, each made of blood-iron. Not only can I see her face, but even at this distance, it seems to shine. Her gown spills down around her, like a black waterfall on the stairs.

A crown gleams in her dark hair—its spiked tips are also the red gold of blood-iron, I realize with a jolt, which gives the impression that the crown has been dipped in blood. She glides up to the carved-oak throne and stands there a moment before sitting down regally, every inch the queen. Around me, people leave off their conversations and head for the dais, and a crowd coalesces around her, lords and ladies lining up to kiss her hands and saying words I can't hear.

I'm startled by the touch of Liam's hand on my cheek, through the gossamer of the veil. A silk bandage peeks out from below his sleeve. His skin is much warmer than mine. I don't know why this surprises me.

He turns me to face him. He's smiling, but I can see the tension in his eyes, feel it in his racing pulse. I let him lead me toward the open floor, away from the timelender, who has gotten too caught up in the grand entrance of the new queen to notice that I fled the line.

I want nothing more than to push through the crowd and run up to Ina's throne shouting everything I couldn't only a few hours ago. That I am her ally, that she can't trust Caro, that her handmaiden might try to control her just as she did the Queen. That she and I were born together in a town called Briarsmoor. That our birth mother's name was Naomi.

But instead I mimic the actions of all the other couples around the ballroom, putting one hand on Liam's shoulder and letting him pull me close—his hand on the small of my back, the fingers of my right hand interlaced with his. I can tell from the tightness of his jaw that he's afraid.

I glance to either side, sure that at any moment someone will see that I don't know the steps and recognize me for an imposter. And I'm fearfully aware of Caro at the front of the room. Even though I can't see her, her presence exerts a kind of dark gravity. But Liam catches my gaze and shakes his head. He leans down to whisper in my ear, and his dark curls brush my cheek. A chill runs through me.

"Don't look around," he says, a little curtly. "Don't be nervous. We just need to make it to the door and slip out without being seen."

My dress falls all the way to the floor, masking the traveling boots that I still wear beneath. I've managed to tug my hair up into something that resembles the elegant updos that the other women wear, braided crowns to hold up our veils. But I still feel conspicuous, set apart from everyone else. Only people with centuries running through their veins know how to dance like this. I fumble along as best I can. The couple from the bloodletting line swirls by us, resplendent now in the dance. Through the woman's veil—lighter than mine—I glimpse her face, smiling shyly up at her partner.

A pang of loss for something I've never known goes through me as the musicians tip into a plaintive chorus. In another world—in another life, that could have been me. I let myself imagine it, dancing here as an honored guest, the thought fizzing in me like a sip of madel. I wouldn't be wearing a veil. No one would be, because there would be nothing to mourn, only to celebrate. Ina wouldn't be cold and distant on her throne but dancing among us, as joyful in her queendom as I knew her to be as a princess.

And Roan would be dancing with her. Liam and I would

dance past them and smile, too—maybe touch and smiles and shared laughter would be possible for me, and not just possible, but easy, flowing, free, instead of locked and forbidden.

Instead of deadly.

But that world is not this world. There is a vein of sorrow running beneath everything, all the beauty here, showing itself in our veils and the mournful song of the violin and in Ina, so close and yet so far away, untouchable. There's so much hollowness in me, the space left by everything I've never had—everything that until recently, I could never have imagined missing. I'll never dance like that with Liam or anyone, without a care in the world.

Not until Caro is dead.

Not until I learn how to kill her.

Suddenly, the need to escape swamps me, and it's all I can do to keep from sprinting for the door.

A young man with bronze skin and striking gold hair spins past us, his arm brushing mine, a woman in purple silk laughing in his wake. I see him smile warmly at Liam as they pass. Liam nods, though his smile is strained. The man nods back, then melts into the crowd and disappears.

"That's Elias," he says in my ear, once we're a few feet away. "He'll meet us outside."

I can't stop myself from snapping my head around to stare after Elias, my mouth going dry. Without knowing it, I have brushed past someone from outside Sempera, someone who doesn't have time in his blood. Only our country bears this curse.

When I catch another glimpse of Elias between dancers, I search for something strange in his broad shoulders, his laughing smile, and find nothing. At first glance, he appears normal—albeit handsome, clearly wealthy, and graceful—but am I just imagining the slight supernatural grace in his movements, like the blood in his veins is somehow lighter than the rest of us? Is it a blessing or a curse, never to know how much time you have?

"Can we trust him?" I whisper to Liam.

"As much as you can trust me."

The song changes again, to something louder and faster. I glance surreptitiously around the room so I don't have to meet Liam's eyes as we inch closer toward the door to the balcony. Only a few minutes, I tell myself, heart racing, and then I will slip away, camouflaged by the other guests. Only a few songs of this too-tense, prickling closeness, and I will be gone.

But as we move toward the door, we get nearer and nearer to Caro, her silent shadow of a presence beside the throne.

Liam leans down to whisper again. I make myself not react, not shiver at his nearness.

"At the end of this song is our best chance," he says. Outside, I can see a stripe of sunset-painted ocean. As we watch, two women detach themselves from the waltz and slip through it. In the background, Caro looks for a moment after them. My heart races.

"You'll have to pretend to enjoy my company," he adds in my ear. If I wasn't so nervous, I would laugh at how cold and irritable he can sound even as he guides me through a graceful dance. But there's no room in me for laughter, only fear.

He changes the direction of our dance, angling us directly toward the door. I'm caught off guard and fall behind a step, which makes Liam pull me closer, tightening his hold on the small of my back. My breath catches, but Liam either doesn't notice or pretends not to.

Then I realize we've crossed most of the dance floor and are nearing the propped-open glass door that leads outside. Liam's grip on me tightens and I force myself to smile, to hold his gaze, to project casual grace as we reach the edge of the crowd, just as the song ends. My pulse flutters as questions race through my mind. Have the guards gotten free? Are those Caro's eyes on me, up on the dais? I daren't turn around to check, but needles prickle the back of my neck. Liam steps away from me, keeping hold of my hand, and though I hate to admit it, it's all that keeps my fear at bay.

Together we walk onto the garden-balcony, which hugs the curve of the palace. On the far end, the balcony stretches over the cliffs. The earth below is all craggy rocks and sand, though up here is cultivated with slender trees and enormous flowers surrounding us, almost lush enough to make me forget the sheer, salt-stained cliffs that flank the palace. But the constant low thunder of the waves below us is enough to make me remember, and my muscles tighten up with fear and adrenaline. Freedom is so close. I can hear the waves that will carry me away.

I glimpse the water through the trees. The cove is dotted with boats, small pleasure craft and stately yachts, flying the pennants of Sempera's five most powerful, land-owning families, in addition to a few other crests I don't recognize. My eyes land immediately on a sleek craft flying Connemor's colors—red and gold—Elias's ship, which will carry us away. A dozen yards off the shore, it sits incongruously in the dark, bobbing with the waves. I don't know how we'll get in the boat without being seen.

Liam keeps hold of my hand as we walk, passing a few others who have drifted from the ballroom as the music from inside gradually surrenders to the sound of the waves. One woman's head turns to follow us as we go by. She's thrown her veil back, revealing a strong, bronze, lovely face, and I see her dark eyes linger on Liam. It's more than a casual glance. My chest contracts with fear that she's seen something amiss.

But it's nothing, I tell myself. Liam is tall, handsome, striking in his finery. It's unsurprising that gazes would follow him.

We're so close to the sea, I can taste the salt on my tongue. My legs ache to burst into motion, but Liam's hand is firm around mine, forcing me not to run. To act like any other young people escaping the dance, enjoying the gardens.

And that's when everything goes wrong.

The music from the ballroom stops, not the gentle fading out of a finishing song, but abruptly. I had stopped hearing it, blended as it was with the waves below, but my ears detect silence where they couldn't detect sound.

And suddenly I know, with certainty, that Caro has realized I am not in my cell. My hand flies to my leg, feeling for the hilt of my knife beneath my dress, and it's only the knowledge of the two women strolling behind us that keeps me from whipping the blade out.

It takes Liam a heartbeat longer than me to hear the threatening silence—but when he does, his eyes fly wide, and I sense his body stiffen. His gait falters.

"Should we run?" I whisper, though there's nowhere to go but down or back into the ballroom.

Liam shakes his head, a barely perceptible motion. His face is white in the gathering dark. "She doesn't know where you are," he says, his voice so low I have to strain to hear. "Just that you're somewhere in the palace. We can still leave without being noticed."

I nod, but Roan's blood flashes in my memory, and my limbs scream at me to run from Liam, to put as much distance as possible between him and me—dangerous, deadly me. It's all I can do to keep walking. My fingers twitch with the effort not to go for the knife. Instead, I pull the veil farther down over my face.

As we walk, the hush gives way to a clamor of confused

voices, as people begin to pour from the ballroom out onto the balcony. Liam's grip on my hand tightens. Behind me, I can hear confused voices, people shouting over one another in an effort to find out what's going on.

The Queen's murderer?

Here?

Escaped?

Fear seizes me suddenly, stronger than anything since Caro held me in her arms, and my knees fold without warning, the world swaying around me. Liam doesn't miss a beat. He tucks an arm around my waist and pulls me to him, as if he's just supporting his sweetheart who had one too many glasses of madel. He pulls me along through the crowd. All the tension between us momentarily forgotten, I press against him, trying to steal resolve from the places where his body presses against mine.

I can see the end of the balcony, where it slopes downward to the lawn. Just a short drop—

But then the soldiers appear. A dozen of them stream from a side door in the palace, all broad shoulders and shining breastplates fanning across the marble balcony. The guards step forward to meet the coronation guests, grabbing men and women roughly by the arm. A glass falls to the ground and shatters. I watch a guard speak to the woman who dropped it. She hesitates for a moment before lifting her veil.

They're searching the guests. For me. Panic floods my veins.

Liam begins to run, pulling me along with him. Startled guests jump out of our way as we race forward, trying to pass the guards before they coalesce into a line. A salt-scented gust of wind blows my veil up, off my face—

Then my eyes are full of light, pouring down from above. A door has been thrown open to yet another smaller balcony above us, and torchlight floods the lower balcony, illuminates my skin. Caro and Ina emerge. Both their faces so familiar, but Ina's is hardened with wrath. With hatred. And Caro's, twisted into a terrifying smile.

All around me, people stop moving and look up, mesmerized by the light streaming out of Shorehaven. Then, Ina points a hand straight at me.

Shouts rise up. The soldiers close ranks ahead of us, their gold chest armor like a line of blood-iron barring the path of escape.

No, I think as hundreds of faces turn toward me at once. They see me, all of them—and they see Liam, standing beside me. Too close.

One thought crystallizes in my head. No matter what happens to me, Caro cannot have Liam.

I pull out my knife—and lunge for him.

8

Even in the midst of the chaos, I catch a glimpse of Liam's face. All the haughty distance he wore in the ballroom is torn away. His open mouth and wide eyes steal my breath. Pain spikes through my body.

I need to make it look real. In the air, I arc the blade over his chest, shoulder to ribs—aiming for the place where I know he has my leather journal tucked in his pocket. I sink the tip of the knife into his jacket, but it only pierces the fabric and the leather journal underneath.

It works. All around us, people scream. He stumbles back, hand to his chest, and I start after him, knife raised dramatically high again, keeping my eyes trained on his the whole time. As he backs away, putting a hand on his sword hilt, I see the understanding come over his face.

I slash out at him one more time—the attack is too wide, careless, but I can't bring myself to get any closer. I'm grateful when a guard drags Liam back and charges for me instead. Inches ahead of her outstretched hands, I turn and surge forward, brandishing the knife as I run.

Guests scramble out of my way, but the guards make for me, closing in from behind. I run with everything I have, ignoring the burning in my chest and feet. Hundreds of gazes heat my back, and I can feel Caro's presence, imagine the stirrings in the air of her awful power that I saw at Everless.

And I'm not fast enough. A huge guard slams into me from behind, throwing my body into the balcony railing so hard that I almost tumble over the edge. The air leaves my lungs, but through the pain I slash blindly at his arm with my knife. He curses and jumps back—but by now I'm surrounded, ringed by five guards all two yards away, my back to the ocean. Behind, the balcony overhangs the water. Below, huge, sharp, pale boulders tumble down a slope to the sea cove. Elias's ship bobs in the dark water, its sails fluttering, waving good-bye.

Trapped.

I have no choice.

I lash out with my power, trying to freeze the guards in time like flies in honey—but it's as if they don't exist in the world of time. My attempts to stop them slide right past them, like water around oil. Panic grips my heart, and I look up to the distant figures of Caro and Ina on the upper balcony.

Desperately, I search out Liam's face in the gawking crowd. He's halfway down the balcony, surrounded by a knot of solicitous guards and guests, staring helplessly at me.

"Arrest her!" Ina cries, her voice battering the backs of the guards.

As the guards step forward, advancing on me, I glance over my shoulder at the sea.

It's far enough down that a leap wouldn't be certain death, but wouldn't be safe either. I could break a leg and have Caro drag me back to her dungeons, utterly helpless this time. Or there's the possibility that I could break my neck, and everything would be over in an instant. But if I stay here, deliberating, the guards will take me back to Caro. And Liam has already freed me from her captivity twice now.

Would she be so careless as to let it happen again? Or will this be the time she finally breaks me?

No. If I can't kill her now, I have to get away from here until I can finish what I started.

I throw the knife toward the lead guard, realizing too late that she's the same one who helped Liam get me out of my cell. Luckily I haven't the skill or strength to aim true, and it flies over her shoulder and clatters harmlessly to the marble floor. But more screams rise from the crowd, and the guards exchange alarmed glances. I take the moment to bunch my gown up around my thighs—I wish I could tear it off, but there's no time—and haul myself over the railing so I'm standing on the outer edge, the sea churning far below me, with only a jagged cliff face and stacked boulders in between.

More screams and gasps. Caro's eyes bore into mine from a distance, two calm pools in a sea of panic. I look down only long enough to get a sense of where the boulders are, and immediately vertigo slams into me. But I've made my decision.

I turn around and step off the ledge.

Wind fills my eyes and ears. The waves and tiny, distant boats blur on all sides of me. I barely have the presence of mind to bend my knees and slow time slightly—imperceptibly, I hope—before I hit the stone with what feels like bone-shattering force. My ankles slide out from beneath me with a sickening crunch of rock and flesh, sending me hard to my side.

For a few long moments, I lie there, gripping the stone beneath me with all my might so I don't slide into the ocean. Above me, I see a multitude of faces against the night sky, peering down at me . . . and the guards, already fastening rope to the ironwork of the railing, preparing to rappel down after me.

I push myself upright, still dizzy from the fall, and look back and forth between their small silhouettes and the water. There is nowhere for me to go but down the boulder, toward the sea. Already I'm soaked through with icy, salty water. The velvet of my dress clings uselessly to my body, the skirt shredded by the sharp boulders along with the palms of my hands.

I could try to swim to Elias's boat, but even from here I can tell the tides are too strong, the waves white-tipped like some hungry beast snapping at me.

The thought of drowning—of being driven to my death like a panicked animal—sends a flood of adrenaline coursing through me. With every ragged breath, time rages stronger in my blood, screaming to be let loose. I shut my eyes, trying to gather the faded magic in my blood into a storm. Time can be a cloud, expanding out of me, capturing everything in its path. It can be a battering ram. And now—

I look up at the descending guards once more, my breath sticking in my throat. I memorize where they are against the night sky. And then I close my eyes and imagine wielding time like a whip, a glowing line of light arcing over the ocean and the rocky beach. I imagine it weaving into the ropes, aging the fibers, ten years in a moment, fifty years, a hundred, grasping for my magic more deeply than I've ever had to. It saps my strength from me; and I have to remember to breathe, my chest aching for want of breath. But even at this distance, I feel it working, feel myself throwing off the invisible chains that Caro put on me— and I know that the soldiers' ropes will start to fray and snap.

I don't consider what this means until the first soldier plummets toward the blackened sea.

Shouts come from above. I open my eyes as the guards start

to scramble down faster, dropping onto the boulders. Another isn't quick enough—the rope breaks, sending him screaming down. I don't hear him land among the crashing of the waves, but nausea rises in my throat. Another person, two, probably dead because of me.

But even as the thought crosses my mind, I'm turning my attention to the boulders that hold up the three remaining guards, imagining them as they will be after centuries of these waves beating down, smooth and shrinking and eventually tumbling into the sea. I concentrate with every bit of strength I have. My grip loosens on my own perch; if a wave were to hit me, I wouldn't be able to stop myself from being washed away.

But one of the guards loses his grip and slides down, only barely catching himself on a lower boulder. The other two—a hulking man and the captain with the braid, close enough now for me to see their terrified faces, scramble down toward me. The woman gets closest, catching herself on a boulder separated from mine by twenty feet of water.

"Jules," she yells.

But I can't answer. All my attention is now taken up with keeping my balance, fighting the waves that grab at my ankles like living things. I've stopped eroding the boulders, but a deep, terrible creaking has started up among them.

Like the crude wooden dominoes Amma and I used to play with as girls, I can't stop what I've started. And the boulders begin to crash down, tumbling over the sandy, sheer slope from the castle, taking others with them as they go. Only one or two at first, and then half a dozen, and then there's a terrible moment where I know what will happen in the instant before it does.

I will time to stop, but I'm spent, my strength gone. Nothing stops.

One by one, all the boulders on the cliff begin to tumble down. If they seem to be moving slowly, I can't tell if it's my power or just sheer terror warping my perception. But they are falling, with a deep, monstrous grinding and screaming, one after another. The stone shakes beneath my feet, threatening to give way.

I turn, screams from the balcony above pummeling my back, and leap from my boulder, into the sea.

The cold hits me first. Above water, it was a balmy spring night—but the sea has kept a jealous hold of deepest winter, saving it so it can wrap around me now. Like hands made of ice are gripping my limbs and pulling me down, reaching down my throat and groping for the warm vital things that keep me alive. I can't move, not even to pull myself toward the surface or fight the waves that spin me around, head over heels, heels over head. I'm spinning, bubbles rushing from my mouth and nose, and I can't tell if the silver glimmering in my eyes is moonlight on the water or my brain manufacturing images in a desperate plea for air.

I'm vaguely aware that boulders are falling into the sea

around me, each hitting the water with a deep, resounding, water-muffled *boom* that rattles my bones. The impacts make the water snarl against the existing currents, tossing me like a rag doll between them. There's nothing I can do to avoid the boulders, no way to know where they are going to fall—no air.

I force my limbs out and try to swim in the direction I think is up, and my head breaks the surface for a moment—I catch a glimpse of the woman guard, swimming toward me—before a wave drives me down. For all the ancient magic and memories tumbling inside me, I'm helpless against the water. When I break the surface a second time, I don't even have time for a breath before I'm dragged farther under. Panic blooms in my mind as my limbs start to burn, ice creeping in. Black spots waver at the edges of my vision. I am going to die like this, drowning.

I don't want to die.

I *cannot* die.

A sudden, wild surge of power fires my body, starting in my heart and racing outward. It makes me cry out in a rush of useless bubbles, throw my hands and feet wide and start fighting the currents again. Time seems to leap through my veins.

But I can't control the ocean—it's too vast, too wild. I can feel the thousands of years already winding through its waters course through me. All I have left is my own body, and I retreat into it now, pulling my magic inward, willing my seconds not to tick away, pleading with my heart to put off the moment of

9

I am vaguely aware of someone hauling me upward, out of the sea. Hands lay me on a hard surface on my side and start pounding my shoulder blades until I cough up the seawater I swallowed. I'm lifted and settled on a bench, a blanket tucked around me—too weak and frozen to move or even open my eyes, to do anything else but splutter out seawater and gulp down air. There's indistinct footsteps and voices around me, and the wrathful beating of the waves through the wood of what must be a boat floor, like they're furious to have lost me.

Then—pain. Mountains of it spiking through my body, solid and jagged and impassable. I cry out before I can stop myself.

Someone lifts my head into their lap, then gently wipes the seawater from my face and tucks the blanket tighter around me until the pain recedes into a faint pulse. *Caro*, I think distantly, her twisted tenderness.

But these hands are large and warm and gentle, only half familiar. When I finally open my eyes, it's not Caro above me. It's Liam, brow lined in concern, his face very pale.

"You're alive," he whispers, for the second time since the soldiers dragged me to Shorehaven.

I manage a weak laugh. "I think so."

Behind him, I see the woman guard—not a guard, I suppose—quickly raising a dark sail that blends into the water, so black it seems woven from the night itself. Beyond her, I see Liam's friend Elias drape more black cloth over the deck, to cover the boat's sides. A red-and-gold flag is crumpled at Elias's feet.

"Jules, this is Danna from Connemor," Liam says, following my gaze to the woman. "She pulled you out."

Danna nods curtly at me. She might have saved me, but I don't suppose she's forgotten that I accidentally cast her into the sea trying to escape from the palace.

"And, of course, this is Elias," Liam adds.

"It's good to finally meet you, Miss Ember," Elias calls over to me. There's a hint of strain to his voice, but he has a musical accent, and a wide white smile even as sea wind snaps his hair. He picks up a coil of rope and tosses it to Danna. "I've heard much about Sempera's legendary Alchemist."

My cheeks flush. I want to ask more questions, but I'm too shaken and exhausted to speak. I don't push away Liam's hands when he helps me to sit up. I'm shivering violently, even under the blanket. It feels like my insides have been scraped out and replaced with salt water.

He climbs around to my other side so he's facing me. Behind him, the shape of Shorehaven looms, farther away than I expected, the lights of the ballroom just a distant glitter in contrast to the ruin of the beach, where the boulders have fallen into the sea. Dust hangs in the air.

The wind on the cove fills the black sails with a soft *snap*, carrying us out toward the open sea. It's quieter here, away from the crashing of waves on land. Relief trickles into me as I watch the smoking palace recede farther.

As we skirt the palace, small lights blink to life and begin to crawl around the cove—Caro's forces in boats, I know, searching the water for me, or my body. My heart flutters, as if it knows it's being searched for. I cup my hand over my chest, trying to hush that incomprehensible magic that connects me to Caro.

"How long has it been?" I croak.

"An hour." Liam produces a map. Of course he has a map. "When Shorehaven is out of sight, Elias will drop us off on the shore where we can hire a carriage. With the havoc at the palace, people will be less likely to notice he's gone missing."

My throat is dry. I try to follow the route he's tracing along the map, but my sight blurs, my breath hitching as I try to stay in control of my emotions. "And is the same true for you? Will anyone at the coronation realize you're missing?"

Liam looks up, his eyes blank.

My stomach sinks. I know him well enough by now to know that he prefers to say nothing than to lie.

"You were under for nine minutes. And still unconscious when Elias picked me up along the shore," he tells me, his voice raw and strained.

Nine minutes. Without thinking, I squeeze Liam's hands to assure myself that I'm present. I'm above water. I'm safe.

"I thought I was dead," I say, hearing myself as if from a distance. "How am I not dead?"

"You saved yourself." Liam's voice is low; I only understand because of how close he is, our faces a foot apart. Something inside tells me to move away, but it's all I can do to stay upright and keep the blanket wrapped tight around my shaking body. "You weren't breathing when Danna pulled you out. Your heart wasn't beating. They didn't realize at first that you were— stopped. They thought—"

Here his voice breaks, and I realize he's shivering too. His normally tied-back hair has come undone and hangs in damp curls around his face.

A sudden, warm impulse washes over me, overpowering as a wave, and I lean forward and wrap my arms around him, pressing my face into his shoulder, wanting nothing more than to feel safe. I feel his whole body tense up, and then, slowly, relax. His hands come up and rest on my back and briefly, I consider stopping time.

I pull away. My voice comes out small and raw and frightened when I speak—not only of Caro, but of Liam's touch. "I—I thought I might die."

A soft pained noise escapes from somewhere in the back of Liam's throat. He closes his eyes for a moment. I glance over my shoulder at Elias and Danna, but they've retreated to the bow of the boat, Danna steering while Elias examines the dark horizon with a pair of binoculars. His body remains still, staring fixedly ahead; it's a valiant attempt to give Liam and me privacy.

"I'm sorry," I say. "For what I did on the balcony. Attacking you."

Liam blinks, brushing his hand over the journal, which is still tucked into his pocket. I can't read his face. "You had to."

"The wind is with us," Danna calls. "We might make Ambergris by tomorrow, if it holds."

"Ambergris?" I sit up so quickly that Liam flinches. "That's where we're going?"

He tilts his head at me. "Then to Connemor. Shouldn't that be where we're going?"

My head sinks into my hands as I have the sudden feeling that if the boat weren't underneath, the weight of this decision would plunge me to the bottom of the sea. Though we are far from the castle now, skirting the shore and heading south, I imagine that

Caro is looking out one of the Shorehaven windows—one of those distant pebbles of gold light—her eyes trained directly on me. "I have to stop her. She told me that as long as she's alive, she won't stop hunting people I love."

Liam puts a hand on my arm. "I know you want to take Caro down, but Jules, you're too important to throw your life away."

"Are you so certain I'll fail?" I shrug off his hold.

He lets out an exasperated sigh, the picture of the haughty lord that he is. "That's not what I meant. You need to keep yourself safe. Someone else can take care of Caro."

My gut screams that he's wrong, so wrong. "Who? We're not all Gerlings, Liam. I don't have someone to do my bidding."

He quickly runs a hand through his hair, and I know immediately that I'm right. "Killing Caro—that's just not you, Jules. I once watched you nurse a baby mouse back to health after someone chased it from the kitchen."

"That was a long time ago," I say coldly. "You don't know me as well as you think you do. I already tried to kill her."

Liam stiffens. At the other end of the boat, Elias drops an oar. "You—you what?"

Only once my words are out in the air do I realize how mad they sound. Liam, Danna, and Elias have all stopped to stare at me, eyes wide and unbelieving. I swallow the sudden lump in my throat. "The guards took me to her right away. I had my knife . . . at first, I thought I had killed her—she bled so much—but her face started changing, then all the blood went back inside her, as if I'd never stabbed her in the first place. I can't make sense of what happened." I shiver, remembering Rinn, the woman I met in Briarsmoor, who'd spent every day for seventeen years reliving her death over and over.

I sit back against the boat's rough wood railing and focus on only the black blanket of sky and water around us, trying to recall exactly what I saw. I see the image of Caro's face, scrawled with shock below me. The sound of a scream, *my* scream, sends a shiver of fear along my skin. I close my eyes. There was something else. Something just in the corner of my eye, a flash of dark, like a shadow blinking its eye. If I only turn, I could see it—

"That just makes things worse, Jules. You can't kill her. She's the *Sorceress*." Liam lets out a huff of frustration. "She's the Sorceress, and you tried to kill her with a blade."

His words cut my remaining scraps of courage to ribbons. All Caro's power; all my history, lost to me. I'm just a peasant from Crofton. Tears prick my eyes. But Liam doesn't stop.

"You and Caro have been locked in this battle for years. Trust me, I've spent half my life studying it. The best solution is to run, live out your life in hiding. In *safety*."

The tears fall now. Liam's hand twitches, and I wonder if he's considering wiping them from my cheek. I could flee to Ambergris, to the safety that Liam has arranged. Board the ship and let it carry me away to Connemor, a shore where time is still indivisible—a land where Jules Ember could forget the name *Alchemist* forever.

But if Caro burned all of Sempera to the ground and didn't find me—what would stop her from coming after me across the sea? Could an ocean stop the girl who's waited eleven lifetimes to break me? Would it stop Caro from cutting Liam's throat, if she discovered what he had done?

My heart beats the answer against my chest. *No. No. No.*

Amma's voice sounds in my head. *Seize the day, before it seizes you.*

I will not—I cannot—escape to the unbound land.

I battle against the lump in my throat—a tangle of thoughts I can't give voice to—to speak. "She destroyed my home. She killed my friend. I'm not going to Ambergris."

Liam inhales sharply. "Jules—"

"When you told me I was the Alchemist, you said I had the wisdom of my previous lives. I've been fighting her for years, like you said—there must be some knowledge locked inside me that will help destroy her."

"Yes, but . . ." He trails off, lips pressed into a line. I can read the thought on his face—I *don't* have the wisdom of my previous lives. They flit through my mind like shadows.

"My memories come back when I visit places I've been before." I think of the grim impressions I got of being tortured in the palace. "If I go to Connemor, I won't be able to learn more

104

about them. There must be some knowledge that will help me defeat her, but it's here in Sempera. It's here too," I grab the leather journal from inside Liam's jacket, letting my knuckles brush against his chest. "Knowledge so dangerous and important that my father would die for it."

The words linger in the cold night air. I nourish a small hope in my chest: saying the words can make them true.

Liam's mouth opens, then closes. "What will you do? Where will you go?"

Elias shouts from across the boat immediately, like he's been waiting to speak. "There's always Bellwood."

The name sounds familiar; it takes me a moment to place it as the school where Liam spent his childhood away from Everless. "Bellwood?" I ask.

Elias shares a look with Liam, something unspoken passing between them. Then, Liam's face smooths over, a resigned expression sealed in ice.

Elias's face, however, is melting with mischievous joy. "I just thought the Alchemist's ancestral home would be a good place to start rediscovering yourself."

The word *home* tugs at me, despite my confusion. I nod. I don't know where to start, and Bellwood is as good a choice as any other. Before Liam can object, or question me further, I ask him, "What will you do?"

Liam fixes his eyes just over my shoulder, staring out to the

Semperan shoreline as we pass it by, as if he'll find an answer there. Eventually, he says, "Come with you."

It's what I feared he would say. "You can't just go missing. How will you explain that? You—you have responsibilities at Everless." I can't fully keep the emotion from my voice. It trickles in, and I can only hope that Liam interprets the roughness as irritation and not wild, desperate hope.

"You are more important than Everless."

I clench my fists. How is it that his words can make me cold and start a fire in me all at once? "If you return to the palace now, and leave me, she might not suspect you."

"You made your choice to stay, Jules. Let me make mine now."

Before I can respond, he stands and moves away from me. I want to scream at him not to follow, that he'll die; at the same time that I want to plead with him to stay with me until it's over, one way or another. That I've had eleven chances to defeat the Sorceress, and failed every time. That as far as we know, this is the Alchemist's final chance. That I'm as confused as I am frightened, of Caro, of him—of the possibility, creeping in the distance like a stalking wolf, that somehow, this is another trap of Caro's—

But most of all, that I'm afraid of what secrets lie locked within me.

Instead, I only say, "To Bellwood then."

10

Once we are out of sight of the palace and in calmer waters—so still that Elias is afraid to proceed too far, lest his sailboat get stuck for lack of wind—we part ways with him and Danna. I've changed into one of Danna's sensible dresses, long and gray, a significant improvement over the stolen gown, even though it hangs loose on me. Danna will continue north—to get money and supplies from allies of Elias's family, I gathered from the snatches of conversation I overheard, while Elias will return to Shorehaven to show his face and gather news. But my eyes kept drifting closed when I didn't concentrate on keeping them open.

Liam and I load into a little lifeboat, and he rows us toward shore. My knees press against his back, and my own back scrapes against the rear lip of the boat. Now it feels like we're only minutes away from capsizing should a breeze pick up and hit us at the wrong angle. His arms move with the fixed determination of clock hands, and the muscles in his back brush rhythmically against my knees.

Soon I become lulled by the motion, exhaustion rapidly overtaking me. Our only illumination is a scant bit of dying moonlight, which turns the profile of Liam's face into a sculpture of bone white and inky black. I long to touch it—to feel his warmth and remind myself that he is not a statue but alive, full of heat and energy—but I don't.

Instead, I find myself drifting off into half dreams. In my last scraps of awareness, I both hope and fear that I'll meet Caro there, in the dark of sleep. But I dream mostly of Amma, sparklingly alive: of sneaking into the woods with her and kneeling by the creek, playing with paper boats we folded from parchment I'd stolen from Papa's stash, fantasizing about the future day we'd finally be able to visit the sea.

We hit land with a soft thud, and my eyes peel open. After rowing all night, the darkness of the sky is beginning to part for dawn, and a pang goes through me as I think of Amma. Our friendship was a chorus of *somedays*. *Someday* we'll go to the seaside. *Someday* we'll outgrow Crofton.

Amma's somedays were stolen from her.

We climb out—my legs a little wobbly beneath me on the soft moss of the shore—and then set our boat adrift with a strong shove, turning our backs to the waves as the boat grows smaller and smaller on the brightening horizon.

As we walk, salt-sprayed boulders giving way to rocky plains dotted with seaside towns, I try to focus on the task ahead of us. Destroy Caro. Caro, the living, breathing Sorceress of legend, who's walked Sempera for centuries, accruing knowledge and power that are lost to me. I flinch, remembering again how I drove the blade into her body, the soft whisper of metal piercing flesh. The sensations flash through my mind over and over as we walk, and suddenly I'm overwhelmed. I stumble to the bank of the stream that edges along our path. Kneeling, I scoop cool water over my flushed face.

I catch sight of myself in the water's surface—and hardly recognize the face blinking back at me. My cheeks seem sharp as two blades glinting in the stream's reflected light. My mirror face wavers in the slowly moving stream, seeming to shift and re-form with every passing second. Imagined whispers rise up from the forest—*murderer . . . witch . . .*

I steel myself, adding, *Alchemist*. It's what I'll have to be, if I want to end Caro's reign.

A hand grasps my shoulder, making me jump. I whirl to see that it's only Liam. "Are you all right?" he asks.

"Fine," I mutter. But my mouth is dry, my gut empty. Liam extends a hand to help me up. I ignore it and push past him, back to the dirt path.

The wilderness and towns slowly give way to the beginnings of a city—Montmere. It's nothing like Crofton or Laista, which are surrounded by woods and fields—it's a proper city, with roads and rivers feeding into it. My mind flits back to sitting with Amma, a map of Sempera spread across our laps, her grandfather running his finger along the rivers and towns, telling us about his travels as a younger man. Montmere is at the heart of Sempera, its oldest part, where the Sorceress and Alchemist were said to roam. Bellwood sits at the center of a tangled web of its narrow roads and rivers. Despite the early hour, carts and carriages rumble past us on the road we're walking alongside, and I smell aromas of bread and fish, coffee and fruit, and hear the sound of clinking blood-irons trailing in their wake. Shutters above us are thrown wide to take in the breeze, and there are no beggars haunting the side of the street, no soft chorus of *an hour, an hour.*

Liam's given me his cloak to wear. I pull up the hood, stealing glimpses of the neat, hilly cobbled streets from below its rim. Even though I have to duck my head whenever anyone passes by, I can't help but feel a light, buzzing feeling in my chest. Montmere is strange, and yet something about it tugs at me, as though I've been here before. Vaguely, I recall reading a history book in the library of Everless that theorized it was the birthplace of the Alchemist, but the thought makes me uneasy, and I push it away. It's the kind of place I'd always begged Papa to take me to as a child, when we still lived at Everless, when I wanted to devour the world.

We hear a clatter ahead of us, heavy footfalls and Shorehaven-accented shouts. Instinctively I veer into an alley to our right, Liam behind me, and we stand with our shoulders to the wall. Fear clouds my mind. But the soldiers pass.

"Do you think they know we're here?" I ask Liam quietly, when we're back on the street.

Liam shrugs, but I see the worry creasing his brow. "I doubt it. It's just that they're everywhere."

Ina's face flashes in my mind, the way she looked at me when I confronted her in her room. Rage bordering on hatred. The thought of her hating me sends sadness and dread stabbing through all over again. But worse than that is the possibility of Caro controlling Ina like a puppet, like she did the Queen before her and threatened to do to me. I remember her words from the blood-soaked day I confronted her at Everless—how she whispered in the Queen's ear and stole her mind to control her—and cling to the hope that Ina's mind is stronger than the Queen's, that Caro has not yet invaded her head with the tendrils of her magic.

After the soldiers' voices fade away, Liam leads me onward, uphill, to a quieter part of town, where the wide streets are nearly empty. A high stone wall runs along one side of the street for several blocks, beyond which I can see the tops of trees and hear the faint call of songbirds. We follow it as it curves gently, until we reach a large gate of oak wood and wrought iron, boasting a single word spelled out in twisting brass inlay:

BELLWOOD.

As we draw closer to the gate, I see that it's covered with a series of slits in the metal. Liam doesn't hesitate. He withdraws three day-coins from his purse and puts them into three of the slots: the third, seventh, then the first. I hear a muted grinding of gears, and then the gates click softly open. A combination lock.

Liam pushes the door open. Beyond it, I see a stretch of bright green grass, clustered with brick buildings shrouded in ivy. All around, trees the color of ash have started to bud with small bursts of violet and yellow, giving the entire place the appearance of being strung with garland. Seeing no one, he beckons to me, and I follow him inside.

I feel half dead on my feet, but I hope I look presentable. My hair is tamed and covered with Liam's hood. In Danna's dress, I could pass for a student, or so Liam's told me. I have no idea how scholars dress, or how they act, or if I resemble them in the least.

Fear has kept me awake and moving, never fully fading. The daylight feels like a new threat—but Bellwood, and whatever is hidden there, will hold a way forward. I have to believe that, trust in the past, or I won't be able to keep putting one foot in front of the other.

"Are you sure this is safe?" I whisper as we slide inside,

walking under the scant cover of the fruit trees that line the road.

Liam scrapes a hand through his hair. "Safer than anywhere else," he says, walking faster. "For what it's worth. And we'll be able to keep track of Caro's mischief from here."

Old resentment stirs in the back of my throat. "Is burning down an entire village *mischief* to you?"

"No. But it is to Caro."

I grit my teeth, biting back anger as if we're once again in the cellars of Everless.

"Come on, we should be inside before the first bell tolls at eight."

We race the rising sun up the hill, toward the neat collection of buildings, veiled in ivy and all surrounded by a low wall of red brick, topped with burnished iron spikes. Liam grew up here— after the fire that destroyed my father's forge, and his parents sent him away from Everless. This is where he transformed into the boy who's spent his life studying the myths of the Alchemist, and who's risked his life more than once to keep me safe.

The sky is dripping with light now. We stay in the shadow of the outer wall, Liam slightly ahead of me. I increase my stride, determined to stay at his side.

"Everyone ought to still be asleep," he tells me quietly. "But we'll be careful, just in case." He can't hide here, recognizable as he is. The thought makes my stomach churn uneasily. How long until Caro and Ina put two and two together, realize he's helping me? Have they already?

"It's beautiful," I say, anxious to break the silence between us. "What was it like, growing up here?"

Liam looks at me, his expression surprised and uncertain, as if he's not sure whether I really want to know. When I hold his gaze, a small smile steals onto his face, making my heart flutter.

"My parents meant it as a punishment, sending me here," he said softly. "Far away from Everless, the feasts, the hunting trips, the luxury. But I never experienced it that way." He surveys the gold-limned silhouettes of the buildings, an unfamiliar softness in his face. "I *wanted* to learn. I liked the classes, the scholars. First-years weren't allowed in the library—too many old books that can fall apart if you look at them the wrong way—but I would sneak in at night anyway to read the stories."

I let myself fall just a step behind him, so he won't see me staring. I don't know if I've ever heard him say so many words in one breath. It makes me miss Everless with a fierce ache. And maybe it's just the rising sun, but there's a glow in his eyes that I can scarcely tear my gaze from.

"How did you meet your friends?" I grasp for words, wanting him to keep talking. I realize there must be an entire world of people he knew here, people he respected and studied with and socialized with. Maybe even people he loved.

His smile comes back all at once, now even more light-filled.

The change in him takes my breath away. "Elias and I met in year one. It was in our very first class," he says, the corner of his eyes crinkling. "Tenets of Semperan History. We got there first and sat in the very front row, not in the back like everyone else. No one had told us that the scholar for that class had terrible breath."

I let out a laugh, too loud, but I can't help it. With the happiness in his voice, I feel like we're shedding the weight of years, that we're children and history has changed to make us friends. The side of his mouth tugs up, and he glances at me.

"I always wished you could have come here too, Jules," he says quietly. "You would have loved it."

I smile crookedly at him. "You're only saying that because you know I'm the Alchemist."

"No," he replies with surprising conviction. "*You*, Jules Ember, you would have loved it." He waves his hand. "The biggest library you've ever seen. Staying up late with your classmates, trading stories, just like you used to do at Everless with us and the servant children."

My heart twists with memories, a bittersweet feeling. A longing for the life I never had, but also a warmth because Liam is right. Even now his words call to me, painting tableaus of happiness in my mind. He knows me better than anyone alive, I suppose. "Maybe so," I admit, trying to tug down the feelings that have risen up in me like a flock of birds. It won't do to become nostalgic for the Gerling estate, not when I can't go back.

"But yes, the Alchemist is said to have walked all over this city when it was nothing but wilderness. This was your home." He clears his throat, changes his tone as if he's said too much.

"I'd always planned to return to Bellwood after Roan's wedding, though my mother had a different idea," he says as he guides me across the campus—over an arched bridge beneath an array of draping tree branches, across a wide-open square of green, along cobbled paths, around tall brick buildings that look both old and timeless. "Don't worry. No one will wonder why I'm here—"

Voices behind us make me jump. I whirl around, my muscles already tensing, and Liam's hand flies to my arm, as if to pull me behind him—but it's not soldiers. It's students, two girls and a boy, stumbling with too much madel, laughing and weaving as they emerge from a building, only a few paces away from us.

"Long live the Queen!" the brown-skinned girl shouts in greeting, raising an imaginary glass at Liam. "Let's see how long this one lasts!"

Liam freezes like a hare who catches sight of a fox, but they keep walking. The girl's gaze lingers on me though. Despite her smeared makeup and tripping walk, her dark eyes are sharp and penetrating, freezing me to the spot.

"She saw me," I whisper after they pass. "She saw my face."

Liam's frowning, but he shakes his head to dismiss me. "Don't worry about her." His eyes follow the trio away. "Even if she were to recognize you—and I doubt it—no one takes Stef seriously."

I think of her powerful gaze. "Why not?"

He lifts a shoulder in a shrug. "She's the illegitimate daughter of one of the Chamberlaynes."

The name sends a shiver over my skin. The Gerlings are the most influential family in Sempera, and widely known to be cruel to their servants. But according to rumors, they are almost considered kind when compared to the Chamberlaynes.

Liam continues. "Her line is full of hedge witches. And you heard her, she has a bad habit of spouting treason when she's had too much madel."

"A hedge witch?" In most parts of Sempera, hedge witches are tolerated as an amusement for the superstitious—an amusement that drained poor towns like Crofton of their meager blood-irons, according to Papa. The old Queen was rumored to collect powerful witches, though some claimed that she had them killed if they displeased her. I shudder, remembering how close this belief hewed to the truth. What would Semperans say if they knew that the Queen kept the Sorceress by her side—or rather, that the Sorceress kept the Queen at her side, under her dominion, disposing of her with a cold thrust of her knife.

"I'm surprised to find a hedge witch at Bellwood," I say, trying to push the thoughts away. "Don't you need money to attend?"

Liam's cheeks flush. He clears his throat but doesn't say anything more. We walk a little farther before he finally slows.

Ahead of us is an ancient-looking ruin, a shell of a building about the size of Everless's carriage house, with crumbling stone walls, two half-fallen spires, and one standing tower, like a small castle. The decaying structure is surrounded by a circle of bare earth—or maybe ash—as if both grass and snow have conspired to shun this place.

Yet something about it calls to me, pulls me toward it, and I have to hold myself back from moving forward and putting my hands in the ashes.

"Is this . . . ?"

Liam nods. "The Thief's Fort. Where the Alchemist once lived."

My breath catches. Before us, the ruin is a gray, three-pronged smear against the cool blue sky. I try to imagine what it must have looked like before it fell to pieces, a refuge—a home.

"What happened to it?" I ask as I step over the edge of a ragged hole in the wall, into the shadow of the interior. It's untouched by sun, and dust—or maybe ashes—muffles the sound of our footsteps completely. It seems strange that wind and rain hasn't washed it away. What remains of the walls suggests a large, round space, ringed by a courtyard with semi-collapsed archways leading off in different directions. A staircase winds steep along one wall but ends with nothing at the ceiling. As I wander, Liam follows at a distance. I'm aware of his eyes lingering on me. My skin prickles with warmth in spite of the chill—the temperature seems off in here, warmer than it is outside.

"The Queen burned it centuries ago. Most of the secrets of blood time were lost," Liam replies. He considers me for a moment. His gaze sends more waves of warmth through me. "Most of them, anyway. Some books remained—people never realize how many secrets a book can contain."

I nod. My throat tightens, thinking of the flutter of pages in my journal now, the petals of hidden knowledge pressed inside, flat and dry and lifeless, each more inscrutable than the last. Will being here, among these ruins, help me discover what might be hidden in the book my father died for?

"Look." Liam lifts his hand to gesture to one archway on the opposite side of the room, an east-facing, intact arch that perfectly frames the morning sun. He takes my hand—I start—and leads me outside through one of the broken archways, then back through the intact doorway.

I've opened my mouth to ask him why we're walking in circles—but then my breath dries up in my throat.

The room inside has transformed. Instead of shadows, it's filled with light, summer sunshine pouring in from certain glass-paned archways. The others lead into new rooms, through which I can see bookcases, a porcelain washing tub, a garden bursting with green. Tapestries decorate the spaces between doors and windows. The grimy stone floor has given way to clean, shining tile, covered with a blue carpet in this room, and a table laden with food sits in the center of the room. Strange, half-familiar food, bread and wine and flowers. And outside, through the gauzy curtains, I can see the eggshell blue sky of a spring noon.

"What is this?" My voice escapes in a whisper.

"An enchantment." Liam sounds joyful. He points back to the archway from which we came, where a curtain has materialized. "If you walk through that doorway with a belonging of the Alchemist's, you can get inside this . . . this . . ." He gestures around him, for once at a loss for words.

I think of the frozen town of Briarsmoor, twelve hours behind the rest of the world, its one resident stuck in a loop of life and death like a fly in amber. But that was frightening, grotesque. This feels peaceful, right. It's the same feeling as stepping into our warm cottage to escape a howling winter wind, back when I lived with Papa in Crofton.

"I found it by accident when I came through carrying your journal," Liam says, a bit sheepishly. "I hope that's all right."

"All right?" I echo, confused. "Why wouldn't it be?"

Liam looks at me strangely. "Because this is—was—your home. The Alchemist's home."

I take a deep breath, inhaling the smell of the place, bread and flowers and something else, something achingly familiar. I recall reading about this place long ago, in the Crofton schoolhouse or the Everless library, I'm not sure. About two hundred years after the Queen put down the foreign invasion and took the throne,

Sempera's inequality had deepened so that blood-iron was no longer a glittering promise, but a death sentence for the poor. In the midst of this, a group of scholars tried to unbind the country by uncoupling time from blood. And the Queen burned them, to provide a warning to Semperans and outsiders alike—that the secrets of blood time were hers alone.

Or Caro's alone, I think. The Queen wouldn't have burned this place—burned my home—except by her command. Was Caro trying to find the Alchemist, find me, all those years ago? Or was she simply trying to erase every mark of my influence, everything I cared about, from the face of the earth? For a heartbeat, the loss dissolves in me like blood-iron into tea. It feels like Crofton all over again, the impact blunted by centuries, but painful all the same. My happiness at the magic fades.

"Why is it called the Thief's Fort?" The echo of the Crofton woman who screamed at me floats through my mind again, a refrain I can't get out of my head. *Thief. Snake. Murderer.*

Liam blinks, seeming to read the hurt in my eyes. "I don't know how it began." He speaks slowly, as if choosing his words carefully. "But according to an inscription on the wall, the Alchemist herself called it that too. And her followers, in their writings. She—*you*—reclaimed the name for yourself."

The words kindle a small warmth in my chest, like a struck match.

"Another thing," Liam says. He points up the staircase,

which extends along the wall in both directions. "Down leads to the tunnels, so you can get around Bellwood without being seen. The students do use the tunnels, but not often these days." He lifts his hand, pointing up. "And there . . ." At the top of the stairs, instead of the dead end I saw earlier, a wooden door with bronze detailing has materialized.

Without waiting for an answer, he guides me to the staircase and climbs up. He produces an ancient, intricate key on a leather cord and passes it to me.

A nervous lightness fills me as I take it. I turn the key in the lock—it scrapes a little but moves easily—and brush past Liam to step inside; it takes me a moment to recognize the feeling as excited anticipation, so long has it been since I had something to feel truly happy about. Now, the feeling grows that I'm returning to something familiar and beloved, and though I know I should be careful, I can't stop myself from bounding up the stairs, my fingers skimming along the wall as I go. The walls and stairs are stone bricks, smooth with age, and it should feel cold but it doesn't. Warm sunlight spills in through small windows set into the round walls, turning the dust motes in the air to gold. It feels familiar, it feels *right*, and something in my chest swells buoyantly, tugs me upward.

The sight at the top makes me stop short, Liam colliding with my back a second later. We've emerged into what must be one of the three spires I saw, a stone room bright with afternoon light.

The room is dry and smells like old paper and cinnamon. Instead of a window—half the wall is gone, its ragged edges giving way to a view of Bellwood's redbrick buildings and the farmland beyond it cast gold by the sun. I can't feel any chill from outside. Inside, a deep red rug covers the floor; and in the center of the room is a voluminous bed strewn with green and gold fabrics, a trunk at its foot spilling clothes. There's a small washbasin along one wall, a writing desk across another. Leather-bound books are piled at random across the floor.

"How is this possible?" My voice comes out in a whisper. Liam moves me gently aside so he can squeeze into the room. He stands beside me, looking at our surroundings with reverence in his eyes.

"Look." He takes my hand, making me start, and pulls me gently over to the window. Staring out, I can see the mosaic of rooftops in Montmere, a field just starting to turn green. Liam lifts our clasped hands and reaches them, together, outside the tower. I feel cool early spring air for a second before he pulls our hands quickly back down.

"It's your room, Jules," he says softly. "You built a home here."

I can scarcely hear Liam over the roaring in my ears. The specific memories elude me, swirling just out of my reach, but the feeling is there—that this was my home, that I was safe here.

"The Thief's Fort burned down, but you were able to

123

preserve it as it was that day," Liam goes on, excitement quickening his words and making his eyes shine. "Only people faithful to the Alchemist, who have something of hers, can access it. I had your journal. It's always spring in here—rain, snow never come in. And if you look from the outside, it's just a ruin."

"Trapped in time," I say, marveling that I could have ever done such a thing. Liam nods. I finally tear my gaze from him and look around me. Everything is clean and—not new—but not ancient either, as if I've just stepped out for an errand and am now coming home. *Home.*

Color dances high in Liam's cheeks. "I used to sit downstairs, sometimes, and read. I . . . I hope that's all right."

It takes a moment for the meaning of his words to sink in, and then a laugh bursts out of me. It startles me at first—it's been so long since I've laughed, so long since I've been truly happy about anything. Liam's eyes go wide.

"It's all right," I say hurriedly. "Of course it's all right."

Liam's smile has fallen slightly, and I'm forcefully reminded of his expression at nine years old, at Everless, looking from one face to another to gauge the servant children's reaction to an old fact he'd rattled off. I'd always thought him pompous for this—dangling his knowledge over us like a bag of blood-irons, waiting to see how impressed we all were—but considering the memory again, I see the wistfulness in young Liam's eyes, the desire for connection burning there alongside insecurity.

"It's wonderful," I continue quickly. "I love it here. It feels . . . safe."

His smile widens, making something jump in my chest. "Even though I hate to admit that Elias is right, I think it is safe, Jules," he says. "Caro doesn't seem to know there's anything left."

I manage to choke out a laugh. "How reassuring." I realize Liam is still holding my hand. He brushes his thumb against my palm, so lightly that I'm not sure if I'm imagining the warmth brush across my skin.

My throat tightens. Inside the safety of these walls, I feel plucked out of time—far from Caro's reach, invisible to everyone in Sempera but Liam, standing in front of me. Suddenly and all at once, I want to pull him in.

Nothing happens though, and a twinge of silly disappointment shoots through me. I tug my hand from his. "Is there something here that can help us take down Caro?"

I make myself meet his eyes when he smiles at me again.

"Perhaps. Do you want to see what we came for?"

11

In the lower room, I sit at the wooden table while Liam paces in front of me. His eyes are glittering in the way they only seem to, I've learned, when he's discussing some sort of history. Behind him hangs a simple tapestry: a plain, threadbare map of Sempera rendered in blue and gold. He turns to me, hands spread in front of him, looking for all the world like he's at the front of a classroom about to begin a lecture. For a moment, I'm seven years old again, watching a much younger Liam jog after Roan on Everless's lawn, reciting some arcane fact that gets carried away by the wind. "Elias and I have collected accounts of the Alchemist and Sorceress over the past few years."

Liam wears a grin on his face. It's strange, this much joy in his eyes, untethered to the glumness he usually wears around his shoulders like a coat. I can't help but let a smile tug at the corners of my mouth too. "I thought you were hesitant to come here."

"Well . . . defeating the Sorceress is a puzzle, isn't it? Puzzles can be solved." Clearing his throat, he takes up a pile of paper from a bookshelf and crouches down in front of me, nudging plates aside before carefully laying each page down. Some are ancient like the journal; some are newer, judging by the crispness of the parchment. One with a crude illustration of a girl's face—neither mine nor Caro's—is scrawled on the back of what appears to be a Gerling tax log.

I scan the scatter of pages but discern only drawings and fragments of *fox and snake* stories. Nervousness swirls in me, dispelling the joy I felt watching Liam work. "What am I supposed to be seeing here?"

Liam points, his index finger floating from page to page. "I studied these from back to front—first just for the mystery of the Alchemist"—he reddens, but keeps going—"but then I detected a pattern. Here, here, and here, the alchemical symbols for poison and death have been found in writings you left behind, or other written accounts of knowledge I believe to be passed down by the Alchemist," he says, more animatedly than seems fitting for talk of poison and death. "From what we could gather, all of them are from different lives—at least seven of them. We assumed it was information you were trying to pass on."

"Or remember," I say automatically, something stirring in me.

Liam furrows his brows but continues. "The symbols—they

127

keep appearing in stories that tell of Fox's death."

An odd feeling—envy?—tugs at me, along with a surge of confidence. "I don't remember making up stories of Fox's death—but that can only mean I'm right. I've been thinking of Fox's death. The Sorceress's death."

Liam sits back on his knees. "This story tells of a hound's claw that pierces Fox's hide. This one of a tooth that takes away her life in a single bite. Which isn't so interesting until you know that, in high Semperan, the same word was used for *tooth* and *claw*, which means they might have been referring to the same item. They're simply translated differently by the scholars who worked on them."

He looks expectantly at me, but I don't say anything, dizzied by the onslaught of information. There's bitterness too, gathering so swiftly in my chest that I'm afraid to speak. All this time, while Papa and I lived day to day, meal to meal, Liam sat here, investigating the mystery of me, the mystery of the Sorceress who was hunting Sempera for me, enshrouded in esoteric symbols and layers of secrecy. *He knows more about the Alchemist than I do,* I think bitterly.

"There's more," he says hesitantly.

"Great," I mumble.

Liam is already moving to the wall, where he carefully pulls back the tapestry. Underneath it, the wall is smooth stone—smooth, that is, except for something carved into it. An ancient glyph, strange and yet familiar somehow, the rough shape of a circle with details and flourishes flying out. Recognition stabs through me. I rise and move nearer to it.

At a closer distance, I can see that the glyph is not one shape but several, interwoven into one impossible maze of twists and curls and sharp corners. Simple circles and squares morph into fractured lines that burst into symbols that are—or might be, for all I know—ancient Semperan. All the forms are stacked on top of one another as intricately as needles and straw are wound into a bird's nest, coming together to make the solid form I saw at a distance. With my nose almost pressed against it, I see that the delicate lines are actually chiseled out of the stone. The tool must have been impossibly small and sharp. Inside each furrow is a fine gold powder, which makes the glyph shine softly in the light streaming in through the window.

Uncontrollably, I shiver.

"This is familiar," I say, and glance over my shoulder to see Liam's eyes widen. "Not this one exactly, but something similar was carved above the door of Calla's hedge shop. Crofton's hedge witch. Not this complicated or this . . . beautiful."

The glyph *is* beautiful, almost otherworldly, intricate and complicated like nothing else I've seen. I close my eyes, trying to remember Calla's shop in detail from the time before Papa forbade me from visiting her. I had always believed that Papa was only being strict, trying to ensure that I wouldn't grow up to be superstitious and waste my blood-irons on a hedge witch's trappings, but now I realize he stopped me from learning about the secrets that lay within me. I loved listening to the hedge witch's stories, not knowing what truth they could contain.

"Calla told me that it was meant to ward away . . ." *The Alchemist's spirit*, I remember, trailing off. "But I went back one day and it was taken down."

"My mother ordered routine sweeps of all the towns on our lands, to remove any of the old alchemical symbols. Usually whenever she was trying to curry favor with the Queen." Liam gestures toward the blown-away wall behind us, where the Thief's Fort, broken, appears to lie open to the night.

"So these—" I fix my eyes back on the glyph, trying to decipher a single shape above the many. My mind whirs. "What do these symbols mean? They wouldn't be carved into a wall if they weren't important, would they?"

I raise my hand to touch the wall, then stop, stilled by fear. After a moment Liam joins me at the wall and traces over the lines with the assurance of long familiarity.

"It's an ancient language of sorts used by old scholars and alchemists. Many of these symbols are even older than ancient Semperan, and no one knows where they originated." He points to one simple curved line. "This one denotes water." He pauses, tracing his finger over a circle with a smaller circle inside it. "This looks like a canine head. But this one is time itself. Alchemists—you and your followers—passed down their history however they could, even though the Queen—or Caro, maybe—destroyed it at every turn. They passed it down in pieces, in stories. They had to protect their knowledge from the Sorceress. So nothing was ever simple with them."

"Of course not." But my old stories are already surfacing in my mind. *When Snake had stolen Fox's heart, he swallowed it whole.*

"It took us years to figure out what they all meant, even longer to distinguish all of them. But this one, which is repeated several times, means *weapon*, same as in the papers. And this one, the biggest of all, means *love* or *heart*. But this one—" He steps away from the wall. "This one denotes *evil*. Placed like this, they form something like a sentence: *a weapon against a great evil*."

"A weapon against a great evil? Against *Caro*," I breathe. A thrill drops cold down my spine. Suddenly all my memories seem to dance tantalizingly close to the surface, as if all I need to do is step forward and I will fall in. Something seems to move over my shoulder, in the corner of my eye—but when I snap my head around to look, nothing is there.

Vaguely, I hear Liam's voice over my shoulder. "There are

other symbols that I still don't know the meaning of. It's taken me years to search discreetly, but I can't find any record of them, nor can Elias. . . ."

But his words sound distant, like he's at the other end of a long tunnel. I shudder.

My sight blurs. All except for the glyph on the wall before me, which seems to become sharper somehow, more visible. My breath and heartbeat speed up and I reach behind me for Liam, suddenly desperate for something, someone to anchor me to the moment. But before I can touch him, he dissolves in my sight and his voice fades, replaced by a tangle of others. Voices everywhere, familiar somehow, but panicked.

My vision clears. I breathe in the smell of something sharp and sweet. Liam isn't there. The Thief's Fort is whole but lacks the shimmer it had a moment ago, the light outside the windows matching the light inside. It seems realer somehow. And there are people all around me. Men and women in jewel-toned robes.

And they are in chaos.

They run, shouting, pulling books and scrolls from the shelves and shoving them beneath their cloaks, clustering around the window to stare out into the night. By the door, a dark-skinned old man hands out swords to people as they pass, and near me, a wan but bright-eyed young woman is standing by a table, her hands trembling as she wraps glass jars in cloth and tucks them into a burlap sack. As I stare, a tear slips down her cheek.

What's happening? I try to ask, but the words come out warped and muffled, like I'm speaking underwater. Still, the woman whips around toward me, extends a hand to help me to my feet.

"We have to leave, my lady," she says, voice rough with fear and unshed tears. "She's here. The Sorceress."

Downstairs, there's a mighty crash; someone screams. And through the open door, winding up the stairs, I smell smoke.

Remember, I think frantically, panic stabbing through me before I can even register what needs to be remembered—panic because I know that the Sorceress is here, for me, and that I am not going to leave Bellwood's gates alive. I watch as my own hands reach out to the wall of stone, feel the pain as I trace the symbols over and over with my fingers, until my skin is broken and bleeding, and my blood dissolving the stone underneath into the shape of a message. *Water. Lead. Ruby. Evil. Weapon. Claw.*

My bloodied finger goes to trace one more, in the shape of a crescent moon—and stops.

I whirl around to face the Sorceress. Her dark streaming hair is tangled with blood and ash, though a blue silk ribbon snakes through it. My eyes fall to where her dress is torn, revealing a line of scarred skin—pink and jagged and screaming—directly over her heart. The mark shimmers in the growing heat.

"You thought you could run?" Caro snarls and lunges toward me, stripping the blue ribbon from her hair and wrapping it around my neck in one fluid movement.

And then—

Black, empty. I'm somewhere else, though the space around me is so dark, it seems like nowhere at all.

Pain explodes across my body. Heat pulses in my palm, sharp and persistent. I look down and uncurl my fingers. My aching fist. Both raw and pulsing.

I'm holding a bloodred jewel the length of a year-coin, sharp at one end as if I'd pulled it out of a great beast. The body of the gem is wound with a stone snake that uncurls into a handle. A dagger. *Claw. Tooth. Weapon.* Horror and awe in equal parts rush over me. The jewel spills crimson light over my fingers, like it's really bleeding in my hand. Staring deep into the light dancing on the blade, I see a reflection smiling back at me—

No. Caro smiles back at me. The Sorceress's face, refracted a dozen times in the dagger's glassy surface.

And—Caro is there, really *there*. On the ground below me, head tipped back, eyes wide.

I did this.

And now I must hide it, keep it safe. *Remember.* I must run . . .

An unseen hand grabs my arm, and I scream.

"Jules!" someone barks. A boy's voice, familiar. The scream and roaring die in my head, the darkness dissolves into a pale light and the room swims into focus—

But quiet now, empty except for Liam and me.

Liam is staring down at me, wide-eyed and pale, but not at my face. I follow his gaze down to my own hands and a wave of shock goes through me, just before the pain hits. My fingers are bloodied, the nails torn. My fists are clenched white with streaks of red, just as they were in my vision. Slowly, heart pounding, I unfurl my hand—

To reveal nothing. Nothing but air.

12

Disappointment floods my chest, so sudden and strong it's an effort to hold in a sob. I'm on my knees beside the table, shivering, hating how easily the vision stole away the comfort and warmth of the Thief's Fort. My stomach roils. Liam crouches down next to me, brushes a hand over my arm. I need to push him away—but I can't. I don't.

"What happened? What did you see?" he asks gently.

But the words flow around me like wind, not sinking in. I feel as heavy and confused as when I wake from a daytime sleep to see that the light has faded into dusk. The panicked faces of the people in my dream—lesser alchemists, I realize, my followers—flash in my mind. The Sorceress came here, to the Thief's Fort, to hunt me. Wrapped her ribbon around my neck in an effort to choke me. Did she succeed? How many of the alchemists escaped?

How many succumbed to the Sorceress's smoke?

I breathe heavy, ragged. Liam puts an arm around me and pulls me against him, unclasping his cloak and arranging it so that it drapes over me, a blanket. Warming me, hiding me. I didn't realize until just now that I'm freezing, shivering hard. Liam's heart beats beside me once again; this time I feel the tension in his muscles, the low tumble of words that are meant to give comfort. I should pull away, I know, but I feel like I might fall apart if I do. The Thief's Fort—my home—danced a promise of revelation in front of me, only to snatch it away.

"It's all right," Liam murmurs into my hair. He pulls me in closer, even though I've stopped trembling by now, and wraps his other arm around me, as if he could shield me from harm. I can still feel the tension in him—but there's warmth in him too, offsetting the cold knot of fear in my chest.

My mind is reeling with images, one overtaking another and another and another, flitting behind my closed eyelids as rapidly as the colorful flipbooks Roan Gerling had when we were children. I try to put them in order, make sense of what I just saw. Beside me, Liam stays quiet. Neither of us move until silence has reigned for several minutes. When I speak, it's to say, "I saw something. A weapon of some kind."

His eyes widen. "A weapon?"

"Yes." I look down at my hand, still half expecting the jeweled dagger to be there. With a jolt, I remember Caro at my feet, mouth twisted open in a scream. The same image I saw after I stabbed her in Shorehaven's gardens. "I don't know what the dagger was or where it came from, but I *felt* it. It was as real as holding on to—"

I stop abruptly, realizing that I've taken Liam's hand in mine to prove my point. I hurriedly unlace my fingers from his. Untucking slightly from the shell of his cloak, I gesture to the papers still scattered before us, then to the shining glyph on the wall. "What if it's the weapon you noted in your papers? The symbol on the wall—" I turn to stare at the gold glyph carved into the stone. "Why else would I have such a clear vision of it?"

Liam pauses a few seconds before nodding, clears his throat. "It's possible, I suppose. Maybe something you created in a past life. Is it here?"

I breathe out sharply. Excitement at what I saw and frustration at Liam for being hesitant meet in my chest like hot and cold air. A storm brewing. "I . . . I don't know."

Liam's face falls. "Did you see where it was?"

"No." I squeeze my eyes shut, trying to hold on to the images. But they've already faded. "I was in this room—Thief's Fort was burning, and Caro came inside to find me, but then the vision became just . . . black. Blank, except for the dagger. I knew I had to hide it somewhere, to remember where, but I don't know. . . ."

The words bring a bitter taste to my throat. I fall quiet and let my eyes drop to my pale, bleeding hands. *I am the Alchemist,*

I tell myself. But I don't feel powerful, cowering here, in hiding, with predators circling practically outside our door. What I do feel is a sudden, welling frustration at everything I don't know, don't understand—

At the surging instinct to flee Sempera for good, just as Liam wanted me to do before I went to Crofton, as he urged when we fled Shorehaven.

I stare into the dark of his eyes, my gut tumbling and twisting with doubt. How many years have I lost? How many years did I spend scrabbling in Crofton while Liam Gerling studied the unknown parts of me in musty books? How many years was I condemned to remain a stranger to myself, to the Alchemist buried in shadow inside my mind? Even my ancient home won't welcome me now, not wholly. My fingertips, blood-tipped and ragged where they enacted my vision, ache. My heart aches, too.

If the Alchemist stays sunken in me forever, revealing herself in shards of broken memories, never whole—who am I then? Not Jules Ember. Not anyone.

I stand, backing toward the door. Suddenly the need to be alone—and to get out of the deceptively beautiful Thief's Fort—is overpowering.

Liam gets to his feet too, staring at me uncertainly.

"Don't," I say. "I need to think."

"You can't leave, Jules, it's not safe—"

"Don't!" My voice is louder now, a half shout.

Liam blinks, the hand he'd reached out for me falling to his side. I see the hurt that fills his eyes, but still, I turn around and practically run down the stairs.

Outside, I gulp down the cool spring air, though it does little to dispel the confusion. More than anything, it's the smell of smoke that lingers in my nose, and the sound of screams in my ears.

How many hundreds of years ago was that night, that fire that burned down the Thief's Fort and scattered the lesser alchemists to the wind? How many people died then, as now, because of me? Their loss—because they *were* lost, I know it in my bones—still tears at me. *They followed me*, whispers some conscience older than my body. *They trusted me.*

This was different from the other visions I've had, at Everless and on the road. I wasn't running through the woods or chained in a dungeon, helpless, following a preordained path as surely as a wheel on a cart. I was *there* in the Thief's Fort, there with the lesser alchemists, sharing their terror and adrenaline. I was alive in the memory, I could move and speak and feel. And after that . . . the weight of the strange jeweled dagger in my hand, as real as the pain of my torn fingernails or the heat of Liam's touch on my arm.

I kneel on the ground and breathe in the cool grass, desperate to feel the huge, real press of the earth underneath me. The images and sensations of the memory fade a little, replaced by the pleasantly damp smell of the soil, along with the sound of the wind through the trees. The memories had been hanging in the air of that little room, coating my lungs, but now I've walked outside the range of the cloud.

I lift my head, turn to look back at the Thief's Fort. I left Liam in there with lamps burning, but from the outside, as before, it appears only a lovely, empty ruin.

Suspicion creeps into my mind. This could all somehow be a cruel trick of Caro's—another part of her twisted game. Like how she manipulated the former Queen, when slipping tendrils of her magic into her head . . .

Or is it not Caro at all but just my own weakness? Am I falling apart, going mad, without the strength to hold centuries of memory?

No. The shape of the glyph floats behind my eyes, written in burning gold with my own blood. The glyph and the Thief's Fort—together they pulled me down into the memory, the shapes and lines weaving together over me like a net.

A message left behind—for me.

The dagger. It was in my hand; I can still feel its heat, its light, an inaudible scream of meaning from my past. Its handle was a snake—that can't mean nothing. I flex and curl my fingers, as though by sheer will I might make it appear for me. Squeeze my eyes shut and try to see myself carving those strange shapes, to see more of what happened before, what I was trying so desperately to remember. I try to wash away the blackness of the final memory, to pull back the thick dark curtains in my head, to reveal any indication of where it took place.

But it's no use. Memories dance tantalizingly around the edges of my mind, shades of meaning winking in and out like fireflies at dusk.

A commotion of voices in the distance snaps my eyes open. I realize with a lurch of my stomach that I've wandered far from the Thief's Fort. There are pine trees all around me, blankets of needles under my feet. Faintly, I can hear the distant noise of the city. *It's not safe*, Liam had warned.

Fear floods me. I shouldn't have run from Liam, not when memories are clouding my senses like this.

Then up ahead, in the direction I think leads to the main gate, I spot a figure. It takes me a moment to recognize the silhouette as a person, because she—a girl in scholar's robes—isn't moving. She's sitting on the grass, facing away from me, hunched over something on the ground. It's clear from the stillness of her body that she's utterly absorbed in whatever she's doing. A patch of sunlight lingers behind her, the inverse of a shadow.

I know I should run, but instinct pulls me forward. It's dark in the trees, and cold. Dark enough, I hope, that she couldn't make out the details of my face.

I'm debating whether to call out when a twig snaps beneath my foot. Before I can think, the girl jumps up and whirls around, scattering the things laid out on the ground around her—I see the shine of metal, the white of bone.

A hedge witch's trappings.

"Who's there?" the girl calls out. I recognize her as one of the drunken passersby from before—the girl, Stef, who Liam said was from a family of hedge witches, who shouted mockingly, *Long live the Queen*. In any case, she's far from drunk now. Her dark eyes scan the woods, and her posture is tense, as if she's ready to run or fight.

I could stay still, or try to slip away. But the memory still has its claws in me, snarling in my ear. An idea blooms in my mind—a dangerous, desperate one.

Before I knew that I was the Alchemist and Caro the Sorceress, Caro, Ina, and I visited a hedge witch in Laista. That was the night before everything changed forever: Ina was seeking a blood regression, the countryside ritual where you can fall back through your own time and let lost memories float to the surface, moments to be thumbed through like pages in a book. Like so many dotting Sempera's isolated towns, Laista's hedge witch was a fraud—but her smoky shop brought forth memories in me, vivid details that had been buried. Those recovered moments led me to Briarsmoor, where I discovered the truth of my birth.

If Stef is really a witch, maybe she can help me where Liam can't. Where I can't even help myself.

So I step forward, into the puddle of light between us and call out to her.

13

"Stef."

I hold my breath as Stef whips her head around to stare at me, the recklessness of what I've just done sinking in. Too late to take it back. Her sharp, unblinking gaze sparks fear in me like a flint stone striking rock. Maybe her flippant talk about the Queen earlier was just a show. If that's the case, and she recognizes me as Jules Ember of Crofton, wanted for the Queen's murder, I may have just doomed myself for desperate want of help.

But thankfully, she doesn't recognize me, or at least if she does she doesn't show it. Her eyes travel slowly over my face, her mouth flattening into a suspicious frown.

"I heard that you're a hedge witch." An attempt to be conversational. I make my voice bold and bright, the way I imagine a student's would be if this were only a diversion.

She glares at me. "Who did you hear that from?"

"From Liam Gerling," I say, remembering the lesson Papa taught me and Everless drove home: to tell the truth as much as you can, so the lies will be harder to see. As I speak, I try to surreptitiously peer down at the things scattered around her feet, my heart quickening at the sight. Bits of metal twisted into strange shapes, carved trinkets that could be pale wood or animal bones, a small brass bowl of powder.

Her eyes widen in surprise, then narrow again. "High company. I've never seen you before."

I shrug. "So are the rumors true?"

With an air of brisk efficiency, Stef gathers up her items in the piece of burgundy velvet they're sitting on. Plucking a string of leather from the grass, she ties the fabric into a pouch and secures it to her belt. "Which rumors?" she shoots back, never taking her eyes off me. "There are a few. You'll have to be more specific."

"That you know about lesser alchemy. And that you have no love for the Queen." I add the second statement impulsively, then stop, my heart racing. Can she tell I'm trying to feel out her loyalties?

Stef regards me levelly, looking just as wary as I feel. But I detect a glint of mirth in her eyes. At my boldness, I hope. "I had no love for the *old* Queen. I haven't made up my mind yet about the little orphan Queen. But I doubt my life will change anyhow."

My stomach clenches at the jab at Ina. I push down the anger. "What about the alchemy?" I ask. "I'm in need of a service, and I can pay."

She gives me a flat stare. "If I did have whatever it is that you're looking for, why would I tell you, stranger?"

My heart picks up. "Because I need a witch's help. It's—important."

"What is it, then?" she says evenly, rising to her feet.

I brush my sweating hands on Danna's dress. I see Stef's eyes flicker as she notices.

"Remembering things I've forgotten," I say. "I want to do a blood regression."

Stef takes a step toward me. She's tall, dark-skinned, with long braids falling over her shoulders. Her green robes look perfect despite the fact that she's been sitting on the forest floor. "Blood regressions are for bored noblewomen or desperate fools." Her eyes race down my body, then back up to meet my gaze, assessing me unflinchingly. "You're no noblewoman. It must be important if you're coming to me for help. But if that's the case, how could you have forgotten the memory in the first place?"

My heart beats faster. She seems to be studying my expression, and I desperately hope that she's been cooped up on campus studying for the past weeks, that she hasn't seen the flyers with the sketch of my face plastered all over the city. "They're the stories of someone who's gone." Not a lie.

"We've all lost people. Remembering their stories won't bring them back." Stef's face remains stony. Then, in a quieter voice, she adds, "People forget in order to survive."

In spite of her words, there's a cautious note in her voice that ignites hope in me, a curiosity shadowed in her face. Now I'm the one to step forward. "Please. I'll pay you for your time, but I really need the help."

"You'll have to find it somewhere else." Her voice cools. She turns her back to me—apparently having concluded that I'm no threat to her—to finish gathering her things. A small bowl, a short knife shining in a bed of flowers. "Did Liam Gerling also tell you that the old Queen executed half my family for practicing magic?"

I swallow. "No."

She turns back to me, a sad smirk brushed across her face. "Well, I'm not looking to go the same way."

"Yet you're here, in the woods, practicing magic," I respond quickly.

She whirls on me, her eyebrows arching high, but says nothing. The silence emboldens me.

"I'm sorry to hear that about your family," I say quietly. I move two fingers in a circle over my torso, making the sign of the clock, a traditional sign of respect when mourning the dead. "All I need is a single blood regression. Like I said, I can pay."

Stef's mouth twitches. "If you've heard rumors about me, I'm sure you've also heard rumors about my parentage. I'll admit that being the daughter of a Chamberlayne allows me certain discrepancies"—her hand unconsciously travels to the pouch on her belt—"but I'm not going to risk myself doing blood regressions for strange girls who follow me into the woods. Now—good-bye." She turns and walks away, green silk cloak flaring behind her.

"It's Jules!" My voice cracks on the shouted word.

The echoed shout—*Jules, Jules, Jules*—seems to fill the trees. Immediately, I wish I could take it back. I stand there frozen as Stef slowly turns around again to face me. My name hovers in the air between us, a venomous snake that's expanded its hood, ready to strike. A sign of warning. Of danger.

"Jules," Stef echoes slowly, thoughtfully. She takes in my face again and I think I see her eyes widen slightly, almost imperceptibly. I remain still. "Jules Ember, I don't suppose?"

My silence is answer enough.

Stef's breath hisses out through her teeth. She moves forward, her feet silent on the ground, but I don't miss the way one hand drifts to her waist. I tense, preparing to use my magic if she draws a knife from her cloak. But she just comes to a stop an arm's length away from me.

Stef's smile curls across her face slowly, like a ribbon over heat. "Did you really kill the Queen?"

Sweat trickles down my back. I shake my head. "No."

Her face falls. "Oh. That's a shame. If you had, maybe I'd consider helping you."

"I was going to," I blurt out. Enough of the truth has already spilled out of me—what does it matter if I let the rest out too? "But she was just a puppet. Someone else was pulling the strings." I clear my throat, swallow down my fear. "*That's* who I want to kill."

"You?" she asks. Eyebrows lift again. Confusion and curiosity even a hint of fear war across Stef's face—but the reasonable side of her must win out, or she must not believe me, because she turns on her heel. "Good luck with that," she calls over her shoulder.

Frustration twists my gut. *Yes, me,* I want to yell. *Who else? Who else but the Alchemist?*

There's one way to show her. My body moves faster than I can change my mind.

I raise my hands, throwing my mind out into the air. Before I think too hard about what I'm doing, I find the trees in the air and stop time around them, so that the branches around her go still, despite the breeze. The world quiets around us, the song snatched from birds' throats. Stef stops walking.

One hand floats up to tug on one of the tight braids framing her cheeks. The seconds thicken around her, like honey. I can't read her expression. Emotion twists her face, equal parts awe and fury and—

Recognition.

With a shudder, I let the magic go. The wind whispers around us again, the birdsong bursts back into the air. The sounds are frenzied for a moment, hurried, as if they're catching up.

Eventually, she says, "My mother told me you'd come one day . . ." She trails off and takes another step toward me, her voice dropping into almost a whisper when she finally speaks the name, "Alchemist."

The undercurrents are still there, awe and anger both.

My heart drops into my stomach. To hear that word from a stranger makes a thrill race up and down my spine, alongside terror.

"Your mother?" I respond, immediately wishing I could take the words back, they sound so young and foolish.

Stef ignores my question. She doesn't seem to notice or care. "It's true, isn't it?" She looks at me hard, then takes my still-open hands into hers, flipping them over as if they'll reveal some great secret—or trick. Then, in the span of a breath, her face changes from surprise to fury. She shoves my hands away, hard. I clasp them to my chest.

"If you're the Alchemist, that's all the more reason for me to stay far away." Her voice rises above the birdsong and whisper of the breeze. I remember how close we must be to Bellwood. Stef, though, doesn't seem to care. "You've been a plague on my family. Hasn't there been enough collateral damage in your fight with the Sorceress?"

My heart twists as her words sink in. I recall the Alchemist's followers who I saw less than an hour ago, in my vision in the Thief's Fort. Were Stef's ancestors among the dead? But I still need help—and I've already committed, I remind myself bitterly, remembering Amma's words—so I take a deep breath.

"It's true. I'm not asking you to be a part of anything now," I say. "I just need one blood regression. Like I said, I'll pay you."

Stef studies my face for a moment, her own brow creased in concentration. Then she crosses her arms across her chest. "Five years."

I inhale sharply. The amount makes me wince. How many people in Crofton died for less? But though I haven't seen it first-hand, I know that Liam has enough blood-irons in his satchel. With a lurch of my stomach, I agree. "Fine. Five years."

"These are real rites, practices dated back centuries, prac-ticed for centuries by my family. No magic as powerful as yours, but," Stef says shortly, eyes flicking to my hands again, "not a hoax or a party trick. You might see nothing, or you might see something that you don't want to see."

I nod my understanding. "Let's get started."

Hood drawn over my head, I follow Stef into the student dormitories so that she can collect the items required for the blood regression. A sense of triumph rings through me, drowning out fear. I'm delaying my return to the Thief's Fort, in no rush to face Liam. I swear that, even at a distance, I feel the air growing warm with his anger at me—for running into danger, for rashly betraying my identity to Stef. But didn't he say himself, on a wintry night in Laista, that I race openhearted into danger? Liam knows that the answer is yes. Always.

I'm surprised to find that the dark, sunken hallways of the dormitories that lead to Stef's room don't appear much different than the airless servants' corridors at Everless. But, devoid of the servants who rush through the hallways of the Gerling estate, carrying laundry or nursing aching limbs, the dim tunnels of Bellwood feel lighter. History hangs in the air, saturated with a muted sense of joy.

Stef has her own room. It's small and close, lit only from one narrow window looking out over the city. I have to duck so as to not hit my head on the eaves. A square desk sits in one corner. She opens the bottom drawer and pulls out a wooden box, which is full of items.

I hang awkwardly back, curious but not wanting to pry, as she fills her leather pouch with a mixing bowl the size of her palm, a wooden pestle, several bundles of herbs. She hands me a worn pamphlet scrawled with ancient Semperan. It's clearly old, its texture soft under my fingers. It smells faintly of metal and ashes, or the bittersweet perfumes that all hedge witches seem to have in their shops. Then she strides across the room and lifts a wooden floorboard to reveal a row of gleaming wine bottles. She tucks one into her cloak, murmuring, "I owe you one, Ruthie."

Once she's concealed the pouch and the bottle, Stef straightens up and looks at me expectantly. "So—where to?"

I feel the blood drain from my face. I wouldn't mind taking Stef to the Thief's Fort—it's *my* home, after all—but Liam's there. Even though she knows I'm the Alchemist, it's dangerous to let her see that Liam's with me.

"I'm one step away from getting expelled as it is," she says pointedly. "I won't do magic in my own room. Where are you staying?"

Doubt pricks me, but I won't back down now. Seize the day, as Amma said.

The silence between us is stiff as I lead her to the Thief's Fort, the quiet seeming to crackle with danger. A stream of students passes us in the other direction, laughing. Dread rises in my gut. I feel as if I'm back at Shorehaven, toes hanging over the cliff, nothing below me but jagged rocks and a great fall. Stef's eyes, too, dart side to side. *Nervous*, I think, and this knowledge releases some tension in my muscles. I'm the one to be feared here—not her.

I have Stef wait below while I climb the stairs. The Thief's Fort is my secret to tell, but Liam will have to leave before I let her in. No one can know he's with me.

But when I enter pass through the archway, into my patch of stolen time, Liam isn't there.

He's probably out looking for me, that's all, I tell myself, trying to dispel the fear gathering in me. But an image of a soldier dragging him away makes bile crawl into my throat.

Not knowing what else to do, I call for Stef to come upstairs. When she reaches the Alchemist's room, her lips part, her eyes widening to devour the space, lingering on the summery image of Bellwood that appears outside the broken wall, spilling sunlight over the floor.

"My mother told me about this place when I was a girl. I never knew . . ." Her eyes scroll over the broken wall with wonder, a smile forming, quick and fleeting but real.

"Earlier, you said that she told you about me. What did she say? Did I—" I pause on the strangeness of the words in my mouth. "Did she know the Alchemist?"

Stef doesn't answer right away. Instead, she goes to the table and begins to lay out her things. Eventually she tells me, "As a girl, yes. She grew up on stories of the Alchemist and Sorceress like any child does—though our stories were passed down, not found in books. But when my grandmother died in service of you, my mother stopped dreaming of you. The stories she told me were more like warnings."

"Oh," I say softly. Lamely. I wring my hands, guilt burning in my gut. But at the same time, I can't help but feel a twinge of envy. What if instead of hiding the truth behind lies, Papa had been honest with me when I was a child, after he saved me from the Queen—from Caro—in Briarsmoor? What if Liam had told me about my past instead of tucking it away for himself, like a handful of blood-irons slid underneath the mattress? Would I have shunned the truth, like Stef? Would I have run?

Or would I *be* the Alchemist, stronger and more powerful than my enemy?

Emotions bloom in me, tangled and hot. Stef grew up with magic, and I feel the urge to unburden myself to her. "I only found out about my past recently. I don't know anyone from my past, other than the Sorceress herself—"

"The less I know, the better." Stef interrupts, waving her hand to quiet me.

"Right, of course." I press my lips shut, trying to keep the sting of disappointment from showing on my face.

She sighs. "It's hard to shed the old ways. My mother used to tell me that every single thing in Sempera—perhaps everything in nature itself—once held magic. That still, to this day, you can bleed magic from a stone, if you know how to do it."

Motioning for me to join her at the table near the window, Stef gathers a black leaf shaped like the tip of an arrow, a bright-red fruit half the size of a plum, and a familiar string of leaves pearled with silver in the palm of her hand. Her voice is brusque, but I think I can detect a note of excitement underneath. "Spadesmark, from the oldest tree in Sempera, to connect you to the past. Hour's blight, a poison in high volume, to shed the present from your mind, and finally—"

"Ice holly." I try to keep my voice light. "It only grows in spots where the Sorceress has worked her magic."

I know that because Caro told me herself. In my mind, she smiles.

"Strong magic always leaves something behind," Stef says flatly.

Stef tears the spadesmark, hour's blight, and ice holly into pieces, and lets them flutter into the brass bowl that sits at the tip of her knees. Taking a pestle, she grinds the mixture impatiently, turning the bowl as she jabs. Then, satisfied, she places the pestle on the floor and uncorks the stolen wine with a soft *pop*. The sweet scent blooms between us, filling the room.

Slowly, she pours the dark red liquid into the bowl,

floating the plants on a shining mauve surface. At first, nothing happens—but soon, a thread of pale green smoke grows from the mix. The potion is nothing like the liquid that Laista's hedge witch kept in a bottle in her shop. Just as I think that the strange curling smoke resembles the stem of a flower, the end stretching toward me bursts into color: a crown of five golden petals encircling a pulsing red center. My breath catches in my chest. "It's beautiful. I've never seen anything like it."

I watch in awe as Stef plucks the smoke flower from its stem with her index finger and thumb. The nearly translucent bud seems to float upward, toward the vaulted ceiling—a bird gripped by the tip of its wing.

"Listen closely. Focus on what you want to remember," she instructs.

I open my mouth to protest—there are so many shadows swirling in my past that they all burst into my head at once. I do my best to push them away, to focus on the object that felt more real: the jeweled dagger. I need to know what it is, where it came from. Where it is.

While I try to keep everything from my mind but the image of the dagger, Stef starts whispering in ancient Semperan. My mind latches on to the sounds, begins to reel and spin, growing as thin as the smoke surrounding me . . .

With her free hand, Stef tilts back my chin and opens my

mouth in one gentle motion, then drops the smoke flower inside. The smoke dissolves instantly on my tongue, sweet as honey, then cold as ice, then hot as flame—

And though I sit perfectly still, I feel myself plummeting down, down, down.

I feel stone pressing in on me on all sides. I'm in a small room, smaller than the Thief's Fort and devoid of light. I have my hands pressed to a wall, and I'm concentrating, pouring time into the stone, willing it to erode and crumble, until it gives way, pouring dust over my hands.

I'm jerked upward, enveloped in smoke, dropped into a new memory. Caro stands on a dark plain, her face in shadow, and raises her palms toward me. Her eyes are wild, streaked red with tears. Blood slicked over the palms of her hands. I turn and run from her.

Then—I'm still running, but the dark bursts into sunlight with the force of an explosion. My curls are flying around me, and I'm not crying but laughing, being chased. A pebble sails past my head, splashes the surface of the river next to me. I bend down, panting to draw a childish shape onto a boulder with a stick charred black at one end. Suddenly, the water rushes up in a great wave—

Too powerful, a voice calls from nowhere, and the flashing images dissolve into utter, starless black. The rubied dagger appears swirling in space in front of me, as if it suddenly born from nothing at all.

Then something tugs violently at my mind. I feel myself rising to a watery light, panting, ready to strike—

But only Liam's face is before me, his eyes flashing fire.

14

I freeze. The anger simmers on his face—and confusion too, underneath. Liam is swaying on the balls of his feet, as if to leap. His gaze flies from me to Stef. He looks every inch the cold, arrogant lord that I knew at Everless. It makes my stomach drop.

He rounds on Stef. "What are you doing here?"

"What are *you* doing here?" she shoots back. She's already on her feet, too, her stance that of a warrior's, shoulders squared and eyes defiant.

I pull myself up unsteadily, still dizzy from the onslaught of the slew of memories. "Stef, Liam is traveling with me. Liam—she's helping me do a blood regression."

She cuts her eyes at me, accusing. "You said you'd heard rumors from him. You didn't say you were *traveling* with him."

"I didn't say I wasn't." I feel as young as the taunt makes me sound. Head spinning, I lurch forward over the table.

"Why would you share the Alchemist's secrets with a Gerling, of all people?"

Liam scowls, and I know Stef's touched a nerve. "I'm not my family. Jules knows she can trust me. Can you say as much, hedge witch?"

"Don't talk to me about family, lordling," Stef almost spits. "My grandmother died in the Alchemist's service. My father won't recognize me because he's ashamed to have a hedge witch as a daughter, so he sent me away, to a school where everyone whispers about me. Jules"—she whirls to me—"you have others who will support you who don't support the crown. You don't have to rely on a Gerling—"

"Liam saved my life," I say. "I trust him."

Stef goes still. A tense silence settles over the room. Liam's eyes are hollow and his mouth tight—frustration, I'd guess, at losing control of the situation. Eventually, his face softens and he glances at me, giving a small nod of acknowledgment.

"Stef," I say, my voice rough. "I want to try the blood regression again. Please."

A grimace curves her mouth. Quietly, more to herself than to us, she says, "Mama and Grandmama would be horrified to know that their Alchemist had entrusted herself to a Gerling."

"Jules." There's a strained quality to Liam's voice, like he's trying not to snap. "I don't think—"

"Tell me what you saw," Stef cuts in, her voice tight.

Liam falls silent too, both of them looking at me. I close my eyes, as much to shut out their curious gazes as to describe the series of images. When I finish telling her about the slew of images I saw, ending with the dark blank surrounding the dagger, I'm shivering with heat and cold. Stef is staring steadily at me, the only trace of hesitation on her face the slight tension in her pursed lips. "Jules, I don't think another blood regression is going to help you."

"But—it has to," I finish weakly. Hot, desperate tears sting my eyes. "Why would you say that?"

Shaking her head, Stef pulls a glass vial from her leather pouch and fills it with the remaining liquid in the brass bowl. "Memory can take many forms—but it's never blank, empty, and altered as you described. It sounds like a dream."

"No," I say bitterly. "I wasn't dreaming. It's not a figment of my imagination. Liam, tell her what you found in your research." My voice comes out pleading.

Liam shifts uncomfortably. His face reddens. "Records of the old stories speak of a weapon that will kill the Sorceress. There are symbols inscribed on the wall"—he points to the glyph carved into the stone—"that suggest the same."

Though Stef's eyes narrow, it's clear that she listens to him. She turns back to me. "I don't think it's a figment of your imagination, Jules, I didn't say that. I only know that your mind seems . . .

163

scattered, somehow. Affected by magic."

"Affected? What do you mean?"

"When you removed the Sorceress's heart, you removed pure magic from her, then cut it up into pieces. It's like"—she gestures, searching for the word—"cutting the sky into pieces. No one knows how that magic might change you." She pauses, staring out the window, eyes blurred in thought. "It may just be that you're too far removed from this weapon to see it clearly. But to the Alchemist, memory is moments, and moments are time. Who knows how your magic could interact with them."

While I consider this, Stef's attention alights on my journal. Her hands still, and then she's moving. She crosses the room to sit in one of the chairs, holds the journal in her lap, and begins to flip through its pages.

I reflexively move after her. It's odd to see a near stranger leafing through the journal. I want to snatch it away, but I resist. Her movements seem idle, but her eyes are focused.

"Let's try something—an old trick. Give me your knife," she says suddenly. The journal tips down, and I see she has it open to a blank page. The cream parchment curls with age.

Liam stiffens. "Jules—"

I touch Liam's waist, and he falls quiet. I find the knife I've left on the bedside table. My chest is tight with something, not quite hope but akin to it. I'm afraid to consider it too closely, in case it dissolves.

When I pass the knife to Stef, she catches my wrist and holds the tip of the blade to my left thumb.

Liam curses under his breath, but she's already pressed the blade down, already brought a bright bead of blood welling up. She presses my cut thumb to the top of the parchment.

Liam lurches forward, but stops when I tilt the paper from the page so that he can see what's happening. My blood isn't soaking into the parchment and ruining it but branching down the paper in thin red threads, splitting up to follow what seems to be predetermined paths.

Words. The blood is forming words, swirling down to form lines and letters in a familiar hand. The Alchemist's hand, my hand, as it appears in the journal. My breath leaves me.

Seek the river of red.

"'Seek the river of red,'" Liam says softly, reading upside down. His eyes flit to the stack of books on the desk, and I know he's considering how many other secrets might be hidden there. "How did you do that?"

Stef answers, calm. "That's certainly not the business of a Gerling."

Liam's breath leaves his teeth in a hiss of frustration. "If this is a trick—"

"It's not a trick. As I said," she says steely, "my family has been in the service of the Alchemist forever." She lifts her eyes to mine. "I don't want to get mixed up in whatever this"—she waves her hand, contempt in her voice—"is, but I'd never harm her."

Liam and Stef continue to bicker softly, but all I can think is: *Seek the river of red.*

My blood swells. I feel the knowledge swarming in it, the secrets singing in my veins just out of reach. I must have written this note, laid this magic in a past life. Many rivers run through Sempera, most of them named for the towns they run through, but I don't know anything about a river of red. I close my eyes and picture the maps of Sempera that Papa would teach me to draw as a child. *We should know our own land.* With a lurch of my stomach, I wonder if he insisted on it because he knew that one day, I'd have to run.

The images tug at me somewhere deep inside, but when I try to follow them down, I come up against another infuriating blank wall. Their words buzz in my ears. "Stop," I snap.

Liam and Stef fall quiet, then Stef rises to her feet, the journal in her hands.

"I have a proposal, Alchemist," she says.

"What?" My cheeks prickle at the title, but Stef holds my gaze.

"Let me read this," she says. "In payment, instead of the blood-irons."

I look at Liam without meaning to. He looks pained, but he must have learned his lesson earlier, because he remains silent.

I swallow. "Will you take care of it?"

"The best." Her voice is steady. "I'll bring it back later tonight."

I nod.

Stef inclines her head in thanks, then sweeps out without saying good-bye.

After the door falls shut behind her, Liam lets out a long, slow breath. "I don't like letting that journal out of our sight," he says stiffly.

"She already knows I'm the Alchemist," I say. Any secrets beyond that feel small and unimportant in comparison. "And besides, she found the bit about the river of red—maybe she'll find something else."

Despair trickles into me along with hope. I stand up, cross over to the open wall. "It must mean something. Do you know anything about a river of red?"

"Maybe there's something in my papers . . . ," Liam mumbles, retreating to his stack of books on the shelf. He takes them down one by one while I stand by the window, trying to pull any scrap of meaning from what I saw during the blood regression. Though the image is shimmering—fading—I recall the stone soaring past my curls, into a river at my feet. Drawing a snake and fox on a boulder. *Just like I doodled in the margins of my journal, as a child.*

I shake my head, trying to loosen a buried answer, but nothing surfaces. Moving back to the window, I watch Stef stride through the field below, back toward the dormitories. From this height and distance, her green cloak resembles a leaf tumbling through the grass. The sun melts over the horizon. She turns, shading her eyes with one hand and looks back at the tower—I wave in greeting, realizing only a second later that because of the time enchantment, she'll see nothing but an empty window.

"Jules," Liam says, startling me. "There's no mention of a red river in scholarly versions of the myths, other than the river Caro drowned you in during your first life." He bites his lip. "It's quite far, bordering a town called Pryceton. It's Chamberlayne territory, and I know for certain that they're keeping the town heavily guarded. I don't think we should travel there unless we're absolutely certain that the risk is necessary. But look at this—"

Guiding me gently by the shoulder, he leads me to the map of Sempera, pointing to a thick blue thread that cuts the country in half. "Here's where you're thought to have been killed by the Sorceress." He points to a spot marked with a deep red pin. His finger traces the blue, then stops only a few inches away from where Bellwood is labeled on the map, tapping the spot for emphasis. "The water glows red when the sun is rising or setting, like it's been cursed. Or at least, that's what the legends say.

"How far?" I ask.

"Only an hour or two, if we cut through Montmere."

"I once lived here," I mumble, thinking of the Thief's Fort, hidden by me for later use. Maybe there are more scraps of me hidden close, scattered in a moment of desperation and survival. I look down at the dried blood on my thumb, remembering the unfamiliar message in my own handwriting. "It's a place to start."

15

I can't think of sleep until Stef reappears with my journal. Her eyes as she hands it to me are thoughtful. I want to ask her what she read, but I feel strangely self-conscious, so I just thank her and bid her good night.

After she's gone, Liam and I spend the night at Thief's Fort: me, curled on the bed next to my journal, and Liam on the other side of the room, on the floor, using his cloak for a blanket. He has his own rooms at Bellwood, but he refuses to let me stay alone.

The next morning, after he brings back a plate of fruit and rolls, we leave Bellwood an hour later, both dressed in plain, hooded brown scholars' cloaks Liam borrowed. I try not to notice how the plainness of his dress makes Liam look more handsome—how, stripped of his Gerling colors and finery, he looks more himself. Freer, though he's still weighed down by a hungry kind of grief.

Montmere's smell—horse dung and baking bread, turned earth and a film of smoke—is comforting after the faint incense smell of the Thief's Fort, that I didn't realize was present until we left. My heart twists. Being on the road again makes me feel too open, like a target waiting to be pierced by an arrow.

But even still, my veins are thrumming with eagerness. We are going to find the weapon today, I tell myself, or information that will bring us closer to it. Then we can return to Shorehaven, and I will get rid of the Sorceress for good. I'll finally be safe, and so will Ina, so will Liam.

I stop that thought in its tracks, before it can grow into something dangerous.

Some of the doorways we pass are scattered with wilted violets, or draped with purple cloth. My heart lifts a little—these are remainders of what must have been a celebration of Ina's crowning. We come across a tall, thin wooden post in the middle of the road. It's covered from top to bottom in ribbons, each fixed around the post with a different-size knot.

"One for every year of her rule, miss," a frail voice calls out. I flinch, keeping my eyes averted—I didn't think anyone had observed us—but the old woman only stares back at us with a kind smile. She extends her hand, which is bursting with ribbons. "Add one, and Queen Ina will reign for another year. They're only an hour-coin."

I reach into my purse and draw out an hour-coin. At first, I only want to blend in—but when I take the silk ribbon from the woman, I know that it's more than that. I miss my sister and want to do something, anything, to feel closer to her. To promise her that I'll end this soon. For both of us.

Hood pulled low over my face, I approach the post. The same longing I felt at the coronation ball stabs through me. I wish, as I lay the silk over the wood, that my action was just a simple celebration. My sister is the Queen. I believe she will be a good one—as much as possible in this corrupted land. But instead I have to hide a tear from the ribbon seller as I tie a careful knot and step away.

Liam chooses a merchant's road that skirts the outside of Montmere, arguing that merchants are used to strangers—and minding their own business. "I know the river is on the other side of town, but I'm not sure of the way after that. We'll have to find someone to tell us."

As we walk, I can tell—*feel*—the weight on Liam. I can feel it in the way he walks, shoulders stooped like he's carrying a heavy load on his back, even more dour than usual. I realize that in the past few days we've spent together, he's never once spoken of his home or family, except when I've brought them up.

"What news do you have of Everless?" I ask him as we walk down the empty road. I've kept my questions to myself, not wanting to upset him. But Everless is a part of my childhood too. I care for the people there. The halls of Everless wind through my fate as surely as the blood through my veins—along with its secrets.

Pain crosses Liam's face, there for a moment and then gone. "It's in shambles, if you really want to know," he says, his voice brittle. "My father is draining the coffers trying to hunt you down. Ivan has the run of the place, and he's under Caro's thumb. Without Roan . . ." He trails off.

Sadness, heavy and cold, settles in me. For all his faults, Roan held the people of Everless together, loved by all. It must be a darker place without him.

Maybe, if we survive this, Liam can change Everless for the better. The thought warms me in spite of the crisp morning air, a small candle of hope in my chest. I want to nourish the flame of it. Together, Liam and I, we could—

I can't allow myself to think of that. So instead, I ask, "What do your parents know?"

"Before I left for Shorehaven, I told them that I was going to resume my studies at Bellwood after the coronation." He looks forward, his throat moving as he swallows. "I didn't want to tell them anything in case . . . in case Caro returns to Everless."

The thought of it makes me shudder. "Why would Caro return?"

Liam gives me a level look. "Because she expects that *you* will."

My stomach sinks. I knew that my presence at Everless would put everyone inside in danger. But this extra reminder that I can never go back—it just makes me feel more alone.

Up ahead, I spot a small figure, far down the stretch of the road and rapidly approaching. My chest tightens but then I release a breath when I see that it's only a child, a boy with the same scampering walk as Hinton, the young servant boy from Everless. He has a yellow sash slung over him—the uniform of a young page, hired to shuttle news and messages within towns.

"Ask him about the river," I whisper. I veer off, ducking into a narrow opening between two houses, acting like I'm just returning home. I listen as Liam walks past a few yards. A moment later, a child's voice hails him. "Good morning, sir!"

I peek around the corner. Without looking at me, Liam subtly moves so that he's facing me, and the boy has to turn in the other direction. I slide back into the alley, pressing my shoulders against a rough wooden wall.

"News of the day?" I hear the boy say hopefully. "Only an hour-coin, sir." Then, a moment later: "Queen Ina continues to receive supplicants from all over Sempera," he reads. "As her first orders of business, she has introduced a temporary tithe in addition to promising to alleviate hunger, and to grant a reward of five hundred years to the person who brings her the traitor Jules Ember."

Hidden in the shadows, I flinch. He says it rather proudly. The boy goes on with his news, loud and self-important. "There are reports of strange weather along the eastern coast—"

"I have another question for you," Liam says, cutting the boy off. He looks quickly up and down the road, then turns back to the boy. "I'm a traveler here. Can you tell me—is there a swimming spot around here, where the river runs red?"

At this, the boy stiffens.

"Pardon me, sir, but I wouldn't go looking," he says. "The Alchemist's spirit roams there. If you touch the water, it'll wash away your years. It almost happened to a friend of mine, I swear—"

My heart pounds in my ears. Could the message hidden in my journal lead to somewhere so close? There's a short silence, in which Liam reaches into his pocket and there's the flash and faint clink of another coin. "But if I did want to find it," Liam presses smoothly. "Where could I go?"

After another moment, the boy shrugs, then raises his hand and points past Liam, past the houses and toward the thick set of woods that engirdle the town. "Out there," he says, subdued. He turns the blood-iron over and over in his palm. "Walk straight and follow the river south until you get to a clearing with a little waterfall. That's where the light hits, they say. But truly, sir, I wouldn't go."

"Don't worry," Liam says lightly. "I won't. Thank you for the news."

The boy turns to leave, and I pull back into the alley as he passes. I give him time to get a little distance down the road, and then return to Liam's side.

We start off silently so as not to draw attention to ourselves. After a half hour of slipping off the road and around buildings in the direction the newsboy pointed, the town is behind us and the woods stretch in front of us, silent and dark, like they're somehow repelling the light of the rising sun. We pause at the edge of the woods. The dark seeps into me, like smoke rising to the sky. My throat tightens.

My fingers twitch with the sudden desire to reach out and take Liam's hand. Instead, I curl them into loose fists and walk forward into the trees first, Liam half a step behind me.

Shadows fold around us immediately, immersing us in a sudden and strange silence. The sounds I've come to expect from woods, the gentle swishing of leaves and the conversation of birds, are there but softened, as if held at some distance from us. Even though we've just stepped into the trees, the undergrowth is thick, and I'm suddenly grateful for my long-sleeved dress and cloak and boots. They protect my skin as I soldier forward through branches and newly green leaves and thorns.

After only a few minutes, we find the river as the boy described—though it's really more of a stream here—and follow it south, opposite of its flow. The air grows cooler and thicker. Heavy, charged like the air at Everless.

Then, certainty takes hold of me, a feeling similar to the one I felt when we entered Thief's Fort. *I've been here before.*

I deliberately let my mind unfocus, allow my feet to take me where they will while my hands clear away branches. There is no path through the underbrush except for the faint trails left behind by deer, but I don't fully feel the branches as they scratch my hands and arms. I'm not in any memory or vision—I'm still Jules, my thoughts unfogged enough for a faint sense of fear to curl through as we go farther and farther in. Behind us, the sight of town filtering through the trees has faded completely.

My nerves begin to fire, slowly at first, but faster with every step until it feels like someone cast a net of flame over my entire body. What will we find when we reach the river of red? If we don't find the weapon, we'll have nothing, no hope to defeat Caro. And if we do—

And if we do, I'll have to use it. I'll have to end her.

The thought is unexpected, the words—*end her*—recalling the sensation of my dagger sinking into Caro's side. I shudder, stomach and heart twisting. The thought of doing it again is horrifying. My own feelings are a dark maze. I must kill Caro—I have to—and yet the thought of doing so seems impossible. Both because it makes me sick to imagine, and because the weapon I need—the strange, glittering dagger in the Thief's Fort—is nowhere to be found, despite the fact that as far as I can tell, it was only ever in my possession.

A strange idea sinks in. What if I hid the weapon on purpose? Not from Caro—what if I hid it from myself?

But it doesn't make sense. If I stole Caro's heart, I must have been trying to harm her. To kill her, even, to stop her from wielding her power over all of Sempera. She's my enemy.

After what seems like a long time of silent walking, the soft burbling of the river at our side, we come upon a clearing in the woods, a glen filled with dappled light. Though the sun must be high in the sky by now, the weave of branches overhead filters it, casting a net of shadows over us. Ahead, the stream slows and broadens into a wide, gently flowing sweep of water. At the other end, just as the boy said, is a small waterfall. It crashes down, spraying a silvery mist into the air that makes the trees glitter.

My breath catches. The scene is beautiful, and I find myself turning automatically to Liam, wanting to see the image reflected in his eyes. He's taken off his cloak as we walked, and his shoulders shift beneath the white cloth of his shirt as he pushes his hair off his forehead. His lips are parted, his eyes wide—and I take the moment just to look at him.

"Do you think it's here? The weapon?" he asks.

I can't help but smile. He's asking me now, and not the other way around. "I don't know, but we'll soon find out."

My feet tug me forward again, toward a large boulder sunk in silt, half in and half out of the water. I gather my skirts up with one hand, kicking my boots off so that I can wade in and examine it from all sides. I can feel Liam watching me, but I'm too excited by the pull in my chest as soon as I step into the river to care about how odd this must seem. The cold water sends a pleasant shock up my body.

And then I see it—a pale mark on the dark rock, a set of shallow scratches forming the shape of a coiled snake and a fox, sitting side by side.

My heart catches. Entranced, I reach out to touch the image. When I brush my fingers against the damp stone, the air shifts around me, the air seeming to contract and expand again, my senses flooding with the smell of wildflowers.

Another embedded memory.

I look up to call to Liam, but he isn't there. Instead, a girl stands at the edge of the water, on the other side of the stream. Skinny and panting, with her dark hair damp around her shoulders, her face is more familiar to me than my own.

My old enemy.

Caro.

16

Liam is gone. I've stepped into another world—another time.

The glen has shifted; it's the same and different at once. The trees are slender, and instead of forming a thick ceiling overhead, they form a sort of airy lattice, letting in bright splashes of sunlight over the water. Birds sing hidden in their branches. The scent of warm earth and wildflowers drifts lazily on the breeze.

Then, the small part of me that's able to observe my surroundings as Jules Ember is pulled down by a wave of feeling. Not my own.

Panic storms in the Alchemist's heart, *my* heart. It hammers at my ribs, thunderous and steady, trying to break away from me and escape. My blood races through my veins, and disordered, incomprehensible images flash sharp through my mind. A grand hall with a shining wooden floor. A table spread with metal and glittering powders. Caro—Caro beside me and a man handing me a glittering vial. The smile, ear to ear, that split his face.

Then—guilt. Waves of it, crashing over and over. I collapse to my knees at the edge of the water, panting. A sharp pain in my thigh.

I look down to see the rubied dagger biting into the fabric of my pants. Shock courses through me. The blade isn't sheathed but tucked hastily into my belt. The twisting snake handle is warm beneath my fingers and almost seems to vibrate, like something alive. It's beautiful, elegant, sharp, and—

There's blood smeared over the blade. A slick of wet, glittering red.

"No, no, no," I murmur softly. Hands shaking, I plunge the dagger into the water at my knees. Blood blooms in the water. When I pull the blade back, it shines again, and relief floods me—but within seconds, my fingers scrub a blood spot that didn't wash away, a red droplet snugly kissing the hilt. I submerge the blade again and scrub, but each time I bring it up again, I find fault with it. Each time, I wade farther into the water, until I'm up to my neck in it, until suddenly, I'm crying, shoulders heaving with quiet sobs.

A twig snapping somewhere behind me makes me stop. I look up, alert. A hound is staring at me with coal-black eyes.

My chest squeezes. Panic.

Then, a figure steps out from between the trees just behind

the hound's rigid tail: Caro, dark hair cut short. Up to my neck in the water, I see her before she sees me, moss-colored eyes scanning the clearing, her head slowly rotating as if *she's* caught my scent.

Caro sees me and stills, then walks casually toward the edge of the water. "Antonia." Her voice is light, casual, but I know better than to trust that. "I thought I'd find you here."

I don't move, eyes flitting between Caro and the hound. "Has Ever sent you to punish me?"

In response, Caro merely sighs, then kicks off her boots at the shore and hoists her skirts.

"No. You're always so dramatic. I've only come to find out what in the heavens is going on with you. What happened back there?" she calls, her voice carrying across the water.

"Were you hurt?" I say, trying hard to keep my voice even.

"Hurt? Me? You could never." Caro smiles, but it immediately falls flat. "In case you're wondering, Ever is fine. But you startled us, Antonia."

Underwater, I grip the dagger tightly. "I'm sorry. I—I lost control."

She smiles at me again, but I can tell it's less bright than it was a moment ago. Suspicion lurks behind her eyes. Even as she takes a step forward, cocking her head playfully, and rakes a flat hand across the surface of the glen, sending a wave of shining water my way.

I jump back, laughing loud, but it sounds hollow and forced in my ears. Caro steps forward. A chill goes through me that has nothing to do with the cool water or the summer breeze playing over my damp skin.

As if reading my thoughts, she beckons her to me. "Come out, Antonia. Come home."

"Or what? He'll send the dogs after me?" I bite back, my voice surly and feeble.

"You know that's only a joke," she scoffs, though she can't help but shift from the hound beside her, like she's trying to distance herself from the lie. "He's not upset, I swear to you. What do you expect to happen when you're experimenting with magic as powerful as ours? People are going to get hurt. The strong survive."

Dread seizes me, but I wade back to her and hold the dagger out, handle first. Caro advances gracefully, water creeping up her shift like dark fingers. She takes it from me and holds it like she would hold a fine bolt of cloth. Her lips curve up in a smile as she stares at it.

"Destroy as many rooms as you want, Antonia," she says, a little breathy. "If that's what it takes to create something like this. Look."

She lifts the blade, and for an instant my whole body tenses, expecting it to fall. But Caro just swishes it through the air, admiring the way it shines in the dappled sun, as if it weren't heavy at all. I wish I could take it from her and drop it, let it sink to the bottom of the glen and be lost forever in the soft sand. Fear is pushing at the inside of my skin. A bone-deep knowledge that this is wrong. We shouldn't have this.

"You bound strength into this blade." Caro's voice is awed, almost reverent. "This is exactly what we've been working for. And look what I can do, without it hurting me anymore."

Racing back to the shore, she plucks a bright yellow flower from the soil. I watch as it withers in her open palm, deadening— then as it fills out with strength and color again before it bursts, covering her hands in green-and-yellow confetti. Taking its life away, giving it back, all with the ease of breathing.

When she looks at me to gauge my reaction, her proud, wide grin wilts into a frown. "Why aren't you happy?"

My heart beats faster. "I am happy."

"Don't lie to me." Her voice is light as ever, but it makes fear thrill through me. She takes a step closer and twirls the dagger casually in her hand. Do I imagine that for a heartbeat its tip is leveled straight at my throat?

I blink, and the blade is flipped over again, Caro proffering it to me with her usual smile.

"It's marvelous, Antonia," she says as I take it back. "Your power. Don't be afraid of it." Her hand comes up to my shoulder and rests there for a second, fire-warm through the wet material of my dress.

"I'm not afraid. Maybe you should be afraid," I say quickly.

Caro tilts her head at me. "Why would I be? Power is unstoppable. We'll be unstoppable together someday, you know that."

"Nothing is unstoppable, not really," I say quietly, slipping the dagger into my belt. "You only need to find something stronger."

17

When I open my eyes, steam is rising gently from the surface of the water, which is now warm around my waist. My hair and shift are soaked, but the steam envelops me. Safe. Protected.

Except then the steam grows thicker, enough to make the figure approaching me resemble a walking shadow. Animal panic floods me, pulsing the name *Sorceress* through my blood. She's here. She's come for me.

Then the shape grabs my wrist and I scream, and the scream seems to send waves and waves of cold out into the water, obliterating all warmth. The crackle of ice forming covers the noises of the woods like a fine lace, while the steam around us turns at once to snow. In one motion, it falls to the surface of the water, countless frozen bodies plunging down.

"Jules!"

Liam. I'm no longer in the memory. I breathe, reminding myself that I'm Jules, and of course it's Liam approaching, his lips tinged blue from the sudden cold. Around me, the light has shifted, the trees around me larger and older than they were, seemingly, only a moment ago. I recall the look on young Caro's face—pure, hungry power—and all at once know where I am, *when* I am.

I'm shaking, hard. It's so cold.

"I'm sorry, I'm sorry—I didn't mean to. That's never happened before." My voice sounds more irritated than I meant it to, but within seconds, the water returns to a normal temperature. Now that I have my senses back, I realize we're both standing in the water. Liam's cloak is crumpled on a nearby rock. My mouth drops open. "What—what happened?"

Liam clears his throat. "You waded out into the water."

"I—was running, I think." I glance down. The stream flows around my waist, when in the memory it didn't go past my knees. "I was Antonia again. The memory must have been centuries ago."

Liam shifts. "Steam started to rise, and it was so thick I couldn't see you. I didn't know what was happening."

Now embarrassment does creep in. I feel my cheeks redden. "I was angry. Afraid too." I remember the blood splashed across the dagger, how I'd tried to wash the blade clean as if I couldn't stand the sight of it. "I'd hurt someone. Caro, I think."

A moment passes, and I brace for him to pull away from me. Instead, he steps closer, murmuring something about the cold, though I can see that warmth rushes to his face. A torn feeling floods through me even as I turn half to the side, averting my eyes, resisting the urge to wrap my arms around him. All my senses seem to have been turned up. I feel hyperaware of every little sound and movement, the rush of heat to his neck and face, the soft splash as he moves closer, stopping only when he's slightly more than an arm's length away. Water creeps up the white fabric of his shirt. Mist lands and sparkles in his dark hair, and something warm and restless stirs beneath my ribs.

"What did you see?" he asks. His posture is stiff, his eyes trained carefully on my face.

Caro's younger, laughing face flashes before me, her eyes that seemed to shift between shades of green. "I had the dagger, and I was running from something I'd done. But Caro found me, like she always does."

I shake my head to clear it of the tumble of emotion. Liam gently squeezes my shoulder, and I don't push him away, even when his gaze grows a little softer. Wrapping an arm around my waist so that I can only barely feel his skin through the wet of my shirt, he guides me back to shore. I sit down on a flat rock. He wraps his cloak around my shoulders. When I've stopped shivering, he asks, "Forget about Caro. Did you learn anything about the weapon?"

"Yes," I breathe, grateful for his focused mind, that I don't have to bear this load alone. In as much detail as possible, I tell him of the dagger I'd made—Antonia made—a jeweled blade bound with strength. How it buzzed with power, how Caro tipped the blade against my throat. As I recount it, the image of the slightly younger Caro seems to drift away from me, flattening until it seems like an illustration in a book, rather than a real memory. My racing heart calms; at least until the Caro I know in this life rises up to take her place—cold, cruel, hungry.

"What do you think it means? Is that all we need? Strength?"

"I don't know," Liam says softly.

Could the weapon really be bound with strength? But Liam's doubt is echoed in me, and I soon dismiss the thought. If it were only strength, Caro might have used the weapon on me. No, it would take more than strength to beat the Sorceress.

"It won't matter if we can't find it. Was there anything else at all, anything specific?"

I have to sift back through my jumble of thoughts. "We spoke about a man, Ever." I close my eyes halfway, blurring the clearing around me, trying to bring back the memory. I remember the mix of awe and fear as I spoke his name. "Caro must have been bringing me back to him."

Liam looks down at the water, faint color staining his cheeks. "Lord Ever. My ancestor."

The words hang in the air between us, obvious now that

they're out. The man from the stories—the evil lord—didn't have a name before now. He wasn't in my memories or my childhood nightmares. But it's as though by speaking his name in my memory, we've breathed life into him. Fear tightens my skin, drops of cold form on my spine.

"I'm not proud of it," Liam goes on, curt.

I take a deep breath. He is more than his blood, I tell myself. I've seen Gerlings dissolve years of time into their tea with no more thought than a cube of sugar. Liam is nothing like that. His heart is good.

"Maybe it means something—maybe there's something at Everless," I say. My skin tightens as if in warning. *I can't go back.* "There's no river, but a lake—"

"Ivan is there." Liam cuts me off abruptly. "My father is there. Everless is probably even less safe for you than Shorehaven. Besides, I've scoured the place and there's nothing but useless china and dusty blood-irons. We can't risk it." There's just the faintest note of regret in his voice. His shoulders draw in a little, and he looks away, at the waterfall, wiping the slight sheen of mist off his face. "Lord Ever is dead and buried. There's nothing we didn't know from the stories already."

"Maybe the stories are wrong," I say automatically.

Liam's cheeks redden, a warning—but I don't take back what I said. I shouldn't have to. I continue, "The stories have been helpful, but they're not infallible."

"I didn't say they were perfect, but they led me to you, didn't they?" He abruptly changes the subject. "Did you see anything at all about killing Caro?"

"Well . . ." My mind works, turning the remembered moment over to inspect it from every angle, as if it were a blood-iron coin. I look down at my hands, contemplating what I learned. The hands of the Alchemist when she was Antonia, that crafted strength into the blade. The same hands that wove time into blood.

"I bound strength to the blade," I reason out loud. "It's only proof that the weapon I saw *does* exist. Bound with strength, or—I don't know, something strong enough to kill the Sorceress. I said as much to Caro. I practically threatened her."

Liam shakes his head, staring somewhere into the distance. "Jules, no histories tell of a weapon like you described. Not even in Sempera's bloodiest war."

"Just because it's not recorded somewhere doesn't mean it didn't happen." I need this to be true—because I know there's some hidden knowledge out there that will help us destroy Caro. "The late Queen destroyed the secrets of blood time to keep them to herself, didn't she? Who knows what other secrets have been buried by history?"

"Have you considered—" He stops abruptly, then looks at me, mouth slightly downturned.

"What?" Excitement, even hope, flares in me. I wait for

him to finish, expecting a brilliant twist of logic to fall out of his mouth, some unforgotten fact that will shift everything into focus.

It takes Liam a moment to answer. "Have you considered that these memories might be a lie? Or just another one of Caro's traps?"

I inhale, stung. Part of me recognizes that I might think the same, in Liam's position—but the other, angry part of me wants to scream at him. Because if I don't trust myself—if I'm wrong that the truth isn't inside of me, locked away from Caro's tricks and deception—I feel as though I might fall apart completely. "Why? Because you don't have *sources* on this? Your papers referred to a weapon."

He runs a hand through his still-damp hair, exhales a frustrated breath. "Even Stef said that there was something off about your memories."

"*Off*—" I stand up and shrug his cloak from around my shoulders. My whole body burn ember-hot. "You said Stef didn't know what she was talking about. Besides, we didn't just wander here on a whim. My journal said to seek the river of red. You brought us here, remember? And we *found* something by tracing my past."

"We got lucky, and we don't have time to run all over Sempera putting the pieces together. We came here with a purpose and we failed. We're no closer to finding the weapon," Liam shoots back. "Meanwhile, Caro's dogs hunt you."

"I don't know what to do, besides put the pieces together as best I can." I clench my fists. "Maybe you should have told me who I was sooner."

"Maybe you shouldn't have come back to Everless at all," he says coldly.

I turn from him to hide the tears swimming in my eyes, my shift suddenly cold and clammy against my skin. There's a moment of silence, then behind me, I hear Liam get to his feet. Slowly, gently, he eases next to me and slips my cloak back over my shoulders again.

"I'm sorry, Jules." His words are softer, pleading in a way that strikes a different kind of fear into me than Caro ever has. And what's most frightening—I believe him. "I just can't let you— can't stand the thought—"

Please don't finish, I think, because I already know what he wants to say. *I can't stand the thought of losing you.*

I swallow, blink. The pain and fear in his voice threatens to dissolve my anger. Instead, I crystallize it, turning the anger cold and hard and permanent as stone.

"This world would be better off if your family had never existed," I spit. "None of this would ever have happened."

A moment passes, stretching and unbearable, so long that I think I've accidentally frozen time. Then Liam picks his own cloak up off the ground and shrugs it on, his motions tight and snapping with controlled anger. Guilt and fear twinge through me, but it doesn't matter.

It's the cost of keeping him safe.

Before I can question it any further, Liam turns and strides away from me, directly into the forest.

The simmering emotions between us don't dissipate as Liam and I trudge back toward Bellwood, not speaking. When we emerge from the forest and begin to walk along the dome-shaped buildings of Montmere, we stay quiet. A young girl passes, selling flowers from a basket on her arm. The bloodred roses remind me of the flower in Caro's palm—the way she took away its life and gave it back without effort.

I took that power from her, at least some of it. A strange mix of pride and confusion steals over me at the thought. Now she's dependent on others for her strength. I remember the old Queen, pale and cold to the touch even in life. What Caro said after she fell. *I've drunk hundreds of years' worth of blood-iron, and I hate the way it tastes.*

The sun sets, layering darkness over us gently. In the gathering night, it's easier to let my mind wander. I find myself wishing more than ever that the path were clearer, that I was more powerful, that my past weren't shrouded in mystery. I send up a prayer to everyone I've lost—Roan, Papa, Amma—that when we return to Bellwood, the path to dismantling the Sorceress opens up before us, bright and brilliant and clear.

No, not a prayer—a promise.

I stare at Liam's back, wishing I could say this to him. Under his cloak, his muscles move in grim determination.

Up ahead, the main gate of Bellwood comes into view. Elias is there.

I feel a pang of relief, seeing him safe, alive—but the sight of what's behind him roots my feet to the ground. It's a dark silhouette on horseback, trailed by a group of soldiers. The figure is cloaked from head to foot and moving with an almost supernatural grace that sends ice tearing down my spine.

Here for me, a still, small voice in me whispers.

18

Liam throws a protective arm in front of me before dragging me into a row of shrubs. It's the best cover we have, aside from risking a display of magic. Next to him, I press my face into the damp spring grass to muffle my breath.

I dare not even turn my head to look back toward the entrance gate, but we're close enough that I detect Elias's voice, and even through the sound of my heart pounding in my ears, I think I can hear the strain in it.

"Thank you for the escort, though it was quite unnecessary. Connemor has seen its share of assassins and killers, too . . ."

It seems to take an eternity for the soldiers and the strange man on horseback—so many of them, surely a dozen—to flow into the school. My heartbeat doesn't fade with their footsteps. It's completely dark by the time Liam and I wend our way back to the Thief's Fort. Elias is just beyond the archway, waiting for us to enter.

Upstairs, Liam begins pacing immediately. It's easier to be calm when I see him so distraught. Elias smiles at me even as Liam bursts out, "Who was that—the man on horseback?"

"Hello to you too." Elias's smile falters briefly. "A mercenary Ina's commissioned to find you, Miss Ember. The Queen *insisted* he escort me back to Bellwood—as I'm so eager to get back to my studies."

"Do they know I'm here?" I ask.

Elias pauses. "I don't think so. But this huntsman isn't much of a talker. I have no idea what information he has. No one knows anything about him—where he's from, why she chose him." He shifts on his feet. "Caro seems to trust him a great deal though. She's ordered most of the soldiers to watch the rivers and ports, letting the Huntsman have reign over the interior. I thought it might be a ruse to keep the people calm, but she seems genuinely confident that he can find you."

Ice drops down my spine. What sort of magic or device might Ina—by way of Caro—have given to this huntsman? The soldiers stationed throughout Sempera were threat enough, but the cloaked man, whose very silhouette froze me to the spot—who knows what he's capable of. There are enough threats lurking in my past. The thought of yet another enemy stalking Sempera sends a wave of exhaustion through me.

"There's something else." Elias drops his eyes to the floor sheepishly. "The Bellwood headmaster, Linfort, has requested Liam's presence at a dinner welcoming the Huntsman and his royal soldiers."

The blood drains from my face. "Does he know something? That Liam is helping me?"

"No," Elias says dismissively. "Master Linfort couldn't keep a secret like that to himself if you offered him a thousand year-coins. He just likes to show his prized Gerling off to fancy guests. Don't worry, Jules."

Liam halts suddenly. "We need to leave. Now."

No, I think. In spite of the Huntsman—an extension of Caro—arriving, being inside the Thief's Fort is the safest I've felt since I fled Everless. Plus, the memory from the waterfall fills my mind again, and this time, a new feeling comes with it: a small twitch of power. I may not have faced Caro down then, but her words linger: *Your power. Don't be afraid of it.*

I'm not afraid.

I want it to be true. I don't want to be afraid any longer.

But I know from the look of animal panic on Liam's face he won't accept this.

So instead, I say, "Elias is right. We can't leave now. If you don't show up for dinner, you'll be suspicious."

I'm interrupted by the *pop* of a cork. Elias grins roguishly.

He's pulled a bottle of wine from his bag. He pours a rather large glass and hands it to me. "While you're gone, Jules and I will enjoy ourselves. After all, we've survived the Sorceress so far."

"Ignore him, Jules," Liam says loftily. To Elias, he says, "It isn't the time for your gallows humor."

"On the contrary, it's always that time." Elias stretches, leaning back in his chair. "You Semperans are so humorless."

"Oh?" The challenge comes from me. "What are Connemorians like then?"

Elias smiles at me. "I'm so glad you asked, Miss Ember," he says. "There are our striking good looks, for one. Our happiness—I think that comes from not having winters that last an age. And in Connemor, when you feel something, it's frowned upon to bury it underneath layers of stiffness and formality."

Elias throws Liam a glance. "Don't glower. Isn't it what you always dreamed of, being here with—" Elias's hand rises and gestures vaguely in my direction—then drops as Liam gets hastily to his feet. Blushing furiously, I realize what he meant to say: *being here with the Alchemist.*

Liam's posture is suddenly stiff, his fingers drumming on the table. "I'll go to dinner, but we're leaving as soon as I return. At least one of us should take this seriously," he says.

His barbed words catch on my skin, but I don't object. Once Liam is gone, the tension spills out of me, and I collapse onto the bed. It's easier to forget the small thrill of the thought of Liam sitting here, books open on his lap, dreaming of the Alchemist—of me.

Outside, the bells of the school tower ring out—for special occasions, Elias tells me—then fade into the night. The bustle of birds in the trees has given way to the first of the season's crickets. I tell Elias everything: about Stef, the weapon shaped like the curve of a fang made of gem and stone with a carved metal snake wrapped around it, and the clue found in my journal that I hope will lead to it.

Elias listens to me with interest. His manner, charm underlaid by a serious intensity, fascinates me. After I've finished, Elias pulls out several more bottles of wine and some food.

"Where did you get those?" I ask.

"I stole them from the palace when I showed my face there, obviously. There were quite a few left over after the coronation, which *was* cut rather short."

"Yes, I remember." I laugh.

He tops me off. "Your breakthrough calls for a celebration."

"Breakthrough? What breakthrough?" I keep my voice sarcastic, trying not to betray that I want him to answer sincerely.

"You know there's a weapon out there that will kill her. All you have to do is find it," he says simply. He leans over and squeezes my hand. "Most of all—you're here."

The air has the gentle warmth of summer, and we sit together at the little writing desk, eating bread and cheese and apples. Eventually—and after several sips of wine—I gather the courage to pry. "You and Liam know my story. It's only fair that I know yours."

"It's a boring tale, Miss Ember," Elias counters.

"You helped save my life. I think we can dispense with this *Miss Ember* business." I give him my best smile. "Just Jules is fine, thank you."

His teeth flash in a bright returning smile. "All right, then, Just Jules." His accent softens the *j* sound in my name. "I don't envy you, traveling alone with Liam, even for a few days. I'm surprised you remember how to speak."

The tone of his voice isn't cutting, like when Ina or Caro mocked Liam back at Everless. It's warm, fond, perhaps even a little protective. It reminds me of something Amma and I used to do, teasing each other before anyone else could, because a joke from someone you love has no teeth at all. Grief moves through me. I take a sip of wine to push it away.

It occurs to me that Elias probably knows Liam Gerling better than anyone I met at Everless—maybe anyone in the world—and I feel a rush of curiosity. "You're from the unbound lands; how did you end up on our shores?"

"The unbound lands?" Elias laughs, not unkindly, but I feel

myself blush. "That's an exotic way of putting it, when in fact you Semperans are the odd birds out of all the world. The only land with magic."

"I've never left," I say. "So I wouldn't know."

"Most haven't, in either direction." He leans in. "They're afraid of you." He must see my shocked expression, because he laughs. "No, not *you*, Jules. They're scared of Sempera and its magic. You should hear the stories of this place. Some say that as soon as you step on Sempera's shores, the land itself will drain every drop of blood from you. Fear worked in your former Queen's favor."

That much I know is true. "So your family was brave—they sent you here to be a student, and . . ."

"Well, my family, we're ambassadors of sorts. Scholars as well, though, yes. We had special dispensation from your Queen to enter Sempera when no one else could." Elias stretches his legs out in front of him. I stay quiet, not wanting to give away that I had no concept of such a family. "For centuries, almost all the children in our family have spent time in another land of their choosing, learning about customs, history, trade, before returning to our own shores in order to take up our official duties. The practice is said to make our country stronger. Safer. Better," he adds quickly.

"Better?" Suspicion kicks in me. I can see the reason in it— even through the envy I feel—but, in another way, what Elias describes sounds vaguely like what Gerlings do with blood-irons. In a way, it sounds like stealing.

Elias points outside, toward a large, ivy-covered building with a peaked roof, windows glowing gold in the dark. "Look, you can see the library. Where I've spent most of the past six years."

"What do you study?" I say, a bit too eagerly. But I find myself wanting to know everything about Elias, and this place, his life here. The life he shares with Liam. It's a strange kind of want, part tenderness, part envy.

"Officially?" Elias raises his eyebrows. "Philosophy."

I scoff. I've never heard of a philosopher in Sempera. "And . . . unofficially?" I prompt.

He considers the question, tracing his finger around the wine glass. "Yours is not the only country to be infected by magic. Ours was once too—and we vowed long ago not to let it happen again."

"Infected? " It's an odd choice of words, so similar to Stef's.

He pauses, sips his wine. "Centuries ago, two Connemorians were born with the ability to change forms. It's said that this was only the beginning—that when they were children, they honed their abilities and sought to increase them. I'll spare you the details, but suffice it to say that they succeeded. The power consumed them completely. They became nothing but pure evil."

I nod, rapt. I can't imagine Caro becoming more consumed by magic, more evil than she already is. I shiver at the thought.

Elias continues. "Connemor prevailed against them—eventually, and with great sacrifices. I chose to come to your land to study what I could of blood time. It's best to be aware of what magic lurks in the dark corners of the world."

I think of Caro—how the more I try to learn about her, my past, the more rapidly any knowledge I think I have slips through my fingers. I remember the Queen descending, burning the Thief's Fort as a message, that the secrets of time were hers alone. Slaughtering the scholars who worked here. "I can't imagine that you think being in Sempera is very safe now."

Elias's teeth flash again in that smile. "Don't you know, Jules? Everything worth doing is dangerous."

"A few weeks ago, I wouldn't have agreed with you," I mutter. My old ambitions flash through my mind: a little, well-kept cottage on the outskirts of town. A plot of land fertile enough to keep me and my family fed, and walls to keep us warm and safe in the winter. "So—you're here out of duty?"

"Well, it's not only duty that keeps me here now. It's more . . . personal." Elias takes a swallow of wine, again staring at me like he's taking measure of me.

"Why?" I ask warily.

Elias lets out a bemused sigh. "Because," he says, "my best friend is in lo—"

I half shout "Stop" before the word leaves his mouth. I rock backward on my knees, Elias's words impacting me like something physical.

I sit silently, this information sinking in, the enormity of what I still don't know washing over me. Liam's face flashes behind my eyes. Eventually, I find my voice, though it comes out slow and quiet. "Don't say that. I've lost so many people already, I can't . . . I can't think of that."

Elias scrutinizes me. We sit in silence for a while, sipping our wine and watching the moon rise outside the window. I can almost feel his words settling into me, like black ink mixing with my blood, writing itself into my bones. As if uttering them sends up a beacon to Caro, to the Huntsman, marking Liam for death.

Elias breaks our silence. "I've always thought that maybe if we know the past, we can change the future. But you, Jules, are in a unique position to do exactly that."

"What do you mean?" I tense, uncomfortable by how close his words land to my innermost thoughts.

Elias is quiet for a long moment, his face still in the moonlight; our lamps are burning low. I instinctively feel that he's making some sort of decision, weighing a choice. "You of all people know that the past has a habit of repeating itself—"

A bitter laugh escapes me.

"But that doesn't mean the past *has* to repeat itself. We have to believe that we can change the future. Otherwise, what's the point of anything?"

I open and close my mouth, still unable to find words. His speech stirs something in me, but I'm afraid to look closely at it. Caro's face forms in my mind and floats there, her eyes the deep green of bottle glass, her lips curved into a smile. The thought of breaking the cycle of death sends a shudder through me, deep as my bones.

"At the very least, just know that I want to help you, Jules. Because Liam is family." He takes a sip of his wine. Another roguish smile alights on his face. "Or maybe I'm just bored. Still, think of what might be possible, what things you could achieve," Elias says, playfulness and deadly seriousness tangling together in his voice. There's something familiar in his speech. I realize with a lurch that Caro said similar things to Antonia. "If I had your abilities—"

"You don't," I say sharply. "You don't have my abilities, and you have no idea what it's like."

I expect Elias to laugh again, but he doesn't. Instead, he stares at me, inscrutable as ever. "Then, Just Jules," he says calmly, "what will *you* do with them?"

An image materializes, fast and sharp, like a hot poker to my skin. A future—but a future where I've failed, where Caro has her heart and life back, where the bodies of everyone I've ever tried to love are buried underneath the cold earth.

If there's a purpose to my being alive, it's to stop that future. I take a deep breath. "I'm going to find the weapon that will kill Caro. And if Caro finds me before I do, I'll die before she can capture me again."

Elias's brow creases, but his face at my words isn't the abject horror that Liam's would have been. And all at once I realize why I need him.

"Promise me," I say fervently. "Promise me that if she finds me, you'll kill me before she can take me away to experiment on, to drain my blood, to torture anyone I love in the hopes of breaking me, until finally, she does."

Elias shifts uncomfortably. "Jules—"

"I just—" I stumble, throat hot with feeling. "It's only a matter of time before Caro figures out that he's been helping me, if she hasn't already. You must know that if she breaks me, she'll have her powers back; her reign might never end. And who knows to how many shores it will spread."

Elias blinks, looking stunned for the first time. He casts his eyes down. But he doesn't say no.

"Promise me. If not for Sempera, then for your family. I know that you want Liam to survive this," I say in a forceful whisper.

He takes several large gulps of his wine while my heart beats wildly in my chest.

"It's possible to survive and not truly live, and I don't know if Liam would truly live without you," he says softly. He drains the rest of his wine and a drop spills onto his shirt, leaving a trail of red. "But all right, Jules. You have my word."

After his words fade from the air, it seems there is nothing left to say. But it turns out that I don't have to say anything, because something small and glittering materializes from nowhere and arcs above our heads, cutting the heavy silence. For an instant, I think it's a shooting star, but then it hits the tapestry across the room and drops to the floor with a clink. The face of the late Queen, etched in blood and iron and time, stares up at us.

A blood-iron.

Elias pushes back from the table and retrieves the coin. A look of wonder and fear slides across his face as he flips it over and back again in the palm of his hand.

Elias goes to the edge of the floor, looking down into the night. But he shakes his head. "It's too dark—"

Soft footsteps sound from below, then on the stairs. A shiver runs up my spine.

Then someone pounds on the door.

19

"Who else knows about this place?" I ask, seized by a strange mixture of fear and possessiveness.

"No one." Elias stands fluidly, impossible to startle as always. But I don't miss his hand going to the dagger handle underneath his fine waistcoat.

He crosses to the open wall, looks down, and shakes his head. No one there.

I turn to the door, my heart beating fast. For the first time, I feel vulnerable here, the fort's enchantment suddenly seeming scant protection. I hear faint footsteps through the stone walls, light, quick. Then a knock at the door. I glance at Elias, thinking that the Huntsman is at Bellwood.

He shrugs. *Up to you*, his eyes seem to say.

My mouth is dry, but I won't hide like a field mouse in the

Thief's Fort, the Alchemist's home. Whoever is coming must have something of mine.

I reach down to touch the knife handle at my belt and close my eyes for a brief moment, calling on the time in my blood, readying myself to lash out if I have to. Then I open the door and step back, everything in me freezing up for a heartbeat when I see a slender female form in the shadows. *Caro.*

But no, I realize as I make out her details—tall, dark-skinned, dressed in a scholar's robe. Not Caro. Not the Huntsman. Stef. She cocks her head at me, her eyes traveling down my arm to my hand, poised on my knife handle.

I drop my hands hastily. "Sorry," I say. "You startled us."

Stef lifts one shoulder, a silent apology. "I thought the coin would be warning enough. I didn't want to interrupt a private moment with Liam Gerling." My mouth gapes open. Stef turns to Elias. "Connemor. Not too wrinkled yet, I see."

Elias grins, though his posture is still tense. "Not for a few years yet, witchling. Liam's stepped out."

Stef grins at me. "So has Linfort. Which is why we're holding a small gathering in the tunnels. Would you like to break out, now that your warden is gone?"

Defensiveness curls through me, and I draw breath to defend Liam—he's only trying to do what he thinks is best—but Stef raises an eyebrow at me before I can speak, as if she knows what I'm going to say and she's not impressed.

"Come on," she says. "It's a neat trick you did with time in here, but it's what, ten steps across, with a load of echoing, empty hallways?" She paces to prove her point, her cloak sweeping the floor as she reaches the wall and exaggeratedly pivots. "Don't tell me you're not itching to get out," she adds.

I nod hesitantly. I can't help but be a little pleased that she wants to spend time with me after the disaster of last night, and after reading the strangeness of my journal. What's more, she's right—my skin is itching with the desire to get out of the Thief's Fort, to forget about the river of red and the memories it carried, and the Huntsman. Stef grins and looks over her shoulder at Elias.

"I wouldn't mind," Elias says, one corner of his mouth tugging up. "But there's the minor problem that Jules is the most wanted person in all of Sempera—"

"And nobody knows she's here," Stef cuts in. "And they certainly won't expect to see her at a party. Look." She rummages through her satchel, until she comes out clutching a bundle of velvet. Crossing to the table, she unrolls it. At first I think it'll be more hedge witch magic, but the fabric unfolds to reveal a set of glass vials filled with face paint and compacts of powder, brushes strapped into pockets.

"You can join us," she tosses over her shoulder to Elias, "but I'm not wasting any of my paints on you. You're too pretty already." She turns back around to me and grins. "Sit down."

I grip the back of the chair, nervous energy thrumming through me. "Do you really think that will work?" I want more than anything else to get out of the Thief's Fort, but the idea of stepping out with just a little face paint to disguise me feels like being naked.

"I know so," Stef says.

She pulls out the chair impatiently, and I sit down. Elias looks on, a small unreadable smile on his face, as Stef works this mundane kind of magic. I don't have a mirror, so instead I watch a satisfied smile gradually crawl onto Stef's face, and onto Elias's an expression of bemused appreciation. I can't help but think of the day I joined Ina and Caro to go to Laista to celebrate Ina's wedding, how they painted my face and transformed me. The warmth that existed between us, before I found out the truth and everything splintered.

After a while, Stef puts down her tools. Open powder compacts and tubes of paint litter the table. Stef tugs on a lock of my hair, watching as the red-brown curl springs back up. Her eyes suddenly brighten, and she goes into that case again and brings out another mysterious bottle. She dips a comb in—it smells like roses—and when she runs the comb through my hair, it makes the strands fall straight and shining.

She pulls a small mirror from the velvet case and turns it toward me. "Different enough for you?"

My mouth drops open in surprise. I take the mirror from

her so I can look more closely.

There is nothing drastically different in my face, but somehow I just look different. Older. My cheekbones and brow are more pronounced, while the hollows in my cheeks and under my eyes have been filled in. This girl that didn't spend her afternoon splashing around in a river, or hiding from a huntsman. My lips are red and full. I look twenty-five years old, flush with blood-iron, strange and sleek and new.

Liam would be furious if he knew what I was considering, but something in me wishes that he could see me like this. That we were really just students, and on any given night we could slip out and go dancing. Even though I know that's not possible, I can't help but want to grasp at it.

"That is impressive," Elias admits. He meets my eyes. "Jules, I'm not your keeper. If you want to go to the party, we can go."

My heart beats fast. "I want to."

Stef leads Elias and me across the darkened campus, a noticeable bounce in her step. Though it must be late by now, there are still people about—trailing toward the dormitories from the building Elias points out as the library, or drifting in groups along the paths, their laughter rising into the night. My skin prickles, but just as Stef promised, no one pays us any mind. She leads us to one of the dormitories; once inside, we descend a set of stairs until we come out in a dark, stone-walled tunnel.

I laugh nervously. "Where have you taken me?"

"It's all right, Jules." This time it's Elias who speaks. "There are tunnels all over beneath the school. They were meant to help people get around in the winter, but now we mostly use them for other reasons." He smiles, the torchlight from the walls shining off his white teeth. And sure enough, when I listen, I can hear voices somewhere off down the tunnel, music, laughter. Stef trots off in their direction, and Elias and I follow, until we come out into a larger space where several tunnels meet.

It's filled with students who've shed their scholars' robes and now mill around in dresses and waistcoats. A long table against one wall bears an array of bottles, ale and wine and madel, and two girls in one corner saw out a song on a fiddle and drum, and people circle them, calling out the names of the songs they want played—"The Queen's Guard"; "An Hour for Love." People greet each other, laughing and embracing.

The music reverberates off the walls, folding in on itself, and people sway to the beat, bodies pressed together. Nothing like the genteel beauty of the ball at Ina's coronation or even the madel bar in Laista, it's loud and dark and close and exhilarating. In the dim light it's hard to make out the details of faces, too loud to hear any one specific voice. Slowly, I feel my muscles loosen.

It was reckless of me to come here, I know that, but the noise drives all the fear to the edges of my mind. Stef wasn't wrong earlier. Who would think to look for Jules Ember here?

Elias turns to the table and then back, a drink materialized in his hands. He passes it to me, red wine in an old tin cup, and I take a sip, feeling the warmth flow through me. It's too loud to really talk, so instead we stand with our backs toward the wall, watching the crowd. I haven't the faintest idea how to dance, but I *want* to, as if the music is a magnetic force pulling my body forward.

I resist it, staying close to Elias's side. My eyes land on Stef in the crowd. Lamplight gleams on her brown skin as she dances close with a beautiful blond-haired girl, their feet moving fast in a complicated pattern I can't quite follow. She throws a glance at me over her shoulder and winks, and I feel a grin rise to my mouth.

Here, deep underground where no one knows my name or my face, I can almost pretend that I'll be someone else when I resurface. Not the Alchemist, not even Jules Ember. As if I could transform into a girl just like any other at this party, and when I emerge into the moonlight, it will be to a safe bed and an unbroken roof over my head. A home, a past and a future not swimming in blood, not written in a language that I cannot speak.

After the song winds down, Stef reappears at our side. The blond girl is at her elbow, and behind them are three other students, their eyes on Stef.

"Do your magic!" one of them urges her, laughing. "Summon the Sorceress to bless this party!"

My heart thuds in my chest. I'm careful not to react, though I feel Elias tense beside me at their shouts.

"Wine! Someone get me a pitcher of mulled wine," Stef calls. The blond girl spins away and returns with a wooden pitcher, steam curling from its top. She presses it into Stef's hands.

"Gather round," Stef says dramatically. The students cluster around us, the shoulders of strangers pressing against mine. I haven't been around so many people since the kitchen at Everless, and it's terrifying and comforting all at once.

Stef holds a week-coin in her hand, gleaming bronze in the low light, and there's a soft hiss as it slides from her palm into the wine. I force myself to smile along with everyone else, though my heart is still pounding. Next Stef opens her other hand to reveal a collection of small objects—ice holly, I realize as I look closer, with its strange dark berries, its silvery leaves. A chill trickles down my spine as I remember what Caro told me, that ice holly grew in the places where the Sorceress once walked. I can't go an hour, it seems, without a reminder of her.

Stef squeezes her fist shut, then opens it over the goblet, dropping the silver and blue bits into the wine just like she did with my blood regression. The smell that wafts from the pitcher now is strange, metallic and intoxicating all at once, and I find myself leaning forward along with the others to see what will happen.

"Ice holly and blood-iron together," Stef intones in a deep, singsongy voice. "The powers of the Alchemist and Sorceress, combined."

I suck in my breath, then have to quickly disguise it as a cough when a curly-haired boy turns to stare at me. It's been so long since I've spent time with friends, I have no idea if Stef is purposefully teasing me. I glare at Stef, willing her to feel the heat of my gaze, though she has her eyes closed now and is muttering over the wine in some approximation of ancient Semperan. My fingers dig into Elias's arm without my meaning them to. "What is she doing?"

Elias rolls his eyes. "Nothing. Ice holly sweetens the taste of cheap wine. She does this every party to scare the new students. It's all in good fun."

My laugh rings false in my own ears. I slip my hand into Elias's elbow and tug him away, toward the crowd of dancers in the center. The instrumentalists have started up another tune, fast and light and sweet, and the movements don't seem so complicated anymore now that there's a bit of drink in me. Elias takes my hands and spins me around and around. When the crowds part, I glimpse Stef across the room, sipping the steaming wine, still holding court over her unbelieving followers. I wave in her direction until she raises her head, pausing whatever trick she's in the midst of.

By now Elias is dancing with a group, and he doesn't notice me slip away, making my way over to Stef. My blood feels warm, my heart light. Stef is in a similar place, judging by the pink tinge of her cheeks, her bright glittering eyes as she waves her hands in a complicated dance, cutting up the smoke now rising from her cup. A strange mix of jealousy and sadness rises in me as the people around her laugh along with her movements—her magic is just one more amusement in a night full of them, something to gawk at in between madel and dances.

I break into the circle, grabbing Stef's arm. "I need some air," I almost shout in her ear. The party has gotten louder in the hour since we've arrived, more crowded. "Come with me?"

Stef looks over in annoyance, but her eyes widen when she sees it's me. She glances over a shoulder, dropping a wink at the blond girl. "I'll be just a moment. Don't miss me too much."

Once she's packed her things away—shoving the remaining ice holly into a hidden pocket inside her shirt—I lead her a little way down one of the branching tunnels, laughing as we hurry past a couple entwined in a deep embrace. Once we're past them and out of sight, Stef slows and sinks down against the wall, swiping the back of her hand across her brow. The music and noise of the party floats down the tunnel to us, but here it's quieter and peaceful. I sit down next to Stef, grateful for the chance to catch my breath.

"Did you find anything interesting in my journal?" I ask her, emboldened by the drink.

She shrugs. "I didn't read it."

My brows knit together in confusion. Stef sees this and laughs.

"I just wanted to mess with Liam Gerling." The last two words fall from her lips dripping with scorn.

"Why don't you like him?" I ask without thinking. Then I hear my own words and trip over myself to add qualifications. "I mean, I understand. I didn't either. Until recently."

Stef watches me, a small, knowing smile tugging at her mouth.

Red creeps into my face and I look down at my hands. "Aren't you from the five families too?"

"Not officially. But I take your point." She sighs, tips her head back. Soft music floats into the silence, notes falling around us like gentle rain. "It's just, I thought if I ever met the Alchemist, my mother would be beside me."

I glance back in the direction of the party, the crowd. "Is this really what you want out of your life? Little tricks and secrets that no one around you will ever understand?"

Stef laughs, but there's a bit of an edge in it. "As it happens, I like my little secrets," she shoots back. "I hope you didn't mind that business with the Alchemist and Sorceress and the ice holly. It's habit at this point." She gives me a rueful smile. "I forgot that I had distinguished company tonight."

"It's all right," I say automatically. And it is. Perhaps I should feel more protective of my history, but I feel a sense of kinship with this bitter, laughing witch. "Who knows," I add, trying to sound offhand and not longing. "Maybe the ice holly could have unlocked something in me."

Stef looks at me sidelong. "I wasn't lying earlier, Jules. I don't know how else to help you. I'm sorry. But I thought of someone else who might be able to."

"Oh?" My heart picks up. "Who?"

"My cousin Joeb. He's the son of one of the most powerful hedge witches in our family, Althea. She died recently under . . . mysterious circumstances."

My stomach clenches. "What circumstances?"

"It looked like she'd died of old age, run out of time, but we knew she had plenty of blood-iron stored up. And a relative said that some things were missing from her home, old letters, relics."

Caro, I think darkly. Reality comes crashing down on me, driving out the sounds of the lighthearted joy filtering down the dark hallway. "I'm sorry."

Stef shrugs, the motion small and controlled, and I know she's acting casual for my sake. How many times have I done the same thing?

"We weren't close," she says. "Althea and Joeb were eccentric, even more than the rest of us." She looks down. "But needless to stay, it's made everyone nervous."

"Is Joeb a witch too?"

Stef shakes her head. "Not that I know of. But he keeps records of our family's history, all the way back to the time of the Alchemist and the Sorceress. If you can get on his good side, he might share them with you. Plus, it's rumored that he collects and trades artifacts—most are fake poultices and charms, but he might know something about your weapon."

I laugh. "Trust me, I need all the possibilities I can get."

She smiles crookedly at me. "I'm glad you're here, Jules." She pulls something from an inner pocket of her robe and holds it out toward me, tilting her palm toward the torchlight. At first, I think she has more ice holly, but no—it's a small, smooth, polished gray stone, carved roughly in the shape of a face.

"My mother gave this to me," Stef says, placing it in my hands. It's cool, cold really, despite having been in her pocket. "She said it was a token, meant to remind you that evil doesn't always wear the face you expect. It's kept me safe." She blushes, casts her eyes down. "Anyway, show it to Joeb when you meet him, and he'll know family sent you."

While she gives me directions to Joeb's cottage, I look at the little thing in my hand, trying to keep my confusion off my face. It's the simplest of carvings, just a slight ridge for a nose and indentations for eyes and a mouth, like the stone statue of the Sorceress Papa kept on our windowsill.

A loud noise from the direction of the party makes us both freeze—a few shouts, rising above the general hum, and the next moment the music falters, quiet rippling out. I'm on my feet before I can think, dropping the stone into my pocket and drawing my knife. Stef stands too. We exchange worried glances, and then Stef is off, striding back down the tunnel. I hurry after her, not wanting to be left alone here.

The music has stopped and the room is mostly quieted by the time we get back. Almost everyone stands in a huddle at the center of the room, their backs to us, a murmur of voices blocking out whatever's going on inside. Stef barges forward, throwing elbows to get through, me slipping along in her wake.

And then I see what's captured everyone's attention, who is at the center of the circle.

Liam is here, and when I step into the circle his eyes draw to mine, flashing from cold to livid. Heat radiating off him in waves, he leads me out of the archway, into the tunnels.

"You're acting ridiculous, Liam," I whisper as harshly as I can, though I know that's not true.

Elias lingers in our wake, casually waving good-bye to the partygoers throwing us curious glances. When we're far enough down the dark hall, Liam slows us to a halt and turns to face me. Even though he's angry—fuming, by the rise and fall of his chest—the sight of him brings relief.

"You're safe," I whisper without meaning to.

"Yes. The Huntsman was called away just as we came down to dinner, to conduct a sweep of the dormitories." His eyes flicker. "We need to leave. I shouldn't have let you and Elias convince me of anything different. Do you have your things?"

I grip the strap of my bag, feel the weight of the journal sitting there. "Yes, and I have an idea of where to go next. Stef told me about a hedge witch, a distant relation of hers named Althea. She died recently under mysterious circumstances." I shiver. "Maybe it was Caro's doing."

Liam glowers. "Jules, we have to leave Sempera, not just Bell-wood."

"What about Althea?"

"A bleeder probably got her," Liam says.

It's been so long since I've lived a normal life with Papa that it feels almost comforting to be reminded of Sempera's nonmagical threats. Bleeders, the people who stalk the woods and towns, cutting down people for their time. "No, not a bleeder. She had her time *pulled* from her. Her son is still alive, we—"

"It's not worth an hour-coin."

My stomach curls at the expression, only used by nobles, to whom an hour is worth nothing. "You're wrong. It's Caro. It must be Caro." My mind starts to race. Why else would she target someone who's a stranger to me, and not someone I loved, or who was connected to me? "She's killed anyone who's been an ally to me. Althea's son has his mother's collected papers. Maybe he knows something—about the weapon, or about the river that runs red. And there must be a reason Caro did this."

"A *reason*?" Liam's words are suddenly scalding. "You should know that Caro doesn't need a reason to murder. If it *was* her, she was probably just bored."

I open my mouth to point out that I know Caro better than he does, but my voice dies as Roan's face flashes behind my eyes. She killed him to break my heart, though she failed. Then, I remember another face—the Queen's, tipped back and horribly blank, blood flecked over her lips and teeth. Had she earned her death at Caro's hands?

A small strangled noise escapes Liam. Before I can stop him, he slides his hands up my arms, pulling me slightly closer to him. I can feel him shaking.

"Listen to me," he says, voice raw and aching and desperate. "More soldiers will be flooding into Bellwood tomorrow— they're searching everywhere. It's not safe here. Not anywhere in Sempera. I've arranged a room for us at a local inn, the Green Hour. We'll stay there tonight, then go with Elias in the morning, and get to Connemor as quickly as we can."

For a brief second, I want to say yes, to take his hand and lead him away to some distant shore. The room is already small and cramped with desks. Too cramped for the charge growing between us, the frustrated scream swirling in my throat. Only it's not a scream—it's a question, fully formed and blinding.

Do you love me?

I shove Liam away as hard as I can. "I'm not leaving with you."

"I'm not leaving without you," he responds. In a single second, his eyes freeze over, shadow changed into ice. I recognize the cruel slash of his mouth—and all at once, I know that he's planning to take me away, even if it's against my will, just like he dragged me away at Everless.

But it's not his choice to make.

I back away quickly, throw my hands up to stop his movement. In the distance, Elias is striding out the door. Neither of them can stop the bubble of time that barrels out from my open palms, the invisible bonds that freeze them in place.

I turn my back to them and run.

20

I follow Stef's directions as closely as I can in the dark. Luck finds me—the night is cloudless, and the moonlight shines down on me, illuminating the crude map she made.

Finally, after an hour's walk, I reach an area of patchy farm-land, the earth newly turned in neat rows. It reminds me of the little plot of land where Papa and I lived in Crofton, and my throat tightens. In the moonlight, I make out the shape of a small, decrepit cottage, the light of a single candle glowing behind a canvas-covered window.

Nervousness fills my throat as I raise my hand to knock. When no one answers, I gently push on the door. It isn't latched and swings open easily beneath my touch.

Inside, the air smells of bitter, burned herbs and wet earth. I stop for a moment in the blackness, listening. The only light inside comes from one candle in the center of the room at waist level, sputtering faintly.

Cautiously, I step into the darkness. The moonlight disappears, a candle flame blown out.

As my eyes adjust, I see that someone has created a shrine in the center of the room: an artful arrangement of herbs, colored-glass potion bottles, the single burning candle. Vaguely, I recall similar shrines arranged at the hedge witch's in Crofton, all requested and paid for with blood-iron by a mourning relative. The only difference is that the assortment of offerings in front of me looks more genuine somehow—more purposefully arranged—though I can't put my finger on exactly how I know this. Maybe it's just the fear circling around me now, or my yearning to find meaning in this trip, to trust in Stef, despite Liam's insistence that such a venture is misguided.

I step farther into the room. At this distance, I can see that the shrine is dusted faintly with something that shines like powdered gold. The shimmer draws me forward, and I reach out my finger to gather some of the dust. The flame warms my palms as I stretch my hand toward it, though an odd, unexpected chill passes over my skin.

Then, someone clears their throat behind me.

I spin around.

It's a man—tall and broad-shouldered, but with a starved air about him. It's impossible to tell how old he is. With wild black hair and a pale face etched with wrinkles, he could be anywhere from thirty to fifty. His shirt, which looks filthy even in the dim lamplight, hangs off him. The smell of alcohol washes out when he leans over to light the lamp on a rough-hewn kitchen table.

This must be Joeb.

A small knot of fear forms in my stomach when I register that he's standing between me and the door.

Joeb peers at me with bleary, red eyes and takes a step forward. "Who are you?" His voice is slightly slurred, but still has a low gravity.

"A-an apprentice hedge witch," I stammer, holding out the carved stone Stef gave me. I hope that he's too far into drink to recognize me from the drawings Ina distributed, if he's seen them. "A distant relative of yours. I heard about Althea's death, and . . ." I spread my hands, hoping that he'll fill in the blanks himself, but he says nothing. "I wanted to pay my respects."

Joeb squints at me, scarcely glancing at the stone. "I've never seen you before."

My heart gives a quick twist, as I remember the days just after Papa's death, just how gone from the world I was. I relax slightly. I didn't try to drink my grief away, but I understand why someone would. The man could be kind, I tell myself as I swallow the urge to run. I don't want to risk upsetting him further before I learn anything from him.

"I never met Althea," I say softly. "Though she might have known me."

"Well, she's gone," Joeb says harshly. He casts his eyes on the shrine, then back at me. "You've brought no offering. So what do you really want?"

I gesture lamely to the shrine, already lost in my lie. I grasp for anything that will help me get on better ground with him, figure out what he knows about the weapon without angering him. "To honor her and . . . learn about her."

He strikes a match, reaching past me to light a bundle of herbs. The incense immediately begins to burn, filling the air with sweet-smelling smoke. Blue-gray blooms in the air between us. "No one honors hedge witches in Sempera anymore. Not since the old days, and those have long since passed. So you intend to steal from her." He pauses, letting a grin creep into his features. "But there are people who steal for good, and others who steal for ill. Which are you?"

Steal for good? Is that a veiled reference to the Alchemist? His gaze is too direct, heavy, and yet it reveals nothing. With a lurch of my stomach, I fear that Liam was right. This is all a waste of time, dangerous, and I'm talking to a mad drunk—though his speech is unnervingly focused. I consider leaving right then, calculating whether I'm fast enough to freeze time and dart around him, through the door.

But I can't, not yet; not before I've found out if Althea knew anything about defeating Caro. I make myself meet his eyes, and speak a version of the truth. Bold, to get answers out of him.

"I think I know who killed Althea," I say. His eyes widen and he takes a step back. "And I want to know why."

The man holds my gaze, confrontational, for a moment longer, then something goes out of him and his shoulders relax. "Sit down," he says gruffly, his voice low and suddenly full of grief. He sits down at the table, grabbing a small bottle from a bag that hangs from his belt.

Again, my feet itch to run. I'd come to the door expecting some hidden ally, despite Stef's uncertain warning, but this man's grieved tone—his nonreaction to being told that I might know his mother's murderer—is far more unnerving than physical violence. I came all this way, I remind myself, ran from Liam. And the Huntsman may be still searching the dormitories at Bellwood—I can't go back now. Steeling myself against doubt, I follow the man's outstretched hand and take a seat at the table.

"Your name is Joeb, isn't it?" I ask gently, sitting down.

It takes the man, now slumped over with grief, a moment to nod, like he has to reach down into memory for the movement. As he pushes up his sleeves and pulls the cork out of his glass bottle, it's easier to see the wrinkles that crawl over his skin. The lines start between his knuckles, and are etched all the way up his arms until they disappear under his rolled-up sleeves.

I have to stifle a sharp intake of breath when I realize that they are not wrinkles but impossibly thin scars.

He follows my eyes. "She used my blood every so often." He takes a swig from his bottle. "She always said it was for me. To make me great with magic, as she was once, and her mother before her."

"She was trying . . . to give magic to you?" I ask. Something stirs in me, whipping in my chest like a serpent's tail. "You can do that?"

His laugh is brief and bitter. "If you're powerful, you can do anything. If you're not . . ." He gestures at himself. "I'm afraid my mother's efforts were in vain."

Joeb looks older now that he's not standing over me. A feeling of pity mingled with déjà vu stabs through me—the tiny, cramped cottage, the slowness of the man's movements and words. For an instant, it's like I'm back in my own cottage, a shrine to Papa burning in a dark corner.

I push the thought away, swallowing. I need to focus on getting information out of him. As the orange light from the lantern reveals the room, I look around, squinting to see the details in better light. It's simpler than the setup of the false hedge witch Caro, Ina, and I visited in Laista when we were together at Everless. A small table laden with glittering vials and jars and a wooden scale sits in one corner, and brown bunches of dried herbs still hang over the fire. The air is thick with smoke and incense, the metallic scent of blood-iron and something else I can't name.

Power, a voice in me whispers. Faint, but there.

Joeb speaks, startling me. "Why is it," he says, his voice flat and empty, "that it's only after my mother died we've had this parade of well-wishers? When in life she had to scrabble for every blood-iron?" His words still blur together at the edges, but the meaning—the feeling—comes through perfectly. As he speaks, he sprinkles something into his mug—I recognize the red-gold sheen of blood-irons, but they're not coins, just shavings. My stomach clenches. Is Joeb a bleeder?

"Who else has come?" I ask carefully.

"All sorts," Joeb says indifferently. "Other hedge witches and timelenders, soldiers and madmen. They all leave when they realize there's nothing left to take. Or when they figure out that I don't have her talents."

My heart falls. Stef said Joeb had Althea's papers, which might contain a clue to destroying the Sorceress. My mind spins, trying to think of the combination of words that will help me get information without angering Althea's son. I cast my eyes around—

And it's then I notice the small figurine of the Sorceress propped up against her shrine. Cold seeps into me. "Did your mother worship the Sorceress?"

Joeb spits, then laughs softly. "No. But the Sorceress is a part of our legacy."

"Legacy?" I find myself drifting toward the table, trying to hide my fear while appearing to hang on his words. "What do you mean?"

"There are hedge witches in my family back to the time of the Sorceress. Real hedge witches, not the imposters you find with a sign hanging over their shops," he spits. "My mother's great-great-grandmother walked with the Sorceress and Alchemist. Althea was gifted. But not me, and I've no children," he says bitterly. "Though surely you know some of that already, if you know who killed my mother." Joeb states it so plainly that at first, I don't recognize the danger in it.

My voice comes out hoarse. "I—I'm not sure. I think it was the Queen's handmaiden. A girl a little older than me—dark hair, green eyes—" My stammering dies when I see Joeb stiffen, his eyes sharpening.

"Both," he says slowly. "Both. The dead Queen and the girl."

My breath catches. "You—you saw it?"

"I saw them leaving, when they were finishing with her," Joeb says excitedly. The apathy is gone from his voice, and his eyes are now glinting like steel. "I was too late to save her. She had been speaking ill of the Sorceress again." He leans in, his long nails digging into the table. "I was always telling her not to spread those tales, but she never listened."

"Sp-speaking ill of her?" It's nearly impossible to keep the stammer from my voice.

I stop. He looks at me with a canniness that I don't like. At my indrawn breath, he half rises from his seat.

"You know something, don't you?" he says, animated now. He pounds the table. I jump at the sound. The flame of the lamp flickers, then burns bright again.

My heart is beating fast with the surety that some knowledge, some truth lies here in this cottage, if I can only put my hands on it. "The girl who murdered your mother—she *was* the Sorceress," I say all in one breath. "And I'm searching for a weapon that will kill her."

I stop abruptly, realizing that I've said too much. Calling the Queen's handmaiden an ancient goddess, claiming that I want to strike the Sorceress dead—I must sound mad, despite what Stef told me about Joeb's history.

Slowly, as if trying not to disturb a deer in the woods, I pull the ancient journal onto the table and open it to the page that bears my blood. *Seek the river of red.* "I was hoping you could help me figure out what this means."

I look up to see that a smile is spreading slowly across Joeb's face, a smile I like less than his drunken snapping. When he speaks, his voice is crystal clear. "The river of red, red with blood," he recites, like a twisted child's rhyme.

"Red with blood?" My head swims. "What does that mean?"

He shrugs. "Whose blood has been spilled across Sempera?"

I don't have to answer out loud. The Alchemist's. *Mine.* My gut is screaming at me to leave . . . but I've come so far, only to leave with nothing. "And the weapon? Have you ever heard—"

"To kill the Sorceress? What could kill someone as powerful as her?" His lined face splits in anger, then resolves to a beatific smile. My head is spinning with his shifts in mood. "She's nothing but hunger, isn't she?"

"She's nothing but evil." The words spill out of my mouth, unbidden. Dangerous.

Joeb shifts in his seat, and my hands flex unconsciously, my pulse speeding, stomach turning.

"She wants more than her heart back now," Joeb says. "She needs the Alchemist's soul too. Then nothing will be able to stop her—she'll be able to do things that I can only imagine. Brew immortality. Even control time itself. Not just survive it, move back and forth through it. Take life away with the touch of her hand. She'll rule Sempera for thousands of years, and sit on the throne long after I've turned to dust."

"No, that's impossible." I don't know why I'm trying to convince Joeb of this, but I can't stop the words, or take the pleading edge out of my voice.

"Nothing is impossible." He's risen now, the lamplight making his shadow bleed over the floor. "The Sorceress told me herself. I hear her whisper. In my sleep. In my dreams."

Suddenly, his movements are no longer slow, no longer unfocused. A knife has materialized in his hand, his voice turning cold and authoritative. And yet something in his words makes me obey when he demands that I come forward.

I stand and, trembling, walk to the shrine, Joeb close behind my back. I open my palm with the knife, not even feeling the pain. I hold it out so blood drips over the flickering candle.

The flame shoots up with a brilliant light, a beacon of magic pointed directly at me.

And he lunges for my neck.

21

My blood leaps in my veins, rallying to my defense before my mind can catch up, raging heat flooding my body. I fling my hands out, and the cottage shakes with the force of it.

This time, I don't hold my magic back.

Joeb barrels toward me, hands outstretched for my throat, but I grab his bottle from the table. He cries out as it strikes his head, the blow of it knocking him over and away from me. He crashes to his hands and knees on the floor.

I advance on him, blood roaring in my ears. Now I can feel the time flowing through my hands like a physical thing. As changeable as water and strong as steel. I feel like I'm growing, my strength pressing at the walls and roof, like I could flex my fingers and blow this cottage to pieces—and Joeb with it.

Joeb recovers quickly, exploding to his feet with a feral

growl. Maybe he has more magic flowing through his veins than he let on. He throws himself again at me, and my time can't stop him. His whole weight hits me, bringing us both to the ground with a world-shaking crash. Stars burst around me when my head hits the ground. Impossible light floods my vision even though I've shut my eyes, followed by blinding pain.

A scream sticks in my throat. My hands find Joeb's wrists and force them away from my neck, my legs kicking wildly at air. I grasp at the magic in my veins, scouring my whole body for it, but Joeb is too close, too heavy, triggering an animal panic in me that causes time to slip from my grasp.

"Why are you doing this?" I snarl, trying to scatter the panic with fury. "Your mother followed me, she—"

"The Alchemist's days are over. Don't you understand? The Sorceress will spare me," Joeb grunts, winding his fingers tighter around my neck. The smell of alcohol on his breath mixed with the scent of incense, now acrid and poisonous, fills my nose and throat. I almost pity him. Almost.

I land an elbow to Joeb's ribs that knocks the breath from him, and he rolls away, wheezing. I haul myself up by the table and find my grip on time again. Though he staggers to his feet and crashes toward me, I raise my hands, gathering the time around me into my palms as a seamstress might gather fabric and thread.

The smoke hangs still in the air. The flames of the candle

stop moving. Joeb's chest freezes, though his eyes still glow with life. With fear. I focus on slowing the expansion of his lungs, the beating of his heart, while I let the rest of time advance—and hear nothing but silence as his jaw moves, trying to find breath where there is none.

Suddenly, I know that I could kill him, if I wanted.

Then I let time go. Joeb clattering to the ground. He lands flat on his back, clutching his chest.

"I'm sorry," he chokes out. I almost believe him—but it doesn't matter if he's sorry. "She knew you'd come looking. She said she'd let me live—if—"

He grabs something from his belt, flashing silver, and throws it. The blade misses my face by inches, I feel the rush of air in its passage, and all thought of restraint flees from me. I close my eyes and let time flow freely from my hands, wrap around Joeb as he writhes on the floor. He screams.

Somewhere that feels far away from me, a door slams open, Elias yells my name. But I can't stop, can't even force my eyes to open. Joeb is crying out, his voice changing strangely as I drag him forward through time, aging him so rapidly his breath can't keep up. On and on and on. It's not in my control any longer.

Hands grip my arms, just as Joeb's wail cuts out. Finally, I wrench open my eyes to see Elias in front of me, face painted with terror. His hands still curled around my arms, squeezing. Behind him, a crumpled form lies still on the cold stone floor.

Shock pours into me as I see how far I've gone—what I've done. Joeb is dead, I know right away: his skin is loose and gray, his eyes saucer-wide and swirling with a cloud of filthy white, a color like soiled cloth. As I stand there, my heart pounding a war drum through my veins, his head lolls to one side. Ashes trickle in a steady stream from his mouth. Thick and gray and plentiful.

Then I'm crawling away, away from the body and the over-turned table. I take off running—where, I don't know. Around me, it seems the whole world has slowed, and I'm not sure if it's my doing.

I don't care. I couldn't stop if I wanted to. My body is making its own decisions, as if it thinks that moving fast enough will allow me to outrun what I've just done. Killed a man. *Murderer.* Does it matter that Joeb would have killed me too?

I can't help but recall what Caro said to me at the palace. That I stole her heart just because I could, because I wanted her power. No—I will not succumb to her tricks and lies. I will not believe the worst about myself.

And yet . . . something in my heart tugs. What am I really capable of? *Why* can't I remember what happened? Why are my memories of past lives so difficult to find?

The town whips by, a dark house and a stray dog and a lighted window passing almost too fast to see, as if my power over time encompasses the whole of me, sending me racing across land while the entire earth is slowed down. Somehow, though it seems only seconds have passed, I'm in Montmere, asking for directions to the inn Liam mentioned, nothing on my mind but escape. Tears streaking my face, I charge through the Green Hour's dark entryway, down the hall to our room.

Then, I'm slamming the door behind me, pulling at my clothes, desperate to get every trace of Joeb off me, every reminder of what I'm done.

When I'm down to my shift and bare feet, I realize that Liam is sitting against the far wall—waiting for me—awake. His shirt is unbuttoned and his hair loose, curtaining his face in soft waves.

My pulse hasn't quieted one bit since I ran from Althea's cottage. It seems to get even louder now, blotting out the sound of my footsteps on the floorboards. Something—guilt and relief, panic and fear, all braiding into the tugging feeling I still refuse to name—carries me across the room, makes me drop to my knees across from him, a sob tearing my throat open.

I reach for him, aching to be touched, to have the memory of death burned away.

Liam's eyes are impossibly dark and soft with sleep. The room is nearly black, but with adrenaline still coursing through me I can see him perfectly: every shadow of his eyelashes on his cheekbones, the way his neck flutters with his pulse, his lips parting with the sound of my name. His fingers, reaching forward to intertwine themselves into my hair.

And I lean forward to meet him. His arms go up around me, and in the space of a breath our lips meet.

Warmth cascades over me. He's warm, almost feverishly so, and my hands are in his hair and his lips are moving against mine. Murmuring my name. He pulls me into the bed, on top of him, holding me tightly against him, quieting my trembling and filling me with an entirely different kind of ache. He tastes like salt and sandalwood, and his hands are soft on my back, moving to grip my waist. He holds me like something precious; the gentle touch of his tongue to my lips draws a sigh out of me—a slow sound, melting in the air that's no longer between us—and it's unlike anything I've heard before.

My heart slows to match his, the strong, steady, just-out-of-sleep beat of his blood, whispering to me from all the places our bodies are pressed together. My frenetic, dancing blood finds an anchor in the steady pulse of his, slowing and swirling and loud and quiet all at once.

I could make this moment never end. Liam wouldn't be afraid, I can tell from the tender way one hand rises to trail over my cheek, the wonder in his gasp as he breaks away for an instant to breathe, then finds my mouth again. He'd stay here with me forever, he will, if I don't pull away.

But I can't. I can't stop the whole world. Not forever.

So though it's among the hardest things I've ever done, I let go. Pull away. Still sitting on his bed, on his lap, really, I drink in the look in Liam's eyes, sleep-fogged and hungry and tender all at once. Allow myself to wonder at how lovely he is. And then lift his hands from my waist and hold them between us, a connection and a barrier all at once, as the awareness floods into his eyes that none of this was a dream.

22

Liam and I sit there, frozen, for what seems like a long moment. Regret tears at me. I wait for him to speak, or even for his face to change from the sleepy wonder it is now.

"Jules. What happened?" I'm not sure if he's talking about the kiss or what happened before—what sent me running from Bellwood, what brought me here, drove me into his arms, the cause of my racing pulse. His limbs are frozen in place, his fingers still curled around the back of my hands. His skin radiating heat. Gently, he traces my wristbone, turning my hands over until my palms face up to reveal the cut Joeb made on my palm.

"You're bleeding." His touch is so gentle that my eyes begin to burn with newly formed tears. "Talk to me. Elias and I—we couldn't find Stef, we've been taking turns searching for you."

I consider lying—but I can't bear the weight of what

happened alone. I *killed* someone.

Adrenaline is still rushing through me from the kiss; it takes only a heartbeat of silence for the delirious thrill of it to turn over into fear. There's something more frightening about this— breaking the silence between us, not holding back the ugly truth of what happened—than anything I've done. But there's no way around the truth but to lie. What's more, what's terrifying, is that I don't *want* to lie to Liam.

I tell him everything.

When I've finished relating what happened, Liam steps out to speak with Elias. After catching him up on Joeb and his attack and death—all that darkness—our kiss remains unacknowledged, and I keep it that way, pretending to fuss over the bedspread and avoiding his eyes as Liam leaves the room. It's only when the door closes behind him that I notice a slip of parchment crumpled on the nightstand. Without thinking, still shaky from adrenaline, I take the note and flatten it to read.

> *Son,*
>
> *Return home at once. The Queen's retinue has arrived, and I can no longer answer for your absence. You well know that she has been taking measures to punish those who are disloyal. I will not have another tragedy fall upon my house.*
>
> *Lord Nicholas*

Dread curdles my stomach at the words. Have I signed his death warrant?

The sound of footsteps outside makes me jump. I let the note fall from my numb fingers just as Liam enters again. "I've asked Elias to give us a few minutes. I didn't know if you wanted company, or—should I leave you, to rest?"

He trails off, a note of hope in his voice that tells me he wants me to stay. Color stays high in his cheeks; his hair is still tousled where I ran my fingers through it.

"Liam." The word escapes me in a rush of breath, like I've been struck in the chest, and I've no idea what to say.

But I don't have to figure it out. He kneels in front of me, reaches out and intertwines his fingers into mine, squeezing my hand as if I'm his only anchor to the world. I press back, caging the sob gathering in my chest.

Caro's taunts echo in my head. I see her teeth bared in mockery, hear her promises to hollow me out and break my heart. I remember the diabolic hunger in her eyes when she put her knife to Roan's throat, thinking his death would break me.

Oh, how she would laugh if she knew what I'd just done.

Liam is still staring at me, his eyes soft, pleading. Waiting for me to say something. He's been protecting me since we were both children, even as I hated and feared him. And all along, I was right to be afraid, even if I didn't know why. All along he would be the one who could break my heart.

Finger by finger, I pull my hand away from his. Tears spill down my cheeks, hot and furious at what I know I must do to save him. The same thing that Papa did, that Liam did, throughout my entire childhood.

I have to lie.

Maybe that's what love is made of. Maybe it's what allowed me to hold on to the Sorceress's heart for centuries.

I get to my feet and move around the room, picking up his clothes where they're folded next to his sleeping mat, tucking them into his leather traveling bag.

Liam's head snaps up at the *snick* of the clasp. "What are you doing?" he whispers.

My voice comes out thick, my throat lined with more unshed tears. "You have to go back to Everless. I"—my words catch in my throat, as if refusing to deceive Liam—"I will go with Elias to Connemor."

Liam stares at me blankly. He stiffens. "You will?"

Through the grief, my heart screams at me to take it back. But I can't. Kissing him was as good as drawing a target on his chest, and if he doesn't go back to Everless now, his father will find him. And then—Caro.

"You were right, I should have fled all along." I abandon the clothes and return to sit next to him. My body feels simultaneously heavy and fidgety, my own helplessness pushing at the inside of my skin. Nothing I can do, nothing, except convince him to go back to Everless, where he can be safer than he is with me. "I'm sure Elias will agree to take me."

"Of course," Liam, says, confused. "Of course he'll take us. . . ."

He trails off as I manage a watery smile. Pity and regret tug at my chest, as I remember Elias's promise to me in the Thief's Fort. That he would kill the Alchemist to guarantee that Liam didn't come to harm. "Liam." I lower my voice, forcing myself to keep breathing so my voice doesn't break. "You have to return to Everless. Pretend none of this ever happened."

Liam looks blankly at me, saying nothing. No matter how much his cleverness usually grates on my nerves—his quick mind constantly fastening on the next answer, before I can even process the puzzle—I miss it fiercely now. The silence is too much to bear. My voice is in danger of cracking, so I don't say any more. I cross my arms over my chest, trying to ease the icy pain that digs into my lungs with each breath.

"You'll go alone?" he asks.

"Yes—" Now my voice does break. I swallow and try again, rearranging my words before I can no longer resist telling him the truth. "It's time to part."

"This is what you want?" he presses.

"It is."

Liam doesn't speak for a long time after that. He only stares at me, eyes working in the pursuit of an answer to a puzzle. Finally, he nods, sharply as the fall of a guillotine, then finishes gathering his things from around the room. I sit there watching him blankly, a ghost of myself.

For a moment he seems frozen, then he reaches out tentatively toward me and takes my hand, squeezes it once before nodding back.

His other hand rises to my face, and he traces my cheek with his fingertips, so quick and light I almost can't tell if I've imagined it.

I stare into his eyes. "Promise me that you'll be safe."

"I'd promise you anything," he says.

Liam withdraws his own small journal from his pile of things, then presses it into my hand, curling my fingers around it with his. He touches his lips to my forehead in one swift motion before quietly slipping out the door, leaving me no chance to even whisper good-bye.

23

At some point I fall asleep, curled against the headboard with my arms around my knees, mattress damp with tears underneath me. A few hours after Liam disappears, when I wake up to watery sunlight, Elias is there at the table, looking somber. But he simply says, "What's the plan, Alchemist?" The hint of a sad, teasing smile plays on his lips.

I let one more tear slip down my cheek. I wipe it away, and for a second, marvel at how different Liam and Elias are. Amma and I were opposites on the surface, too. A flash of her laughter echoes through my mind.

I steel myself and recount my interaction with Joeb to Elias, the twisted child's rhyme he'd offered when I showed him the strange sentence in my journal. *The river of red, red with blood.* I tell Elias how he'd suggested that it was referring to the

Alchemist's blood. The Alchemist's death. Though Joeb attacked me—though I couldn't trust him—he didn't lie to me. He had no reason, or mind to.

"*Seek the river of red.* You think that somehow refers to your death?" Elias frowns. "You've died more than once."

"But we know of at least one death that occurred in a river. At least according to the stories."

Elias leans back. "Caro forcing you to eat her heart in your first life."

I nod. "According to the stories, I offered her heart back by turning it into twelve stones. She fed them to me—she thought I tricked her just like I tricked the lord—then in anger, drowned me in the river."

"And you want to go there?"

I nod. "Even if the stories aren't true they *contain* truths. What if I was trying to point myself to that story, that moment—because something important happened then? Some key to defeating Caro? Maybe it *was* a trick all along, and I intended to destroy her then and there."

I reach into my bag and withdraw Liam's notes. My chest aches to hold them, but I bring them over to Elias and spread them on the table. "The place is never named in the stories, but he found an obscure scholar who speculated the actual site was the Valley of Blythe."

"Then—we go to the Valley of Blythe."

Outside, the morning has dawned foggy and cold, a mirror of the gray landscape in my chest. The Valley of Blythe is several miles outside of Montmere, near a town called Pryceton, and we have to pass through the city first.

Because Ayleston is flooded with soldiers and civilians looking to profit off my arrest, Elias and I try a new disguise: we tear our robes and smear dirt over the fabric as if we spend our days in the woods, until we look passably like bleeders. When we emerge into the streets again to find a public cart, I notice how groups of people gather in the street, wretched looks on their faces. My heart begins to pound, assuming they've caught sight of me—but then, I overhear snatches of their conversation.

"More than a thousand years—"

"May the Sorceress curse the murderess for bringing this upon us, and steal her hours while she sleeps—"

"The soldiers will start bleeding us next week—"

I turn to Elias, but he's already speaking with someone in the crowd. When he returns, he tells me that the Queen has circulated an announcement. Her soldiers are moving through Sempera's towns and will begin bleeding its citizens of their years at random, if Jules Ember is not found by the beginning of the week. It will continue until she is turned in.

My stomach churns with anger. "That can't be Ina. It must be Caro. All the more reason to hurry."

Thankfully, Elias gives Joeb's cottage a wide berth as we leave the town behind and make our way to the spot on the main road where a public hay cart will take us in the direction of the Valley of Blythe.

As we travel, surrounded by silence, the reality of what happened last night sinks into my heart. *I killed someone.*

You had no choice, a voice whispers in my ear.

I let my head sink into my hands. It's true that Joeb was in Caro's service. But looking back, those circumstances don't seem important. He was alive, and now he's dead. Because of me. Because of the Alchemist.

With thoughts like these, the day passes in an agonizing crush—we transfer from cart to cart as the trees grow thicker, keeping our heads down when we pass clusters of guards. The moment of my parting with Liam still manages to sneak up on me everywhere.

Finally, in the late afternoon, Elias and I go as far as we possibly can in the public carts. After we disembark, Elias points out through the trees the shadowy mouth of a gorge, then to a map in his possession. *Liam's,* I realize with a pang. The Valley of Blythe is at its bottom. Something in me gutters like a candle swiftly blown out, and I go cold. All this hiding. All this desperate journeying, and now I will have to finally face my own death—my first death.

But will I find the weapon that will bring about Caro's death?

I take in the view, catching my breath and trying to slow the rapid beating of my heart. Once a shallow plain with a river running through, over the past thousand years, wind and water have carved out a ravine, splitting the earth a hundred feet down.

I see a road running alongside the canyon—empty now, but I spot the marks where wagon wheels have recently churned up the mud. We can't linger here long.

At the bottom, the river is a flat green ribbon. The water is wide and slow-moving here. It's not as far down as I thought at first, but the sides of the canyon are steep and craggy, scraggly bushes and stunted trees sticking out at odd angles. There's none of the hazy magic in the air that I felt in the glen. But still, something draws me to it—makes me scan the walls of the ravine, looking for a way down.

"Are you sure about this, Jules?" Elias asks, peering over cautiously. "If anyone comes by, it will be hard to run."

"Yes," I say, though doubt rears up in me as soon as I stare down into the gorge. But I have no choice—I need to know what lies below, in my past.

"It looks like there's a footpath down the way slightly farther. I'll go down, make sure there's no one there."

I've already crouched by the rim, grasping the branch of one overhanging tree and starting to lower myself down. I can't see below me, but something in me knows that if I stretch out my right foot, there will be a foothold. And there is. That now-familiar trickle of recognition, cold and thrilling at the same time, runs down my spine. *I have been here before.*

I have died here.

A dizzying nausea moves through me and I nearly keel over and throw up.

"Jules," I hear from above, a hint of worry tinging Elias's voice. But I'm already too far down the side of the ravine to pull myself back up, even if I wanted to. I tilt my head up to see him kneeling by the edge—but the path down seems less obvious from below, or maybe it's memory guiding me. Elias's brow creases.

"I'm going to go down to make sure there's no one coming," he says. "It's a quarter mile this way." He lifts a hand, pointing in the direction of the river's flow. His tone is light, but he can't fully hide the undercurrent of worry in his words. "Meet me at the bottom there?"

I wait, clutching the wall like a spider, until the sounds of Elias's footsteps have faded into the soft burble of the water below. I reach the bottom of the ravine and turn around. The water glitters before me, beckoning me toward it.

I died here, I remember again with a shiver.

I want to shout for Elias, and my eyes fix on the small figure of him in the distance. But even as they do, my vision blurs and changes dizzyingly. I vaguely feel my hand reaching into my cloak pocket to retrieve the compass as the sky's color plunges from the washed-out paleness of a spring afternoon to the gilded blue of an autumn evening.

The simple beauty of the river arrests me, even as I stumble up to the bank, legs aching and lungs screaming from running. It fills my eyes, forcing me to squint as I scan the water's edge, searching for any sign of life. But not for Elias, I realize as I see how the trees are no longer budding but barren with the coming winter.

I'm no longer waiting for Elias. I'm waiting for Caro.

24

My waking mind collides with the memory, an explosion of thought and feeling that burns until only one certainty is left in the ashes.

I have to give Caro's heart back.

I kneel at the edge of the river, half hidden beside a flat reclining rock in case anyone should wander by. I can tell by the tint of color in the leaves around me—they're tinged red, like they're bleeding—that we're in the death of summer. The Sorceress has already become a shadow at the edge of my vision, a rumor whispered in dark village streets. She sleeps with the wolves in the eastern forests. She travels from town to town, disguised, letting the poor drink what's left of her blood. I run my hand along a rock next to me, over the crudely drawn image etched into its surface: a snake and fox.

With trembling hands, I withdraw the small leather bag from my skirt pocket and hold it in my palms, so the mouth is slightly open. The bag is surprisingly light, considering what it contains: the Sorceress's heart. Pure power, pure life, cut to pieces.

Inside, the pale gray stones glow, illuminating the night darkening around me. They warm my hands, even through the fabric of the bag. They shimmer in the sunset, flecks of gold catching and refracting between my fingers. Pale threads of solid golden light seem to hover over each stone—a wisp of the Sorceress's heart, vying to be free.

A shadow moves in the distance.

As if in response, heat erupts in the bag. I clutch it to my chest, even though the stones feel like live coals, almost too hot to hold.

A dark, slender shape makes itself known across the river. I look up, call softly, "Caro?"

She stares across the water at me. Her anger apparent in her drawn-up posture, the severe tilt of her chin—and there's a wild hurt in her eyes, visible even across this distance. She comes up to the river until the waves nearly lap at her feet and stops.

She raises her hands, and my skin prickles as her power stirs the air. An instinct rises in me to run and hide, but I force myself to remain where I am. I stagger to my feet as ice lances across the water, a thin, slick path, and she steps delicately across, her skirts trailing in the water. When she steps onto the sand, the ice melts into nothing behind her. For a long moment, the only sounds are river and wind.

I hold out the life-stones between us.

"I didn't think you'd come," I say at length.

"Why here, of all places?" Her voice is cool, controlled. Her eyes flick dismissively to the stones in my hands. "What is this?"

I swallow. Tilt the stones up so they catch the light. "Your heart."

Caro's eyes widen. Something flickers in their depths. She steps closer, until she's only an arm's length away. Until she could reach out and take the stones if she wanted. But she doesn't.

Her mouth turns downward in what could be grief or suspicion. Silhouetted against the light like this, with the setting sun blazing behind her, her edges seem hazy, like she's something out of a dream. Or maybe that's me, weak with fear.

Caro asks, "What do I have to do?"

I swallow down a painful lump in my throat. "Just—eat them."

Caro regards me, her gaze as steady and unforgiving as the sun behind her. Her eyes look dark, her features exaggerated, shadows hollowing her cheeks and bruising beneath her eyes. I reach toward her with my cupped hands, until my fingers almost brush her chest.

Caro's flat green gaze flicks to the stones in my hands, then back up to my face. She delicately plucks just one of the stones from my hands. Brings it to her lips. And stops. "You took everything from me. Everything."

My hands clench. "I only did what was necessary to save you. Please, trust me."

"You liar," she hisses.

Wildfire fury bursts into her eyes. Her other hand shoots out, and she grabs my wrists together, her grip crushing in a way that has nothing to do with magic. I cry out in pain as my fingers splay out, letting the remaining stones fall to the ground with dull thuds. Unsuccessfully, I try to wrench myself out of her grip as she brandishes the stone in her hand—and forces it past my lips, pressing down on my mouth until I have to swallow.

The pain of the stone dissolving on my tongue is blinding. "Caro," I sputter, "Please." But all I can do is thrash weakly as the Sorceress drags me into the river, forcing stone after stone down my throat. My vision goes from red to white, and my tears bleed into the water.

"This was always the plan, wasn't it?" Caro snarls. "You thought to kill me for good and carry my heart with you forever. Tell me it's not true, Antonia, *take it back.*"

Her words blur together in my hearing, the meaning—but not the anger—drowned in the slapping of the waves, the roaring of my own blood in my ears. I try to scream, to fight, but a wave catches me in the face and silty river water fills my throat. My fingers rip at cloth.

I think I can see something glittering red through the smear of river water covering my mouth and nose. A ruby blade set ablaze by the dying sun just above the surface of the river. I reach for it, my vision burning black, but my fingertips brush against nothing, nowhere and everywhere at once, and—

I die.

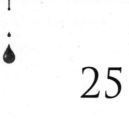

25

I break, gasping, from the water, hands outstretched to fend off the person drowning me, and the bright pale stretch of the after-noon sky nearly blinds me.

That small pain is too much, on top of the fire in my throat and the ache of oxygen-starved panic shooting knives through my body. I fling my arm up to block out the sky—and it's only when my arm actually obeys, landing over my eyes, that I realize something has changed. My limbs ache, but there's strength in them. And there's something solid beneath me—sand—though my head is still half underwater. My stomach turns. My body must have thought it was being strangled and drowned, though it wasn't.

I fling myself forward with a cry of relief and hit the sand hard before rolling onto my back.

I stay that way for a long moment, until the pain in my throat and lungs fades slightly, the sensation sliding from me like the river water from my cheeks and arms. The ravine slides into focus, the water gone to an ordinary green-gray, and there's no sign of Caro.

For a few minutes, it's all I can do to sit slowly up and breathe, try to suppress the panic, my hands fisting around the sand at my sides. Traces of the memory cling to me. I remember the heat of Caro's heart-stones. The fingers that felt like claws around my throat.

A new thought cuts through the disquiet: I tried to give Caro's heart back. The stories are true.

But what does that matter?

As the full memory slips away, the panic polluting my veins starts to get worse, not better, my breath quickening again and tears welling in my eyes. I remember the reason Elias and I came here in the first place—and what I saw just before Caro killed me, glittering above the surface of the water.

The weapon, the fang, the claw. The rubied dagger, the one weaving in and out of my mind like a thread. The one thing that could help me kill Caro, end all of this. But the tighter I try to cling to the memory, to pull meaning from it, the more I doubt myself. I reached for the dagger while I was drowning in the river, in a swath of black. Could it have just been a vision, an image my desperate mind created? Is it lost to time, or somewhere else? Or nowhere at all?

Any remaining hope in me quickly dies when I remember that Liam is at Everless. Caro too. Does she know? Could the weapon be there, despite what Liam said? Is that why she went there, to rid the world of the only thing capable of killing her? I close my eyes, lean against the flattened rock by the shore, dizzy with the questions I have no answer to . . .

And start. Because under my palms, carved into the rock, is something familiar. The crude shapes of a snake and fox. Lightly, I trace the shapes with the tip of my finger.

The world shifts again, swiftly and with a violent tug at my mind. The woods shrink back. Younger. My finger, still tracing the shapes in the rock by eroding the stone—but now, I'm making the rock melt for the first time. I turn it to dust with nothing more than a light touch.

From somewhere behind me, a voice calls, "Hello."

I snap my head around. Shaking, my knees curl into my chest. But it's only a young girl with dark straight hair and eyes as green as the grass, standing a few steps away from me.

"What are you drawing?" she asks.

Slowly, I unfold my knees. She closes the distance between us and bends over the rock. "A snake?"

"That's what they called me. In my village. That, or a witch."

The girl kneels down next to me, glancing at my dress, which is covered in dirt and marred with holes. "Is that why you ran away?"

I nod. "And I'm never going back. You can't make me."

She smiles. "My father calls me a fox, because I'm clever. One day, I'll know as many tricks as the fox. Will you make one for me?"

Warmth fills me, traveling down to my hand as I work it over the stone surface. The girl's eyes glitter as she watches me carve a fox next to the curving lines of the snake.

"My father said you can come home with us." She closes her hand around mine, and our palms spark when they meet.

"I don't have any money. . . ."

I pull my hand away, but she takes it back. "You don't need to worry about that. My father has plenty." She turns and points to a figure standing at a distance, then faces me again, pulling out a small coin purse from her pocket to reveal a shimmer of silver coins inside. The purse is stamped with a flowering tree.

I reach up and pull something from my hair. A blue satin ribbon. "I have to give you something if I'm coming to live with you."

Grinning, she takes the ribbon and helps me to my feet. "You don't have to be scared anymore. I'm special, like you. My father is too. We're not like other people."

The world shifts again in front of my eyes. Back in the Valley of Blythe, every inch of me Jules Ember.

I let out a strangled, wordless cry of frustration, not caring how it echoes up the ravine walls—because I don't want to be pulled into my past any longer, the fractured, broken mirror of it, swimming with shards of me that don't align. When I have no more strength left for weeping, I stumble wearily to my feet and look around, trying to decide what to do next.

Though my mind is reeling, it occurs to me that Elias should be here by now. He should have met me by the riverbank. Elias can help. Elias can make sense of this.

Then—panic. I look to where he said he'd descend. Nothing there but the river, sparkling innocuously in the afternoon sun, nothing there to indicate that these waters had once wrapped around me and poured down my throat, filled my lungs with death.

I plunge in the direction that Elias said held a way down— where he said he'd keep a lookout.

Each step is an effort, my heavy feet sinking into the sand. But still it doesn't take me long to reach a bend in the river, accompanied by a set of narrow stairs carved into the ravine, twisting with tree roots. Where Elias should be. There's no one here. Not a single footstep in the sand.

But I can hear something up above, past the rim of the little canyon. A jumble of voices, men and women shouting and the urgent whinny of horses. They're too far away for me to make out individual words, but I think I hear Elias's voice among them—calm, haughty.

At first, relief—then, shouts in the name of the Queen. A chill rips through me, and I freeze.

As I stand there, rooted to the ground with fear, I realize that the commotion seems to be moving away, in the direction of the tiny farm village we skirted on the way here. A different fear grips me suddenly—what if Elias is captured, what if he's punished, dragged away, because of me? The thought is enough to send me scrambling for the stairs, climbing until I can peer cautiously over the top.

And my heart contracts with panic. Halfway across a field, I see a knot of Shorehaven soldiers circling Elias with swords out. In the center of them, Elias stands with his hands up, head tilted toward a towering figure. The Huntsman.

The Huntsman's knife is pressed to his throat.

I move without thinking, pulling myself over the edge and running, running toward them, the earth rolling under my feet. When I'm close enough that they turn to look at me, I throw my hands out. I call on all my powers of time, make the world leap to my command, no matter what the consequences.

And it does. Time coalesces around me, around *them*. The soldiers slow, gloved fingers reaching to their swords, expressions of wonder and fear splattered across their faces. I freeze them all where they stand, all except for Elias, who sprints toward me—

But something's wrong, because when I meet the Huntsman's eyes through the holes in his mask, I falter—and he stirs, like the flash of a fish under the river's surface, once, twice, then breaks free of my hold on time. He gives a silent order to his soldiers—his hand flashing a signal I don't understand—and his words seem to pierce through the seal I've created. The soldiers fall sideways, out of the path of my time. My hold on them dissolves into nothing.

I'm already moving to gather another attack, but then the Huntsman sprints toward me, seeming almost to fly over the earth. Terror, the likes of which I've not felt since Caro killed Roan, stabs through me.

Almost absurdly, my first thought is to be thankful that Liam isn't here. That I did the right thing, sending him back to Everless. He's safe, as long as he's not found out. I must make sure he remains safe. If I'm captured, if Caro suspects that I love him—

I silently resolve not to be taken alive.

"Jules!" comes Elias's voice. The urgency in it tears my eyes away from the Huntsman to meet his. I realize two things at once—he's drawn his dagger, and his face is full of sorrow. I remember our promise: that he would kill me before he let Caro capture me. I see that he remembers it too.

I stop breathing as he raises his arm and lets the blade fly.

Straight and true. It arcs through the air and I see, rather than feel, the metal bury itself in my chest.

The pain hits everywhere at once. I stumble back. A few feet shy of me, the Huntsman stops abruptly. Faintly, I register that his horse's hooves send a spray of dirt toward me. My vision peels away into black, black, black. Warmth leaves me, along with pain, even when I crash down to one knee.

I think of Liam, walking through Everless's gates. Safe, safe without me.

And something takes over. The time I'd been spinning around my hands to trap the soldiers crawls up my arms through my veins, fills my chest and my head. Time, pure and dizzying, pulls itself over me, a shiver that races up and down my spine. I hear my own heart beating, the buzz of blood in my veins.

The pain hits again, a tidal wave of it, and the world blurs back into color around me.

I stand up.

Though I don't control it, I feel the time unspooling from me, like a snake shedding a layer of skin. The pain in my chest is suddenly lessened, then gone. Blood retreats into my wound. The tears in my eyes, which I hadn't even noticed had spilled down my cheeks, dry up, clearing my vision in time for me to see a streak of silver in the air, shooting back toward Elias.

Time itself shudders. I'm on my feet unharmed, the Huntsman

is racing for me, and the knife is in Elias's hand. He looks at it, dazed, the expression on his face like someone trying to remember.

"He's armed!" one of the soldiers cries.

I'm too stunned, too slow, to stop what happens next, even as I realize how it will unfold. The soldiers step forward as one. Swords flash. And Elias falls, his own dagger thumping uselessly into the clover.

No.

Time explodes outward from me again. I scarcely have control of it anymore, unhurt and alive with fear and rage. Even as it races outward I'm running too, past the frozen form of the Huntsman, past the soldiers in their poses of violence, to where Elias kneels in the dirt, clutching a deep gash in his side.

If I can hold them a little longer, I can save him.

I fall to my knees in front of him and touch his shoulder to bring him out of the freeze. He comes awake, blinking, his face twisting immediately with pain. A wash of gratitude that he kept his promise goes through me, followed closely by a deep, stabbing regret. Another person dead because of me—though it's clear from the confusion with which he regards me that he doesn't remember throwing his dagger.

"I'm going to turn back time to heal you," I say, putting a hand on his ribs, over the wound. Elias winces and nods, and I close my eyes and call on time for a third time, hoping to speed it up around Elias's wound and heal it before he bleeds too much. But my thoughts are too scattered, my heart beating too fast. Images of Amma's body flash in front of my eyes. My bitter inner voice screams at me that I'm a failure, a poor excuse for the Alchemist—that I've done everything wrong since the day I left Papa for Everless. Tears stream down my face. I bite my lip and try to concentrate on Elias's wound, but my hands are shaking with grief and rage and doubt. I'm burned up inside, hollow and useless.

"Jules. Just Jules." Elias's voice is rough with pain, but a trace of his old humor is still there beneath it, somehow.

I look up at him, tears in my eyes. I can feel that his wound is healing, but not quickly enough. Not enough. Blood is trickling down his side and soaking into the soil, staining the crushed wheat red beneath him.

"Only a scratch. I'll be fine," he says, his hand closing weakly over my wrist. I follow his gaze; above us, the soldiers and the Huntsman are paused in midair, descending on us with the speed of gathering storm clouds. "Truly. You need to get away."

"I can't leave you here!" I cry, not caring how desperate it sounds.

"You can and you will." He takes my hand from his side. "I doubt Caro will kill me. At least not right away."

"Small comfort," I growl at him. I feel sweat pop up on my brow as I bend all my concentration toward healing his wound.

But it's not enough. *I'm* not enough.

"Go, Jules. Finish what we started." He smiles a thin half smile.

Leaving him is the last thing I want to do, but I can feel my hold on time thinning. Soon the soldiers and the Huntsman will wake. And things will only be worse for Elias—for both of us—if I'm here with him.

Wherever I go next, I need to go alone.

Elias nods, the humor slipping from his face. "Now go, Jules." His words the last bit of light in the gathering dark.

26

Flight. I'd forgotten how it felt.

The Huntsman's horse gallops underneath me. The pounding of her hooves, the pain in my legs as I struggle to stay seated help me forget what I've just done—we ride for hours before I recall the sight of Elias's wound. I allow myself to cry, blame it on the whipping wind and not myself for leaving Liam's best friend in the arms of the enemy.

Or at least in the arms of the soldiers—because the Huntsman follows on my heels. The only thing that saves me is that I've stolen his horse, which is clearly superior to the other solders' steeds, though I am a poor rider. For hours, he drives me along the small road that runs through the forest, falling back then plunging forward, always keeping pace but never catching up.

The forest rapidly dwindles around us now—and the sound

of the Huntsman behind me fades with it. I slow to a halt, wary of the sound of the wind in the dark, carrying the scent of cook fires in the distance. Though the Huntsman has fallen behind, I've left a trail of hoofprints behind me, serpentining through the woods . . .

I need a place to hide.

The moonlight through the trees illuminates familiar land; I am back in Gerling territory, not far from Laista, and with every stride, coming closer to Everless. In the distance, I see shelter: a small walled area on top of a hill, like a tiny fortress, with green and gold banners billowing at its wrought-iron gate. A shiver runs down my spine at the sight of the Gerling colors.

I've never been here, but I know what it is immediately—the Gerlings' graveyard, walled and only five miles from Everless itself, wreathed now in a chilly fog. The recognition is born not of Alchemist memories, but of the tales Papa used to tell me when I was small, and the whisperings of the other servants at Everless.

It's said that if consumed, any time still remaining in the blood of the dead can kill you . . . and yet, there are always those desperate enough in this country to try and dig up the dead and see. It doesn't matter in places like Crofton—none of the dead have any time to steal—but the graves of nobles are always far from civilization, distant and high and heavily walled. Inaccessible as mountain peaks.

I dismount, legs aching from gripping the horse, and tie its reins to a tree, far enough back from the graveyard that no one will see.

The rest of the way toward the Gerling graveyard, I run. The fog spills over the wall, curling like a finger to beckon me inside.

On either side of the entrance are two nooks, where Everless guards normally flank the gates. They should be there now, ensuring that the Gerlings remain undisturbed by the likes of the living, but I reason that they've most likely been commissioned to scour Sempera for me. I send a word of thanks to the Sorceress for that—if Caro hadn't been hunting me down, I might not be able to enter unbothered. I climb the gate and drop into the graveyard.

Inside, the high walls block out much of the sky, and the morning quiet turns strange and unnatural. Grand tombstones of marble or polished granite stick out of the fog, dark sharp-edged shapes looming from nowhere. Another chill sweeps over my skin as I stand among them. The normal sounds of spring—birdsong, the whisper of wind—are absent; if it weren't for the slow drifting of the fog around me, I would wonder whether time had stopped. For the dead, I suppose it has.

I feel nothing but a creeping sense of unease, like I'm being watched.

A spot of color catches my eye, bright crimson against all

the green and gray. I move closer to it. One tombstone—a taller-than-me obelisk of pure white marble—stands over fresh-turned earth, and about it are strewn flowers of red and white and green, delicate strings of pearls and semiprecious stones, little Sorceress sculptures of copper and gold, and several brass cups of half-drunk wine. The scent of cut flowers and perfume floats above the scent of rain and earth as I draw closer to read the words carved on the tombstone.

My eyes find the word *Roan Gerling* in the mist. It draws me inexorably. So suited to the boy I knew, who was always ready with a smile, a laugh.

My grief for Roan occupies a strange unexamined corner of my chest, a small room I've scarcely entered since I ran from Everless what seems like a lifetime ago—though it's been only two weeks. And yet, when I allow myself to stand still and look, really look at Roan's grave and remember that he is dead, he's gone, the grief slams into me like it's happening all over again. His last confused, whispered plea, cut off by Caro's knife. The dimming of his eyes as he fell, and how heavy and complete and eternal the silence seemed afterward. Dead. Gone. Because of Caro.

Without meaning to, I sink to my knees, all my strength going out of me. I suddenly feel the presence of the dead—feel like they're surrounding me, a crowd of invisible eyes, a silent wind of not-breath. The weight of expectation and a reminder of my failure. That I, who have come back again and again when they have not, can somehow save them, redeem them. Papa, Roan, Amma. And those I didn't know well—Rinn, the woman who taught me my mother's name, caught in her endless time loop in Briarsmoor; Althea the hedge witch, and even Joeb, her son.

Elias, who may already be dead.

Who knows how many more, stretching back through the Alchemist's history.

And yet she hasn't broken me. For centuries I've fought blindly on, neither winning nor letting her break me entirely, and for centuries Semperans have been dying for it.

The memory of my death washes over me again, and I feel a sudden rush of foolishness—of shame.

Liar. You've taken everything from me.

"You've taken everything from me, too." I say the words out loud, though they sit oddly in my mouth. I sit with them, turning them over in my mind. Now that I'm still, the odd moment I slipped into at the side of the river, the one rooted in the drawing of the snake and the fox, resurfaces in my mind. Because the little girl was Caro, of course. And the man in the distance, her father—

Who invited me to live with them.

My stomach drops, and I stand up.

Superstition would not have me stand so close to the graves, would say that Roan's poisoned, dead time can rise out of the ground like a living thing to curdle my blood. But I don't—I can't—move away. Because as the fog burns off in the morning sun, a line of tombstones comes into view behind Roan's. Rows and rows of them. Curious, I follow the rows down until I come across a familiar name:

Lord Ulrich Ever

His gravestone is plain, nearly bare except for a familiar flowering tree, the same shape stamped on the bag of coins that Caro showed me when she found me.

The world blurs. Through the green and gray, I see another face. Papa's. I hear Caro's voice. *My father.*

Lord Ever.

Caro's father.

How could Liam—how could *I*—not have guessed? Yet I feel the truth of it, down to my bones.

A whisper of motion or sound, so subtle I'm not sure if I've imagined it, is what stirs me from my thoughts.

At first, I think I've fallen into another memory, but the sky remains an identical gray wash. I look one way, another, seeking out a sign of another living thing in the graveyard. There is none, but my senses prickle, aware of the dozens of massive tombstones, the remaining fog that could easily hide an intruder. Perhaps it's just another heartbroken friend or lover, who fled at the sight of me.

Then something touches my back, something cold and small and sharp that makes me go rigid.

"*Turn around,*" comes the low whisper, and I do.

To see the Huntsman standing before me.

A scream wells up in my lungs, but I'm determined not to let it out. He stands there, masked and hooded, an arm's length from me—and the tip of his knife a centimeter away from my chest. He's deathly still; I don't even see the movement of breath. As if he's a ghost, a weapon of the dead come to bring the Alchemist to justice.

The Huntsman lunges, flesh and muscle and bone, and it's all too real. I barely dodge in time. I feel the weight and heat of a person under the black silk, hear the knife sing against air, then the soft, sickening thud as it pierces the earth. He lunges for me again.

I stumble back, still stiff and slow from curling on the cold earth. My back catches a tombstone, and I half fall behind it, ducking down so that the Huntsman's next slash with the knife narrowly misses my face. I find my feet and walk backward, not wanting to turn away from him, raising my hands as I go. The Huntsman's shadowed face sucks my eyes in. I can't look away. With a shiver, I remember the figure who tried to drown me. Somehow that span of darkness where eyes should be is more frightening than any face.

He comes at me again with the knife, and this time I knock

the blade from his gloved hand. The Huntsman doesn't miss a beat; he lunges at me with nothing but his leather-clad hands, going for my throat.

We crash to the ground together, him on top of me. Through the black silk of the Huntsman's cloak, I can feel the hardness of armor, leather or metal wrapped around his torso and arms—worsening the pain coming with each blow as we grapple, the Huntsman's metal-tipped boots finding my shins, elbows landing in my ribs, gloved hands reaching for my throat, stronger than my own hands wrapped around their wrists. Ragged breathing escapes from beneath the mask, and I can scarcely hear it, layered as it is beneath my own gasps and the pounding of my heart in my ears.

The Huntsman goes still over me, his hands pushing back at my own in their mission toward my windpipe, small, gloved, ferociously strong. His chest heaves against mine, and for the first time my head clears enough to recognize that his body is smaller and lighter than I had thought.

The Huntsman scrambles off me then, pouncing on the knife where it fell in the grass a few feet away, and straightens up to face me—and then, without letting go of the weapon, lifts one hand to nudge back the hood.

My breath catches in my chest. I recognize that short, curly hair—she undoes the mask, lets the silk fall to the ground.

Ina.

27

I sit up without meaning to, and the knife whips back around to point in my direction. Ina Gold, my sister, the queen of Sempera, stands before me, her face simultaneously calm and lit up with fury. She's breathing hard through parted lips, and color is high in her cheeks. But her hand as she levels the blade at me is absolutely steady.

"Ina." My breath comes out hoarse. Relief and joy and fear twist into a knot in my chest. "Ina, how . . . ?"

"Don't speak," she hisses, a furious whisper. "How dare you? How dare you come here where Roan is buried?"

I close my mouth and open it again, trying to breathe, trying to think. Ina. My friend, my sister. Where can I begin, when she's looking at me with such hatred in her eyes? Regrets roll through me: I thought lying to her would protect her. I did it out of love—but I never should have let her think I was the murderer. Because now the air between us feels thick and impenetrable, the anger and hate in her eyes more painful than all the blows we just exchanged.

"I didn't kill him" is what finally comes out in the end. Out loud, the words sound pathetic, even though I know the truth of them.

Ina's hand twitches, but her gaze stays steady and burning on me. "Of course not," she says, her voice dripping acid. "I suppose he and my mother just decided to murder themselves."

"Ina, you could have killed me. Just now, and back at the river," I croak. My body aches all over, but I push myself off the grass to my feet—slowly, slowly, without taking my eyes off hers. "But you didn't."

"No. You'll have a trial." Ina's eyes travel briefly past me, yards away to Roan's gravestone, and back to me. Again, for a moment, I think I feel the presence of the dead around me, Roan's eyes and Lord Ever's and all the others, the dead here and not here, in this lifetime and the last and the last, stretching five hundred years. Ina only wants the same thing as I do. The truth.

"Roan was my friend," I tell Ina, emotion clotting my voice, but I force myself to swallow it down and be strong for her. She's lost everything too, and I owe it to her not to fall apart. Like Liam first did for me when he told me of the Alchemist, I give her the truth a little at a time. "He was killed to get to me. Because someone thought it would hurt me."

"Who?" she demands scornfully, though tears tremble in her eyes, threatening to spill over. She takes a step toward me; I force myself not to step back, even as the knife comes closer. "I've spoken to the other servants. They told me how you hated the Gerlings. And how so many thought that you loved Roan since you were a child."

I force my voice to remain steady. "It's true. I didn't hate Roan. I never have. The one who killed him . . ." How can I tell her this? How could she believe me? But Ina's eyes stay on me, steady and seeking, so I hold her gaze and say:

"Caro killed him, Ina. She killed him, and she killed your mother too."

The color flees from Ina's cheeks, though she doesn't lower the blade. I watch her face closely, afraid to hope, as she processes my words. Thought is passing over her face like clouds scudding through the sky.

"Why?" Ina whispers at last. Her voice is quiet, but it cuts easily through the heavy, tense silence between us, surrounding us in the graveyard. "Why would she do such a thing?"

I grab on to the fact that she hasn't told me I'm mad, seizing that shred of hope and holding it with all my might. Possible things to say rattle around my skull, each sounding more absurd than the next. But now that I've given Ina the beginning of the truth, I can't stop. It would be wrong to deny her more. I take a deep breath and turn my palms out toward my sister.

"She wanted to hurt me," I say slowly. "It's difficult to explain why, but Caro and I have known each other for a long time. Since before you came to Everless. I can't say I understand it, but I've been trying to." I take a deep breath. "But think back. Can you tell me the first day you met Caro?"

Ina's eyes narrow. She doesn't understand. But as the silence stretches, her face starts to furrow, her eyes widen. I can guess what she's doing, searching through her memories for the first day the pretty, soft-spoken, green-eyed maidservant stepped into her life. And she can't find an answer, because . . .

"She was always there," I say, tentative, letting the end of my sentence drift upward like a question. "She was always there, wasn't she?"

Ina doesn't reply, but I can see my words hit her, see the truth in them in how they make her flinch slightly.

I press on. "Because she's always *been* there. She's been by your mother's side before either of us were born. Never changing. Keeping track of everything. Watching. Waiting."

Ina's silent for a moment more, her hands tightening around the burnished handle of her knife, and I can't imagine what it must have been like for her, growing up alone in a palace, both her mother and her friend disappearing at strange intervals. I remember the manner that the dead queen and Caro had together, the strange, quiet interdependence, orbiting each other while scarcely ever exchanging a word. I imagine Ina got used to the dynamic after seeing it every day, but I can see her questions form now as she turns over my words.

Then, though, she seems to put them aside. She lifts her chin at me. "Waiting for what?"

"Me," I say. It's true, in a way. "Caro and I . . . we're enemies. I didn't recognize her when she first came to Everless, or she me, but eventually she realized who I was." I take a deep breath that hurts my chest, trying to hold back the tears gathering behind my eyes. "She killed Roan to hurt me, because she thought I loved him. And your mother, the late queen, knew it, so she had her killed too, making sure that I would take the blame."

A tear slips silently down Ina's cheek, and I think I see her hands flag a little. "Who are you then?" she whispers.

"Ina," I begin, trying to find a way into it, a way that won't send my sister running from me, or make her reconsider using those knives. "What would you say if I told you that the Alchemist and the Sorceress still live?"

She blinks. "My mother raised me to believe in the old tales, but . . ."

"My father did too," I say, my voice falling into a whisper

without my meaning it to. "And do you believe that the two of them walk the earth still? That they might still be among us?"

Ina shifts on her feet, uncomfortable. "What are you saying?"

"This is going to sound mad," I say. "I still feel mad, but please believe me, Ina." I swallow. "I am the Alchemist. And Caro . . . Caro is the Sorceress."

Ina stares at me blankly. What seems like a full minute passes in buzzing silence.

Finally: "What I felt in the valley? When we attacked you and your friend? That was . . . old magic?"

I nod furiously. The tears press at my eyes again. "Ina, do you know the story where the Alchemist offered the Sorceress her heart back and gave her twelve stones to eat?"

She nods curtly. *Yes.* Her hand lowers a little.

"The twelve stones were the Sorceress's heart, broken down into twelve parts. When I was killed, I was born again."

Ina's eyes flicker.

"I am the Alchemist," I say, with none of the ringing authority that should come with those words. I take my hand back from her and wrap my arms around my waist, like I can stop myself from falling apart. "The twelfth one, the last one. Caro wants to kill me and take back what I stole from her in my first life."

"Her heart," she answers.

"Yes. But first she has to break it. That's why . . ." But I can't go on. The tears that have been threatening finally break free and roll down my cheeks, one after another.

"That's why she killed Roan," Ina finishes for me, her voice soft and unbelieving. "Because you cared for him."

I nod. I can't do anything more, can't ask her again if she believes me and risk her saying no.

"Jules . . ." She takes a step toward me. Reaches her hands out, not touching me, but something has changed in her, between us. Her eyes are soft, still uncertain, but the hatred that burned so brightly has dissolved. Leaving her not the Huntsman, not the Queen, but just a girl, just my friend, pale and bereft.

"I'm sorry I didn't tell you," I say, voice thick with tears. "I should have, I should have tried harder, but I didn't realize, I . . ."

Confusion flickers in her eyes. "Why me? Why would you tell me?"

I almost laugh at that, because it's this part of the truth that feels the most frightening. But I steel myself and continue.

"When we met, you confided in me—you wanted to know the secrets of your birth. Do you still want to know?"

She gives a hesitant nod. "I suppose."

"Do you remember when we went to the orphanage, and the man there told me about Briarsmoor? We were born there, Ina, both of us, on the same day. To the same mother." I draw a ragged breath. "We're twins, and our parents were lost during the time disturbances we were told about."

"The Queen found me there," Ina says. Her voice is still flat, empty of feeling, but I have to count it as a victory that she hasn't run yet, or lashed out at me. She's still here, she's still listening, and that has to mean something. "I had a stone in my mouth."

"A sign of the Alchemist," I say. "And it was me, I had the stone, if there ever was one. But Papa—my uncle—*our* uncle," I realize with a jolt of grief at what Ina never had, "he took me away. He didn't realize the Queen would take you instead, he must not have."

"So Caro thought," Ina says, tripping over each word. "She thought—I—"

"Yes." I dare to take a step closer, close enough to touch Ina, and she doesn't move away. "She was going to kill you, until she found out I was the Alchemist, not you."

Ina regards me for a long moment, fear and disbelief and something else flickering beneath the transparent curtain of her face. My heart aches for how close to the surface all her feelings are. How terrible these last few weeks must have been for her, and I've been running all over Sempera chasing my memories, abandoning her to Caro. But then, swiftly as a gathering storm, her features twist into rage.

"Liar. *Liar.*" The knife is once again at my throat. "Did you think I'd believe that?"

I close my eyes. Maybe this is the end—grimly, I think that

dying by Ina's blade is far better than dying at Caro's. Perhaps the fear of dying addles my brain, because another idea occurs to me. "Ina, can I try to show you the truth? If I can do that, will you believe me?"

She blinks. "How?"

Ina wants to believe me, I'm sure of it. I close my eyes, and gently take Ina's hand in mine. *Memory is moments, and moments are time*, I think, channeling Stef's words, and imagine pulling Ina in.

Slowly—slowly—it begins to work.

Ina in hand, I wade into memories, one after another sifting in and out of focus on the surface of my mind. Caro at Everless, watching the liquid gold of my time dance across the floor; Briarsmoor, first the skeleton of it, then the high keening scream of our mother, Naomi; Roan on his knees, Caro's blade pressed to his throat—

I yank my hand from Ina's and lurch forward, back in the graveyard. In front of me, Ina is staring at me, eyes wide and glassy.

"I'm sorry, Ina," I say, and touch her arm lightly, feeling the hardness of armor beneath the Huntsman's cloak. I know the words can't possibly convey everything I feel, my regret and sorrow over Roan and even the Queen, and how sorry I am that she was drawn into it, that she's been wounded in the fallout. "I'm so sorry for everything."

Her eyelids drift shut for a moment, her chest rising and falling fast beneath her cloak. I can see her trying to master herself, and it twists at something in me. But finally she gives in and lets the emotion spill onto her face. Legs going out from under her, she collapses into my chest, in a way that makes me certain she's been waiting a very long time to fall.

I catch her. I catch her and I don't let go.

28

We sit for hours on the Gerlings' plot. I tell Ina what's happened since the night we visited the hedge witch in Laista. She tells me that Elias will recover—and if only because of her sheer force of shining will, I believe her. By the time we've run out of things to say, the day is faded, the bright moon rising. A dry part of me marvels that twelve lifetimes and everything I've been through since escaping Everless can be detailed in so brief a time.

Ina continues, "I always thought there was something about you. Ever since I met you at Everless. Some secret, some sadness."

The reminder of our time together at Everless—so simple compared to now—makes my heart twist, and I lower my eyes. Maybe, like Ina, I carry my emotions on my face, too, only I haven't experienced any but secrets and sadness, so I wouldn't know the difference. "I didn't know then about . . . about myself.

My father had just died. I was starting to understand, but I didn't know."

"You don't have to explain yourself to me. I don't completely understand about the Alchemist and the Sorceress, but I believe you."

I almost ask her why. The most unbelievable thing of all is this little bit of trust that she's given me. But tears clog up my throat, and I don't say anything.

"At least that explains why Caro's changed since my mother died," Ina says. "All she speaks of now is revenge. She wants me to raise an army, Jules, take soldiers from every town and village in Sempera. She's talked about invading other nations, spreading blood-iron to their shores. She bled time from innocents. She never used to be so bloodthirsty."

"She was." Suddenly I can't meet Ina's eyes, so I look down at the grass. "She just didn't show it until now. Caro said she'd kill until she found the one who would break me. Anyone who I love, or who loves me, is in danger. So many people who have tried to protect me have died for it."

Ina looks at me, then away. "Do you think all of it was a lie?"

"I don't know." My friendship with Caro only lasted a few weeks before I discovered who she truly was at Everless, but Ina had known her for years. I call up the face of the little girl who approached me at the river. Sweet, open. But no matter how hard I try to hold on to the picture of her, an older Caro dispels it.

Ina manages a sad smile. "When I think of what we shared, I'm sure it was real. Some of it, at least. She cared for me."

"She put you into danger, sending you out as the Huntsman."

Ina shakes her head. "I *wanted* to go out and find you. It was my idea to put on this costume." She looks away from me as she speaks. "Whatever terrible things she's done, Caro always saw a part of me that others didn't. She was the only person who didn't treat me like I was some glass doll. It's like . . . she saw the power in me." She pauses, thinking. "That's probably because she thought I was the Alchemist for so long."

"I'm sure it's not," I say quickly, meaning it with every fiber of me.

Ina sighs. "Knowing that it wasn't all a lie makes it worse. She was supposed to be my friend," she whispers, her voice soft and broken. Her cheeks shine with tears.

I stare into Ina's face for a beat too long, still overwhelmed by the knowledge that she believes me—somehow, despite everything, she believes me, like Amma did. She's looking at me with trust and expectation in her face, like I might know what to do next. A sudden, fierce longing for Liam stabs through me. Liam, who always knows what to do next.

"What are you going to do about Liam?" she asks. Can she read the thoughts on my face? "You care about him, don't you? You love—"

"Don't say that," I cut in, hurriedly, and the naked fear in my voice silences her. "Please."

But Ina's never been one to stay silent. Softly she asks, "Do you think he's the one whose death will break your heart?"

I swallow. "I don't know." Though everything in my gut screams that my words are false.

"But what now, Jules? How can I help you?"

"I need to find the weapon that will kill her," I say quietly.

Ina's jaw clenches. "You have to go back to Everless."

I squeeze her hand, wanting nothing more than to ground myself there, next to my sister. It's not that I don't want to go—I want to more than anything—but I also want to stay with Ina for a little longer, not knowing what wrath Caro may bring down on me, when I face her. "You only want me to see Liam," I grumble, to hide what I'm really thinking. Caro knows me. She must know that sooner or later I'll return to the place this all started.

Ina laughs, lets her head rest on my shoulder.

A thread of smoke catches my eye, rising in the air in front of Roan's headstone. Intrigued, I walk forward to see that Stef's gifted stone is sitting in a pool of spilled wine. Dissolving.

Ina follows. "Is that blood-iron gone off?"

"No. It was a gift, passed down from the Alchemist long ago. A token to show you the true face of evil." The smoke hangs in the air above it, unmoving. Seized by an idea, I gather a few more cups of wine from around Roan's grave, pour them into a single cup, then drop what's left of the black stone inside. Just as I would do if I were putting a day-iron into Lady Sida's afternoon tea.

Immediately, the wine begins to sizzle and spark. The smoke becomes thicker, twisting. To my utter shock, the smoke seems to take shape in the air in front of us, crawling slowly into the visage of a man's face. His lips are thin. There are deep, dark sockets where his eyes should be. Ina and I inhale at the same time.

"Is that— Who is that?" Ina asks, breathless. "I've never seen anything like that."

"The face of true evil," I reply, recoiling as the face seems to open its mouth to laugh—then fades all at once, winking out of existence as if it were never there. I blink.

Who else could it be but Ever?

Ina squeezes my hand. It pulls me out of my thoughts. "You're right—I'll go back to Everless," I say, putting intention into the words this time. "If the weapon isn't there, then there might be some other truth there that will help me defeat her."

It makes a grim kind of sense. I need to end this where it all began—both my understanding of all this; and the story of the Alchemist and Sorceress.

"And then what, Jules?"

I look at Ina, and see my own fear and hope reflected in her eyes.

"And end this," I whisper.

Ina looks solemn. "You don't have to face her, not yet, not if you're not ready. You can come back to Shorehaven with me—"

"I'm sure." It's the only thing I am sure of, and I cling to it, even as it makes terror roll through me. The thought of what Caro might do if she discovers that Ina knows the truth rattles me to my core. "I'm ready."

"Well, I'll help you." Ina is still for another beat, then she takes her hands from me. She unclasps something at her chest and then sweeps the black cloak from her shoulders, a shadow made material. Underneath, she's wearing a simple tunic and leggings, like anything Amma or I would have worn back in Crofton. She drapes the cloak over her arm and reaches around to the nape of her neck, to untie the piece of dark silk that had covered her nose and mouth—and holds her old disguise out to me.

"So you can get into Everless," she says in response to my blank look. "They won't stop the Huntsman."

Warmth sweeps through me. No one's ever questioned me so little as Ina just now, even though returning to Everless is the most dangerous thing I've ever done. "That's brilliant, Ina. Thank you."

She bites her lip, thinking. "I'll send a message ahead to call Caro away. I'll think of something. I can't guarantee you long, but—it'll be better than nothing. It'll give you time to search, at the very least."

I look at Ina, really look at her. She's not the guileless, laughing princess who arrived at Everless scarcely a month ago. There's a gravity to her now, an iron in her square shoulders and the way she holds her chin high.

Even in this simple outfit, she looks like a queen.

I realize I don't need to fear for her—or rather, that I might fear for her, but she's not a child to be protected.

My sister holds my gaze, steady and strong. "Be safe, Jules. Sorcer—" She stops short, cutting herself off with a little laugh, then pulls me into a tight embrace. "I suppose I don't need the Sorceress anymore, Jules. I have you."

By the time I mount my horse, Ina has ridden off, the confidence she brought with her blown away with the snapping wind. Everless hovers in the distance, a black stain on the sky. This is where we first bound time to blood. Since then, some ancient, inexorable power has pulled me back to the estate—maybe has been luring me back, over and over, ever since Papa and I stepped outside its walls all those years ago. A silk thread woven through those gardens and towers and corridors, the other end sunk deep into my heart, reeling me back in now.

If there is an answer anywhere in all of Sempera, any weapon buried, any way to end Caro hidden, it feels right that it should be there.

I give the horse her reins and urge her forward, toward the Gerling estate.

29

I ride alone and steady through the dark space between Everless and me. The estate's pull grows stronger and stronger behind my breastbone with every step forward. An odd quiet has pushed every other feeling, every other weakness out of my body. As if my very bones know that I'm nearing the end of the road.

After so much skulking in the shadows, it's strange to travel openly, albeit in the uniform of the Huntsman. The costume fits perfectly: the black cloak is cool and light, and the hood covers my eyes. I travel along the road for the first time in ages as day fades into night. The people and carriages that pass give me a wide berth.

Thoughts swirl through my head, plans and contingencies about what will happen when I reach the Gerling estate. Of everything that passed between Ina and me at the graveyard, one answer sticks at the center of the maelstrom, a center that everything else swirls around.

Everless's secrets will put an end to this, forever.

The sight of the Gerling estate still takes my breath away after all this time, even what I've seen. My first home as Jules, the place where the Alchemist and Sorceress suffered and broke at that first lord's hand, according to the stories. I push the lingering childhood memory away. I have to focus on what's ahead, not what's behind.

I scarcely realize I've stopped riding, stopped dead in the middle of the road at Everless's feet. It looks so dark, so empty, only a few lights guttering in its windows. *Chaos*, Liam had said, the coffers emptied and the servants who haven't been dismissed exist in limbo as the vultures he has for relatives jockey for power. Is he inside there, somewhere? Now that only he and his father and mother are left, what is it like to walk those halls, filled with the echoes of his dead brother?

A cold breeze wraps around me, and my heart twists. Liam, inside now. I focus on a dim, flickering light in his tower of Everless and all at once, my feelings turn into something pure and clean and simple.

I love him.

My horse plunges forward.

* * *

It's as Ina said it would be. Cloaked in the Huntsman's uniform, I ride straight up to the Everless gates. Six guards in the familiar green and gold flank the entrance, three on either side. They snap to attention when the sound of my horse's hooves on the cobblestone reaches them. I feel a bit like I'm floating outside of my body, like I'm observing the scene from a distance, as often happens when I control time. I can see their fear as I come into view—a figure has just emerged from the dead of night. The fear doesn't dissolve when I get near enough for them to see the Huntsman's hood.

Thankfully, before I worry about needing to speak, they salute as one. Another of the guards signals frantically to his compatriots atop the wall. A moment later, the great gates open only for me.

And straight-backed and alone and in the shape of a warrior, I ride inside.

The castle seems to breathe before me, its dark shape like something alive as I cross the lawn, the sound of my horse's footsteps swallowed up in the silence. It's spring—there should be flowers, rioting from the window beds and in the gardens that skirt the castle. Gardeners should be moving through them even now, working their pretty magic in the night so that the Gerlings wake up to a pristine lawn, a seamless quilt of flowers and green. But instead, everything is dark and almost-silent. So quiet that

I can hear the muted sound of the lake on the other side of the castle, waves slapping dull and steady against the rocky shore where only a month ago, I mourned Papa's death.

And yet, it's not empty. As I draw nearer, the shapes of guards make themselves known all around the estate, crawling along the sides of the building and along the top of the walls, nestled in the castle's various little outcroppings and passing before windows. My heart pounds. These are more guards than I've ever seen here before, even when Ina and the Queen first arrived at the end of winter. And immediately I know that they're here for me. Waiting for the rabbit to return to the trap. Suddenly Ina's cloak feels like scant armor.

But I force myself not to show any fear as I draw up to the courtyard that separates the lawn from the castle. The guards ringing the entrance regard me with the same fear at the gate. Once this might have given me a thrill of power, but now it only fills me with dread. I slide off my borrowed horse and hand the reins to the closest guard, who's careful not to touch my hands as he takes them. When I finally pass into the castle, I breathe, and some of the tension flows out of my chest.

I'm home.

Besides the odd guard stationed at a corner or patrolling a stretch of hall, the corridors are completely empty. So much servants' work happens at night—the halls mopped and swept, the fireplaces stocked with wood, the torches kept lit. But none of it is happening now. Everless has changed, even more than when I returned after ten years away. The estate was always harsh and cruel to those at the bottom, I know that. But this is different, the halls empty and dead, the doors closed against a threat darker and more dangerous than any aristocratic cruelty. Despite the emptiness everywhere, I feel seen—watched. A shiver runs up my spine, growing and growing until it swallows up all my plans.

Run, Jules, an old voice tells me. *Run and don't look back.*

I push the voice down, but it remains to whisper at me from a dark corner of my mind.

I steady myself and walk down the main hall. The curtains drawn and dusty, the urns in the alcoves empty of flowers. It unnerves me enough that when I next come upon a guard, pacing the east wing, relief floods me. I catch his arm.

He starts and goes for his dagger but drops his hands when he sees my hood and mask. He's young, the fuzz of a mustache on his upper lift, and the sigil of Shorehaven glitters on his vest. Caro's man, not the Gerlings'.

"Where is everyone?" I ask without thinking, instinctual fear of soldiers driven down by a deeper kind of panic.

"My—my lady," the man stammers. "The curfew you asked for. No resident of Everless is to be out of bed after sunset."

I drop his arm, dread churning in my gut. How much have

the people of Everless—nobles and servants alike—suffered in my name?

I move away from him, forcing myself to keep my head high and my pace even, no matter how unnerved I am. Names, demands drum through my mind—*Tam, Bea.* I feel torn, pulled in different directions—the kitchens, the servants' dormitory, the stables. But one pull is sharper and more urgent than the rest, the certainty digging its claws into my chest. Liam.

I have to find Liam. Tell him what I know. Make sure that he's safe.

Though everything in me screams to find the weapon first, I know that if things don't go my way, this could be my last chance to see him, to tell him how I feel. To say good-bye.

When I'm sure the guard is out of sight, I break into a run. I don't stop until I'm in the wing that holds all of the Gerlings' chambers, as dark and silent as the rest of the estate.

I haven't been up here since I was a girl, and even then only once or twice—when Roan was confined to his room after some small misdemeanor and he would enlist his servant friends to bring him treats from the kitchen. The memory surfaces out of nowhere, and grief for our lost childhoods hits me like a battering ram to the ribs. I lean against the door to weather it—and then freeze, as the sound of raised voices floats from the other end of the hall.

I look over to realize that the grandest, largest door, which can only lead to Lord Nicholas's chambers, is ajar, and a faint light shines inside.

"I ask again," someone growls, voice coarse with drink, who I recognize as Lord Nicholas. "How can you hope to command any authority after these events? The Gerling name is in shambles."

"This is still my home, not Caro's or Ivan's." Liam's voice. Mingled relief and fresh fear flood in, and I drift closer to Lord Nicholas's door almost without realizing. A terrible chill goes through me as something slams in the room, like a cup on a table. Then footsteps, and before I can think or move, Liam storms out into the hall. I only have time to note that he looks haggard, bruise-like shadows darkening beneath his eyes, before he turns down the hallway, occupied by some private grief, utterly oblivious to me.

I move without meaning to, chasing Liam's shadow down the hall—and into his room. The door is wide-open to reveal a large room made smaller by the bookshelves lining every wall, their contents overflowing into stacks beneath the windows. When the door swings shut behind us, there's a moment where all I can hear is the pounding of my own heart, the roaring of blood in my ears; all I can see is Liam turning to see me, his face shadowed in the shifting light of his bedside lamp, but not shadowed enough to hide the fear that blooms in his eyes before he tamps it out.

A shudder moves visibly through him, and he backs away into the center of his candlelit room. I follow almost unconsciously.

I've never been in his room before, and with a pang, I remember how little I know of his life. A thousand greedy observations batter me at once. Everything is messier than I expected. The rug is turned up in one corner; he probably trips over it constantly, head buried in a book. There's a desk and a nightstand, both heaped with papers, and a bed. The covers on his bed are worn but not ragged, and I wonder if he's had them since he was a child. They're also bunched and twisted, which combined with the dark circles beneath his eyes makes me think he's not been sleeping.

"Liam," I whisper.

"I thought I might see you here soon," he says, his voice low and rough. "Come to kill me, my Queen? Or Caro, is it you?"

At first, I'm confused, but then I realize that Liam thinks I'm the Huntsman. He takes a step toward me, his hands open and empty at his side. He's trembling ever so slightly, but his eyes burn with anger and life.

"It's true what people are saying," he hisses. "I helped Jules Ember escape Everless. I traveled with her. I love her."

My breath stops in my lungs as Liam's words land one by one, deep in my chest. *Love.* The impact of that one syllable shakes me, loosing my limbs from their freeze. The lump is still in my throat, but I raise my hands and unclasp my mask. Then lower my hood, taking both pieces down at once, and lift my face to the candlelight.

Liam rocks back. "Jules . . ." My name escapes him in a whisper. "I thought . . ."

My words come too fast, in one rushed breath. "This was the only way I could get in, I—"

In three swift steps, he's crossed the distance between us and has folded me in his arms, pressing his face into my hair. My arms come up around his waist, and I hold him, feeling him shake. It feels like years since we parted—an entire lifetime between us, an eternity of words unspoken. My face into his chest, I breathe him in deep, then raise my head and find his lips with mine.

He gasps into my mouth, one hand flying out to grip the bedpost as the other wraps tighter around my shoulders, pulling me tight against him. I ball my fists in the back of his shirt and wrench it up, my knuckles brushing his bare back, warm, surprisingly soft. As our lips move together, he yanks at the Huntsman's cloak, breaking the clasp, sending the black silk pooling around our feet. I gasp—I can't help it—and he holds me still tighter.

Our last kiss took place in a dreamscape of panic for me and sleep for him, a sense of unreality wrapping around us both, blunting any sense of consequences.

It's nothing like that now.

Dead of night as it may be, both of us are fiercely, achingly awake. This isn't soft, isn't slow. There's something like desperation in the way Liam's lips move against mine, shaping something that could be my name, but my blood is roaring too high to hear it. I answer him, though, catching his lip with my teeth, sinking my fingers into his back in an effort to pull him even closer to me. I can feel the whole of him, the shape of his body pressed against mine. And still I want him closer, for all the times I pushed him away.

I splay my hands on his back, feel his muscles moving beneath his bare skin. He breaks away from our kiss, and a whimper of protest escapes me—but then his lips are on my cheek, my jaw. He tips my head back with his hands in my hair and kisses my neck, his lips trailing fire over my throat, and all the reasons I feared him, feared for him, all the reasons I'd held us apart crumble to dust.

In this moment, I'm not the Alchemist. I'm only Jules, alone and frightened and hoping and wanting, and Liam Gerling is reaching out to me, a hand across the dark. It's been there ever since I kissed him in Montmere—or even before that, perhaps since he found me at Shorehaven, when he rescued me from Everless. There is a part of my heart that is still human, wholly me, and somewhere along the way, that part has come to belong to him.

There's trepidation, fear even, in the ragged breaths we exchange now. There are a hundred small and human ways he could break me. As many in which I could—and probably will— break him. Maybe that's what love is, maybe there's nothing to do except open my arms to it. And so I open my arms, unafraid of the thundering of his heart.

All I know is that I've had enough of waiting.

For a while, I sleep peacefully, the best sleep I've had in what seems like years.

But it can't last.

Too soon, I wake up. For a moment, I don't remember where I am or why—I only know that I feel safe. Happy. But it's a conditional safety, a conditional happiness. An awareness that outside the boundaries of this little space, the world still waits, ready to catch me up again in its dangers.

Liam shifts beside me, and the rest comes flooding back. He's on his side, turned away from me, his shoulders washed silver in the moonlight coming through the window. The sound of his breathing is soft in the dark, the warmth of him tangible even though I'm a few inches away, and I ache with his closeness. I put a hand out, rest it between his shoulder blades. He stirs but doesn't wake.

I want to lie back down again. For once, let myself fall back into dreams. Let this moment last a little longer. But I can't forget the truth. My time until Caro returns to Everless—maybe all the time I have left, I think with a shudder, because I don't know what will happen when I face her—is winding down. And even if I did close my eyes again, I wouldn't be able to sleep, knowing that the key to breaking my heart lies so close.

Awareness presses in on me, the threat of unknown pain tightening my lungs. I can't forget what I must do—find the weapon that will kill Caro. But where do I start?

My heart slows down, each beat suddenly sounding like the ominous toll of some ancient drum.

Only it's not my heart—a sound carries up into the room: the clanging of Everless's gate followed by hurried shouts. I get up, run to Liam's small window, and look out.

My blood runs cold. Caro, returned.

30

I bite back the rising panic as I step away from Liam's window, my heart hammering. Caro is here. Caro is here and she is going to find me. Find Liam.

Think. I need to find some spot of significance, an embedded clue, as I found in the glade and the valley . . . but I have too many childhood memories of Everless—my feet would probably guide me to my favorite hiding spot from my games with Roan, or to the forge that we accidentally burned. Liam said he'd scoured Everless, too, and found nothing.

For a moment, I consider waking Liam. Even with Caro bearing down on me, he'd delight in the puzzle. I could drag him along on this journey, snatch every last bit of time with him I can before Caro arrives. But he looks so peaceful lying there, his brow smooth of the furrows and his eyes free of the shadows that have marked his face—even in sleep—for as long as I've known him. He's lost nearly everything at my hands; I don't want to take his rest from him too.

Besides: something in me is whispering that I have to do this alone.

So I slip out from under the covers. A chill wraps around me immediately, colder than it seems any spring night has a right to be. As if to urge me back into oblivion for another few hours. But this sense of opposition—like Everless itself is aware of me, and is trying to hinder me—just makes me more determined to search out the truth.

Stepping away from the bed, I hesitate. If Liam wakes up and finds me gone, I don't doubt that he'll come after me. He can't be roaming the castle when Caro gets here. For all his bravery, he would be no match for her.

Before I can think better of it, I stretch my hands out toward Liam, letting the memories of a few hours ago sweep over me. I close my eyes and will time to descend on him softly, like a blanket, settling on his skin and stopping him where he is, midbreath. The gentle rise and fall of his back stills, and I shiver. But at least while he's frozen, he'll be safe. It's the only protection I can provide until I kill Caro—or am killed myself.

I find my shift, my dress, my boots. I pick up the Huntsman's mask and cloak and put them on again, closing the clasp as best I can and hoping no one will look too closely at how the cape hangs crooked. I glance back at Liam once more—longing firing every inch of my skin from the inside—but make myself turn away.

If I survive the coming encounter with Caro, the next time I sleep next to Liam will be all the sweeter for being safe. I tell myself this as I slip out into the hallway, taking the sole lantern from his room. If Caro does come looking for him, she'll see the darkness and think the room empty.

I have to tell myself something, or else I'll never walk away.

From the east-facing windows in the hallway, I can see it's closer to dawn than I thought, the soot-colored sky lightening to the color of pale ash on the horizon. These windows look out over Laista and then a stretch of farmland, ringed by woods. I scan the horizon, as if I would be able to see Caro coming, larger than life. But the only movement is a few flickering lights in the windows of Laista's early risers, and far in the distance, a quick flutter in the sky, a flock of birds against the coming dawn.

I turn away and start walking. As when I came in, the halls of Everless are empty of the servants who normally ought to be filling it at this hour. But I don't see guards either; maybe there's enough residual respect left for the Gerlings, in their grief, for Caro's men to steer clear of this residential wing. Maybe.

I wander down two flights of stairs and find myself in the eastern wing of the main floor. I have a vague sense that I'm near the library, but the castle seems changed, making me unsure. The quiet is eerie. It seems as though there should be night sounds—the distant commotion of someone about their chores or pacing their room, the crackling of fireplaces and the creak of the walls as they settle. But there's nothing, as though something has descended upon the estate and smothered all its little noises.

Or maybe it's me. My senses seem to have been jumbled and rearranged, the extremes I've veered between in the last few hours—bliss with Liam, dread of Caro—pulling at me, opening cracks in my perception. My vision seems sharper, and every flicker of motion—a waving curtain, a guttering lamp—makes me whip around. But my hearing is muffled, and I can't feel the floor beneath my feet or the cold air around me. As if my capacity for touch is still being taken up by the memory of Liam's hands on me and mine on him, that wild warmth.

When I think to take stock of my surroundings, I realize I'm near the vault. The carved door to the Gerlings' treasure stands at the other end of the hall, two guards on either side watching my approach with wide eyes. I remember with a sweep of gratitude that according to Liam, the vault is empty, the coffers drained, and hope they won't think much of my being here. One nods to the other, a stiff, quick motion, and they turn smartly on their heels and walk off in the opposite direction.

And I am alone.

Hardly knowing what I'm doing, I drift up to the door of the vault and put my hands on the wood. It's too dim to really see the carvings, but it doesn't matter—I can feel their intricacy beneath my fingers, supplementing the images burned into my memory. The tumbling jewels, the dancing carved women with their flowing silks.

Papa's face flashes through my mind. I never saw his body after he died, never saw the mava stains on his hands, the marks of his trying to enter this vault. His life given to retrieve one little book—or maybe, I think with a thrill, whatever's hiding down there. And here it is, practically standing open.

The conviction fills me: this is where it all began.

Both my journey toward discovering that I was the Alchemist, and the story of the Alchemist—my story. Something draws me on past this carved, shining door, some almost animal instinct, issuing from somewhere deeper than my bones. I close my eyes and reach into my mind, knowing the feeling by now, that means I've been here before I was Jules. Long before.

What's hiding there?

I see chains, I see the bars of some ancient cell. A man's cruel face, heavy and lined, peering in at us through the gaps. But I can't tell what's just the story I've heard so many times, and what's real.

And then, as I think, terror slams into me, surging suddenly from somewhere deep in my gut. Running just as deep as the urge to enter the vault—deeper. The images fly from my mind in a wash of darkness, the memory of a long-ago scream echoing in my ears. Like whatever lies behind this door in my memory is too terrible even to carry with me, like my mind is trying to protect me, hiding part of the memory away behind a thick curtain.

I snatch my hands from the door, my heart pounding in my ears, but the terror doesn't fade. The castle seems to shift and rearrange itself around me, the faint light of dawn retreating, the walls looming closer, the world contracting around my body like I'm trapped in the belly of some great breathing beast. I hear low, feminine laughter as if through a long tunnel; I hear the thunder of horses' hooves. As if Caro and all her soldiers are already here, barreling down the very hallways of Everless toward me.

And still the door waits in front of me, its presence like something alive.

The channel down the middle of the door is swimming with red—maybe just a trick of the light, but it's as if someone has recently put their hands to the spike, letting their blood, their time run down the door. Paying to enter, with—with—

A river of red.

My hands move of my own accord, rising toward the door. I press my palm against the spike, barely registering the pain as blood wells and trickles down the heel of my hand. The world shudders around me as my blood fills up the thin channel, shining like liquid rubies as it races down toward the earth.

Something deep inside the door clicks, the small sound ringing out, impossibly loud in my ears. And when I take my hand from the spike and push against the door, it opens with only the slightest bit of strength. Still moving as though in a trance, or a dream, I step forward into darkness.

I climb the stairs feeling like a sleepwalker in my own dreams, like my feet are trapped on a predetermined course and I'm only observing. And isn't that true—isn't that how it's always been, ever since I came back to Everless, spilling over with desperation and bad dreams? Hasn't my every move been imagined and anticipated by Caro long before I was born, even before she knew who I was? I've never outrun or outwitted her, never had any hope except that when she tries to break me, I will prove stronger. And now I have the sense that for all the stories and books Papa and Liam have armed me with, I am nearing a great and terrible end.

The end of the world plays out in flashes in my mind as I reach the top of the spiral staircase. If I'm not strong enough, if I lose, Sempera will not only remain locked on its course, the course will turn darker under Caro's reign. Bound by blood-iron, time tied to blood until the fragile balance of peace breaks, and we savage each other like wolves under her watch.

Inside the vault, it's dim except for the glow of the lamp—but I can discern enough to see that just as Liam said, the vault is emptied, the shells of chests scattered across the floor. Moved by instinct alone, I trail the lamplight along the walls, searching for any clue that will lead me to a secret dungeon, or door.

Something catches my attention. It's almost nothing—a tiny

imperfection in the stone, but I stop and peer closer. And I realize—it's not an imperfection at all, but a symbol, carved into the wall. A flowering tree, barely discernible by the torchlight. It takes me a moment to remember where I've seen it before, but then—it flashes through my memory, from the memory of the child Caro at the river, and from Lord Ever's grave.

Fear presses in sharp on my throat and lungs, but not enough to stop me. I push down on the symbol, moving more on instinct than anything else, and a small hatch in the ceiling slides open with a deep shudder and groan. Dust rains down on my hood, stinging my face, making tears leap to my eyes. But I wipe the water and dust away and look up into a tiny, vertical tunnel, scarcely wider than the breadth of my shoulders. A hollowness in Everless's tower, a hidden cell in the sky.

My dread is stronger than ever as I stare into the darkness. Not a dungeon, then, but a cell nonetheless.

A sort of ladder is carved into the stone itself, a simple series of hand- and footholds sunk into the wall. The air that hits me is cold though it shouldn't be, and sound seems to fall around me too, a deep and undefinable noise, like howling wind and rushing water and a sighing voice all put together. Low and distant, but there.

I want to turn and run, but where would I go? Hide in the kitchen like the girl I used to be?

No. There's nothing else for me, here at Everless or anywhere in the world that Elias described. There never has been, I realize with a sense of almost-unbearable heaviness.

There's a sense of inevitability as I reach for the tunnel. Hook Liam's lantern over my elbow. Stretch up until my fingers find the first hold. No matter the twists and turns my life has taken, might have taken, I was always going to end up back in Everless.

Like the groove in the wall that opened this passage, each step of the carved ladder is gritty with dust. They're smooth at first as I start to climb, but get rougher as I go—as though people have discovered this place over the millennia and have started to climb up, but at one point or another their hearts failed them and they retreated, pushed away by the black dread that seems to emanate from above like something alive.

The stone is cold beneath my hands and shoulders, when they brush the wall. Colder than it should be. And it seems as though the tunnel is narrowing, though that might just be my imagination, claustrophobia closing in on me as the light from below fades and vanishes, leaving only the precarious flickering of the lantern.

Up and up the ladder goes, until I've climbed as high as I can go. The air takes on the damp, earthy quality that I recognize from the root cellars beneath the kitchen—which should not be the case, being so close to the sun. Then, as my limbs start to ache and my fingers cramp into claws, it changes again, growing colder, the scent of the earth shifting into something strange, sourly metallic like old blood. I'm breathing hard, my panting magnified by the narrowness of the tunnel, compounding my fear, making me feel like I'm announcing myself to whatever lies above.

No one has climbed this ladder in decades, maybe centuries; the dust and settled earth that tumble down with each brush of my boots tells me that. Nor am I climbing toward nothing. All my instincts tell me that, prickling my skin, urging me to flee, whispering that I've gotten everything wrong.

But I don't run. I keep climbing until I feel a space open above me. Until my fingers hit a stone floor.

I haul myself up.

I stand in a medium-sized chamber, the light of my lantern reaching just far enough to illuminate the round shape of its curved walls. The walls and ceiling are stone. The floor is tile, but buried so deep beneath a blanket of dust and earth that my cautious steps away from the ladder leave footprints in it like snow. It smells like earth and ashes and—

It's not empty. A long, wooden table along one wall, warped with age, bears an assortment of even more ancient-looking instruments, the shine of metal and glass dulled beneath dust. But I see the sharp edges of knives, the glitter of strange powders in my sputtering light. Tools of time-binding, I recognize that much, but strange and primeval. Behind that, in cubbyholes bored straight into the earth, dozens of bottles rest—green and brown and blue, some with wine or potion or I don't know what still dark inside.

Last, two narrow beds, each made as if the owners had just stepped out.

I turn around to look at the rest of the room, and see two things at once.

The sweep of wall behind me is carved with a glittering mural of some sort. A snake and a fox face each other, crouched and coiled to fight, their warlike shapes captured in long lines and rough gouges in the stone, marks that have then been filled in with a red, gold, and silver spray, which makes them glitter and shift in the lamplight. But the snake and fox—Caro and I—are far smaller than the other creature that looms above them.

I can't suppress a shiver as deep as my bones. A hound, fur bristled and mouth snarling open, descends on the fox and snake from above—though they don't seem to notice the animal, the way his lips are twisted in hunger.

My mouth dry, I lift the lantern to look closer at the beds in spite of the fact that on the surface, they seem the least interesting. I run my hands along the thick quilts. Guided by nothing but a swimming, longing feeling, my fingers move under the pillow and knock against a hard, cold object.

Heart racing, I pull out a rubied dagger with the snake-wound handle.

I inhale sharply, dropping it onto the bed like it's an actual snake. Blink, because for a moment, I'm sure this is a dream. But the dagger remains there. Waiting for me.

Footsteps sound from below.

I reach down and take the dagger into my hand.

31

Fear spills through me, and I freeze, listening. I grip the twisted handle, trying to push away the nagging feeling that I've done this before.

There's a faint clattering from below that can only be someone climbing up the ladder. The tunnel takes the sound of soft footsteps and amplifies it, so that what drifts up is an unearthly, hollow, echoing thud. Getting louder and louder. And there's nothing I can do, nowhere to go. No escape from this round room but a great fall.

I look at the weapon in my hand, squeezing it as if I could drain courage from it.

My breath comes fast and ragged as the noise from the tunnel grows louder and louder.

But there's no time to wonder, no time to regret. Because

someone is emerging from the vault shaft. In the dim lamplight, I see a sweep of shimmering black skirt, delicate slippered feet flashing beneath them. Even before her face shows I know her, her shape and her movements intimately familiar. *Caro.*

Panic chokes me. In the darkness, she seems to be made of shadows, her black hair loose around her shoulders and blending into her black gown. She turns and sees me and a grin splits her face, her teeth white in the dark. She reaches to her waist and withdraws from somewhere two daggers as long as her forearms. She holds them easily at her sides, turning them slowly so they catch the flickering lantern light. Then she raises one hand, the knife still in it, and something above us moves. A stone disc slides over the entrance to the vault shaft over our heads, shutting out what little light filtered down from below, sealing us inside. A bedroom, becoming a cell, becoming a tomb.

A terrible dread seeps through me as we face each other. Her smile has faded, but her posture is tightly wound, ready to fight. It doesn't make me feel any braver that her usual cold confidence has been replaced by blazing hunger in her eyes.

For the first time since she killed Roan, I feel a twinge of sorrow for Caro, twisted and deep and undeniable—because she, too, has wandered Sempera searching for a way to destroy me. Unlike me, she has been trying for centuries.

I push the pity away. The time has come for our story to end.

I can see the thoughts pass behind her eyes as she registers the room around us. The table with its cruel instruments, the mural, the simple beds. By the stunned look on her face, I know that she has not been here since the break between us.

Her eyes fall to the dagger in my hand, then fly back to me. Her jaw is set, and her eyes wild.

If anything is weighing on her, she seems to shake it off now.

"My guards have Liam surrounded. Your magic won't last long."

In the back of my mind, I register that she's skipped her usual twisted pleasantries, though her voice is still edged with a poisonous sweetness. She raises her right hand with the knife in it, tipping it against an imaginary throat. "Why drag it out any longer? To chat a while?"

I take a deep breath, trying to keep my calm. The air seems to slice my throat on the way down. "No."

"You wound me," she says, her voice seeming louder and deeper in the small space. She takes a step closer to me, her eyes falling to the dagger in my hand. "What is that?"

I hesitate, unnerved by her ignorance. *Feigned*, I decide. "The weapon I'm going to kill you with."

"Living on the scraps of me has blunted your mind, my friend." She laughs, a short bark of a laugh, then sighs. The sounds mingle in the space between us, making my knees quake. "Must we play this little game all over again?"

"Isn't that what you want—a game?" I make my voice like

324

hers, like frozen silk. The ease of it makes my stomach churn, as does the weight of the dagger in my hand. All I need to do is strike out and use it. "Isn't that why you've been chasing me around Sempera for centuries, murdering everyone I love, everyone who's protected me?"

At this, Caro's light eyes go even colder. "*Protected* you? You never wanted to be protected, not when you were Antonia—and not now. If you did, do you think you'd be standing here with me, alone?"

I shiver at the truth in her words.

"Do you think you would have raced back to Everless when you discovered who you were?" she goes on.

"I came back to Everless to protect Ina from you," I spit.

"Perhaps. But that's not all, is it? You figured out who you were. Because every time you died, and every time you lived, my heart was the only part of you that remained true. The part of you that was me. You've always found your way back to the Sorceress."

"It's almost over now," I say, voice shaking.

Her eyes find mine, flash with something like hurt.

Caro has stepped close enough now to press the tip of the knife into my chest. I swallow hard, incapable of moving, of stopping her words with my own, of raising my weapon. If this is another trap, another pretty lie, then she has me ensnared in it like a glimmering spider's web.

"I don't want your heart anymore, Caro," I whisper. "I tried to give it back to you before. . . . I tried, but . . ."

Now I'm fluent in the subtle language of Caro's face, her movements. I can tell by the way her lips turn down that she's losing patience. Know from the way her spine straightens that she's come to a decision.

"How about I try killing Liam Gerling and see where that gets us?" she says with a casual flick of her blade that makes a tear where it presses into my dress.

Desperation cascades through me, and my body takes over, moving without authorization. I spin around and snatch up an old bottle from the table, smash it into her hand, the one that clutches the knife. The blade cuts across my chest, but I ignore the pain. She lunges for me at the same time I lunge for her, neither of us trying to call on our magic to aid us. This isn't a battle of power but of will, I suddenly realize. This is not about our magic. This is about *us*.

We struggle, but Caro finds her strength and with both arms, slams me into the wall with the mural of the fox, snake, and hound.

All I can see for a bleary moment is the hound above me, teeth bared, before I sink the dagger into Caro's flesh.

32

Blood wells up around the rubied blade. Before I understand what's happening, a shimmering smoke begins to rise from Caro's wound, curling into ribbons that begin to wrap around us. Caro's eyes reflect my confusion—but then, the acrid-sweet smell of blood-iron fills my nose, and I think I understand.

The jewel is melting, dissolving where it touches Caro's blood like an hour-coin in wine.

The smoke grows thicker, changing from red to a blue gold to green. Remembering the blood regression, I let the smoke flow into my mouth like water. It's cool on my tongue, and my eyes flutter closed.

"Jules," Caro whispers, her voice soft and surprised, telling me that she wasn't expecting this.

The world falls away as moments cascade through me, flashes

that I only half understand at first. But then, an answer rises in my mind: the blade contains not time, not strength—but memories. Moments pulled from time itself.

A girl finding me in the forest, holding out her hand to bring me home.

Two girls chasing each other, yelling "Fox!" and "Snake!" with no need for magic other than birdsong and the wind singing through the woods.

Lord Ever's grand estate being built, the workers leaving at night, abandoning the empty half-built castle for our use, piles of stones all around and certain rooms still open to the sky. Caro and I, sneaking in at night, running blind through the dark hallways following the sound of her voice, snatching glimpses of the stars. Caro telling me, "Father has room for two, but let's share our bedroom, so we never have to be apart."

Creeping up next to Caro at Lord Ever's workbench, barely tall enough to see over the edge, the way her eyes shine with greedy curiosity as she reaches out for the beautiful, sharp, glittering things scattered over its surface.

Sneaking into the village to play with the other children who live there, joining in their games of chase and sticks and cards without ever telling anyone our names and never leaving each other's side.

Floating on my back in that glen in the forest, Caro beside me, my right hand and her left stretched out and anchoring us together even as the currents try to tug us gently apart.

Testing our magic on trees, holding Caro's hand and squeezing our eyes shut, concentrating to find the current of time running through the wood. A sapling shoots upward, branches unfurling toward the sky like arms opening, leaves bursting into existence in a storm of green, and then the next heartbeat turning gold and falling.

Standing beside her at the top of a cliff, a cold wind whipping our faces, nothing but blue sky all around. Her hair flying out behind her like a dark shining flag, her excited whisper in my ear. "We could do anything, Antonia. We could fly if we wanted."

A new story of the Alchemist and Sorceress unfolds in front of my eyes in a rapid stream of moments, so quickly that I can't count them. In only seconds—or hours, I can't tell for sure—an entire friendship, *our* friendship blooms in my mind. And alongside it, another story takes shape.

Lord Ever, observing. Training. Always pushing, punishing. No matter how strong we grow, he grows stronger.

I chase Caro from the castle, unsure why she's angry but knowing I must comfort her. I catch her arm, see the shine of tears on her cheeks as she turns around. I feel the weight of her head on my shoulder as she falls into my arms.

A spring day, gathered around the table. "We found you alone by the river," Lord Ever's voice drawls, looking at me. "When I told you that I was the last and most powerful sorcerer in all the land, who lives with his daughter in a house of dark stone at the top of a hill with woods all around, you begged to come home with us."

Ever and little Caro taking me to the stone house, which is full of light: sun in the day, starshine at night. Lord Ever says he can sense the power living in me, just like it lives in Caro. "You balance each other—fear and boldness, sweetness and strength," he tells us as he demonstrates how to call on our power to turn lead into gold, how to hold flame in our small, cupped hands. When it burns our skin, he tells us that the price of power is pain. Caro nods, and I notice how her eyes gleam with hunger. Lord Ever sees it, too—and smiles.

Older now, I'm hiding behind a curtain, peeking through the gap as Ever receives his line of petitioners in the great hall. He conjures things with his sorcery—silks and gold, spices and jewels. It's nothing to him, but they happily spill their blood in payment, which turns to shining metal before it hits the flagstones. Caro is at his side, gathering up the blood-iron and bandaging each comer, smiling prettily as they shuffle away. Sometimes she leaves them with only a day, only an hour. I'm playing chase with Caro in the woods one day when I trip over something. A body. The woman didn't even make it back to the village.

In a training session, I lash strength to a dagger and try to kill him. The force of the blade—the force of ten men—hardly makes a scratch. Desperate, I run to a local witch, beg her to help me. She tells me, "The only way to kill pure evil is with pure love." Then, she packs a small bag and flees.

Next, I'm standing by the crystal window in the room that Caro and I share, begging her to make her father end it. Bleached bones litter the moonlit lawn; wolves prowl at the edge of the woods. The villages in the distance are just dead shapes without light or smoke. "We have to do something, Caro. We have to stop this," I whisper. In response, she levels those eyes on me— as bright green as the grass once was—and then turns over and closes them. The bottom drops out of my stomach as I realize how alone I am. I cry, "Why won't you listen?"

In my bed, alone, I resolve to put a stop to Ever myself.

And the last moment unspools in vivid detail—

The lamplight around me has given way to torchlight. Caro sleeps beside me. Our room is dark and quiet around us, her room in the castle that her father built for her. No—*for us,* a voice inside me whispers, and I know it's true. He was a father to me. Once. Whatever I think of Lord Ever now, however evil he is, Caro still loves him.

Which makes what I'm about to do so much harder.

Slowly, I sit up in bed, sliding the rubied knife from underneath my pillow. Moonlight flashes off the blade, so bright I'm almost surprised it's not accompanied by some sort of sound. Breath held, I look down to where Caro sleeps beside me.

The spill of her hair is a dark contrast to the moonlight. She sleeps on her side facing away from me, her shoulders moving up and down in slow, even motions. Her soft breath is the only sound in the room.

She will hate me forever for this.

If she even survives.

No. That can't happen. I won't let fear in, not now. It will work its way under my skin, stop me from doing what I have to do. Even as I sit here, I imagine I can hear wailing from all across Sempera as people realize what a terrible bargain Ever has made them privy to. As they bleed away their time and millennia pool in his veins. He is pure evil, and he must be stopped.

Her father is too far gone. But I can't overcome him on my own. I need Caro's help. I need her power and then, with her power, I can create the weapon that will defeat pure evil.

Someday, she will understand. She must.

I tell myself this as I lift my hand and freeze time around her, arresting her midbreath.

A chill sinks through me as her shoulders still. Her eyes pause, half-opened. No matter how many times I do this—I've been practicing for weeks and weeks, trying to prepare myself— it always sickens and frightens me. She's not dead, but it feels that way as I roll her onto her back, no pulse in her shoulder, no movement under her eyelids.

It's not so hard, now, to bring the knife down—blade shining bright with I don't remember what—and position it over her chest, steadying myself with my left hand on her collarbone. I imagine her as a map, the roads of her veins leading up her arms, through her chest, to the bright space of her heart. Instead of a beat, Caro emanates a kind of steady warmth, positively blazing when she's joyful or angry. I can feel it now through her skin, faint but there, like I'm holding my palm a few inches from a candle.

I squeeze my eyes shut and bring the blade down. Still frozen in time, she doesn't make a sound or movement as the dagger sinks between her ribs. But I know if I opened my eyes, I would see muscle and bone and blood. And then below that, something less human.

There. I pull out the knife, willing myself not to think about the blood, and call her heart forward.

Something meets my fingers, rising up out of her. It's hard and glass smooth, like a jewel, and the heat emanating from it is almost unbearable. But when I wrap my fingers around the shape of her heart, it's light as air. It comes away easily, as if it were always just waiting for me to reach out and take it.

When I feel the last invisible thread of it pull from her chest, I finally dare to open my eyes. The thing in my hands looks akin to a gem, a treasure—and yet its brilliance makes every diamond I've ever seen look like a clod of dull earth. It's bright, far too bright for it to be just torchlight refracted in its glassy body. No,

Caro's heart spills light like a normal heart would spill blood, liquid and tangible, white light filling up my cupped hands and—

The light, the power itself, melts into burnished gold and red and colors I cannot name, until it's no longer a solid thing in my hand but something more like a creature—moving, alive, in tendrils of light and power that wind themselves through my fingers. It burns, but I can scarcely feel the pain anymore as it sinks through my skin and *into me*, heat pouring into my flesh and light shining through my skin. Power. More than I've ever felt, filling up my heart, Caro's strength and mine twisting together to create something more.

I gasp. So much power flows through me. It's easy, almost nothing, to heal the wound in Caro's chest, ribs and muscle and skin knitting together with no indication that there's nothing underneath. Then to vanish the blood all around us, until there's no red left in the room, only black and silver. My hands shake with power, not weakness, as I turn Caro back on her side, as though something larger than me is trapped beneath my skin and writhing to get out.

When I let go of my hold on the strings of time binding her, her shoulders start to rise and fall as though nothing at all has happened, though she looks perhaps a little paler.

Now, to make the weapon. An instrument of pure love.

I look at her face and pull from the depths the first memory

I have of her, a small face emerging out of the dark. She took my hand, and a spark passed between our palms. The first time our power was shared. Closing my eyes, with Caro's heart beating inside mine, I picture the memory in and of itself, making it material, as Lord Ever taught me to do with time so long ago. I imagine drawing it out of my mind and thusly out of time itself, like I plucked hours, days, and years to help Caro weave them into blood.

When I open my eyes, I can see it, a bit of white-glowing mist laced through with lightning. I lift the knife and twirl it, the memory collecting against the blade like spider silk. After a moment, it sinks through the surface of the metal, leaving only brightness.

Moment after moment, image after image, memory after memory. I draw out the recollections of our friendship. Bind them all to the blade, which glows with them.

I will Caro's memories out too—her memories of her father. Bright mist rises from her still brow and joins my memories on the blade. Images flash through my mind, and I don't know if I'm seeing inside Caro's memories or my own, my mind desperately clinging on to the precious things even as I steal them.

Eventually, when I reach down into my own mind, there's nothing there but shadows, piecemeal images I feel but don't understand.

And when I look down at Caro, I feel nothing. I know that she is my companion, that we have spent many seasons here in comfort together. But I also remember her father—turned captor—his greed, how I must be strong enough to stop him from consuming the lives of all of Sempera.

"Pure love," I whisper, squeezing the dagger in my hand.

Lord Ever is awake when I stride into his chambers, fully dressed and puttering over his workbench, a miniature version of the great laboratory downstairs. Bits of bright blood-iron litter the floor around him.

"Antonia." He looks up in surprise, his eyes bright, feverish. "What are you doing up?" He steps around the table, opening his hand to reveal a fistful of rough jewels. "Look—time from children. Who knows what properties it might contain."

His eyes shine, full of plans and avarice.

I draw close to him, holding the knife behind my back, mouth dry and heart heavy. I didn't let go of my memories of him like those of Caro—not all of them. I remember how he sent his heralds out to tell Sempera they could live forever, if they only visited his estate and gave a little of their blood. I remember the bodies littering the floor of the great hall, drained of blood and time, while Ever stood among them, a goblet in his hand and his head tipped back in exultation while centuries flowed into him.

He looks strangely at me now, head tilted. "Antonia?"

Caro's power thrums through me, and my own determination. The dagger thrums in my hand.

He will drain the whole world dry so that the three of us could live forever.

I can't let it happen.

I lift the knife and bring it across his throat. The blade hisses where it cuts, and Lord Ever falls dead at my feet.

Caro finds me in the hall stumbling toward our room, covered in her father's blood, the knife held loosely in my hand. We stop and stare at each other, and a terrible dread sinks through me as the look in her eyes hits me. An awful, blazing anger.

"What have you done, Antonia?" she whispers. I know she can see Ever's broken body through the doorway behind me, the knife still lying in the pool of blood. Anguish fills her eyes but when she opens her mouth, all she speaks is silence—a choked, confused silence. Tearing her eyes away from his corpse, she holds a hand to her chest, loosely cupped as though she's trying to catch something spilling out.

"What did you do to me?"

My eyes burn. My chest threatens to split open—with grief, with magic, with the Sorceress's heart.

"You wanted my power." Her voice trembles with barely contained rage. "You *took* it. How could you?" She flings her arms out as if to attack me with magic, but nothing happens but a weak stirring of the air. She hisses.

Her face twists into a mask of hate, and she advances on me, hands curled into claws.

I turn from her and run.

33

I explode up to my feet in the tower at Everless, screaming.

Caro stands before me—dagger sunk in her, terror inscribed on her face. Unlike when I stabbed her at Shorehaven, the blood does not recede back into her. Her eyes glitter as she looks down at me, with malice and suspicion and what I think is hatred. But how could it be otherwise, given what I've done?

How could I have forgotten?

A weapon of pure love against pure evil.

Gasping, I realize I still grasp the dagger in my fist. I move to pull it out of Caro's flesh, but find that there's no longer any blade to pull out. The ruby has completely dissolved into what it contained: the moments of our friendship, lifted from our minds by the Alchemist, by *me*, right after I stole her heart.

Caro's eyes close, twitching underneath her eyelids, as if dying is nothing more than a dream.

Tears stream down my face. In my first lifetime, I created a weapon bound with love in order to destroy evil, to destroy Lord Ever. And now, I've used it to kill his daughter, the Sorceress.

"Caro." My friend, my enemy. Her name escapes my lips in an anguished whisper. A sharp pain lances through my chest for the girl she was, the friendship lost to us—the friendship that I bound to a blade. The girl laughing, loving, alive.

Caro blinks, once, twice. And I see the fire of hatred grow, then burn out in her eyes, along with the half-life that sustained it. The silver mist around her evaporates with a soft whisper of heat. When there's no trace of it left, Caro pitches forward.

Fear cascades through me, and my body takes over, moving without authorization to catch her. I reach out with my left hand, and she finds my arm, grips it and leans into me.

I sink to my knees with her. Her hand flies to her chest. Our faces are inches apart; close enough that even through the tears in my eyes I can see realization chasing realization across her face, like scudding clouds.

Shock.

Anger.

Sorrow.

Fear.

"You killed him, Jules," she whispers. "You killed me."

I can only nod. I raise a hand to her face, meaning to wipe away tears that she hasn't cried. But she doesn't flinch away. She lifts her own hand to cover my own, and I feel the cold of her skin. My oldest companion. My best and oldest friend.

"Jules," she whispers again. "It's so beautiful."

Fire rises in my throat. "What's beautiful, Caro?"

Caro looks down at my chest. Sweat darkens my dress, but something else is seeping out of the wound her blade left over my heart. Light. Golden, almost liquid, shimmering light, like the pure time I spilled at Everless but brighter. Caro reaches out and catches some of the light on her fingers, and I see her close it into her palm when the answer comes all at once, in a soul-sickening shudder.

It's her heart, broken from mine, like the seal of magic that kept it there. Finally free.

My body rocks. It was never Liam's death that I had to fear, just as it wasn't Roan's, nor any of those who Caro tried to kill throughout my lives.

First and last and always, it was my oldest friend's death that would break my heart.

Throughout every life, the only knowledge that kept my heart intact was forgetting our friendship, removing it from my mind as easily as lifting a pouch of blood-irons.

How could this be true?

And yet how could anything else be true? What else could

explain twelve lifetimes of this, centuries of my heart remaining whole and unbroken?

The answer is here: I hear Caro's laughter again in the glen; I see her hand reaching out to mine in the forest; I see my heart opening up to her, my dearest friend, the only one who could understand me, who could draw me out and help me become who I am.

My vision is dimming, blackness rapidly pressing in around the edges. The brightest thing I can see is the spilled light of her heart, widening in a gold circle around us. Spreading and spreading and spreading, growing thinner but never less beautiful.

I look down at Caro to see if she's watching—but her eyes are blank, and I realize that it's too late. She's already gone.

EPILOGUE

What happens next comes to me in pieces.

I'm slumped against Liam's back, Ina's huntsman cloak turned into a makeshift sling as he descends the vault shaft. Each of his labored steps on the ladder sends a jolt of pain through me, my limbs heavy and cold. But through the haze, I can see gold light clinging to Liam's hair, his eyelashes, playing over his knuckles as he carries me.

I'm lying on one of the oak tables in the kitchen where I labored so many hours after returning to Everless, a pastiche of half-familiar, highly concerned faces hovering above, and Lora bandaging my side, where Caro's heart tore through. The gold light is on them too, clinging to skin like dew, leaping from person to person like something alive. No one else seems to notice it.

Something is changing, I think.

Days later, I'm standing on Everless's summer lawn, watching a river of gold light flow out through the gates. I don't know what it means—only that when I visited a Laista timelender and cut my palm, all that came out was blood; the flames and vials produced nothing. Liam has visited the Everless vaults to find half the blood-iron there crumbled into dust. I wonder whether soon, the whole queendom will be like Elias, unbound, as the magic recedes from Sempera like tides from the shore. Whether now that the Sorceress is gone and the bond between her and me broken, blood-iron will fade away too.

It is here that I finally tell Liam what happened in Everless's vaulted tower. How I watched as the light left Caro's eyes before the heart could burrow back into her chest, which was so long wanting it.

When Ina and Elias returned to Everless together, it made sense: his spine, her fire. My sister oversaw Caro's burial, agreeing to my request that she be buried not out in the Gerling cemetery but in Everless's most interior garden, where the Sorceress's beloved plant, ice holly, grows. Liam helped me set a corner aside for her, far from the pathways where nobles stroll. A place where I can go every day if I choose, to sit and think or weep or talk. It's high summer now, but ice holly already grows over her grave.

I tell her what's happening in the world outside, everything

I never had a chance to tell her, both the good and bad, of the journey that brought me back to her.

When I woke up crying over the loss of my friend, Liam only pulled me into him, cupping his body around mine, careful not to jostle the bandages wrapping my chest where the Sorceress's heart left me. He whispered in my ear that it would be all right, of course it would all right, as tears dripped off the bridge of my nose.

I believed him that day, and every day after that, because nothing remained unspoken between us any longer. No half-truths or lies separated us.

Except for one.

Ina is the only person who would understand. One day, I confess.

I tell her during one of our long walks through Everless's grounds and the gardens, then outside the estate walls to Laista, into the woods and fields beyond. I usually do more listening than speaking on these excursions, trying to help as Ina talks through Sempera's problems of currency, of unrest, of change. I don't envy her these puzzles, nor she mine.

So I tell my sister the truth, what I didn't tell Liam—that on the day in the tower, Caro cupped some of the light of her heart in her palm as her breathing slowed. That I know without a doubt that she swallowed it, and died with a knowing smile on her lips. That it reminds me of how in another life, I swallowed her heart-stone.

That there are ways of defying death, of coming back again.

Ways for her and me and only us. Because we are different.

Or at least, we were.

Something in me—that part that is no longer afraid to hope—whispers to wait and see. That someday, I might be able to speak to my oldest friend again and everything will be different.

Someday doesn't carry the weight that it once did, when every day was hard fought, hard won. My life stretches out before me like sunlight on water. I am healing. With safety, with peace, with Liam and Ina by my side—I don't look forward with dread, but with hope.

I have a future. It's not infinite, but it is enough.

ACKNOWLEDGMENTS

This book owes its existence to a whole host of people whose love, hard work, and dedication are stamped invisibly on its pages. I owe a massive thank-you to the following people:

To the amazing team at Glasstown Entertainment, past and present: Lauren Oliver, Rhoda Belleza, Kamilla Benko, Tara Sonin, Adam Silvera, Kat Cho, Diana Sousa, and Lexa Hillyer, who is ever wise and clear-eyed about the big picture; Emily Berge, my fearless guide to the wild world of social media; and most of all, Alexa Wejko. Alexa, at the risk of being a broken record, this book really should have your name on it too. You're the best!

To the brilliant and long-suffering Erica Sussman, whose margin-note cheers and gasps kept me writing through the worst blocks; to publicity superstars Olivia Russo, Sabrina Abballe, and Ebony LaDelle for showering these books with so much love; and to the whole team at HarperTeen, who worked to shepherd Jules and co. into the world.

To my tireless team at InkWell Management: Stephen, Lyndsey, and Claire, for bringing *Everless* and *Evermore* to the world—it will never cease to be awe-inspiring, thinking of all the places this story has gone!

To the lovely people at Orchard Books: Jess Tarrant, Stephanie Allen, Naomi Berwin, and Nicola Goode; at Blossom Books: Myrthe Spiteri and Lotte Dijkstra; and to all the publishers around the world who I haven't yet had the privilege to meet, but hope to someday soon!

To Jenna Stempel-Lobell and Billelis for two incredible covers.

To my first beta readers: Korinne S., Kaitie C., Katelyn G., and Megan M., whose insight and encouragement helped shape *Evermore.* I hope to meet you in person one day!

To all my writer friends: Patrice, Laura, Sarah, Kit, Mark, Jeffrey, Jeremy, Cristina, Arvin, Kheryn, Lauren, Emily, and more. I'm starstruck by all of you every day, and your friendship and support mean so much.

To my family: Mom, Dad, Rachel, Ben, and Hannah, my first and best fans. And to Henry—did you know you're my favorite?

And most of all, to you, reader. You're the one who makes it real.